MARBECK AND THE KING-IN-WAITING

Elizabethan intelligencer Marbeck must prove his loyalty to a dying queen and a country in turmoil...

Spring, 1603: Queen Elizabeth is dying, and England waits anxiously. The Virgin Queen hasn't named an heir, refusing even to speak. Her cousin James, King of Scotland, is assumed to be her successor, but will the transition be peaceful? Sir Robert Cecil, Secretary of State, fears insurrection and has brought troops to the capital. But from where might the danger come – overseas, or from malcontents closer to home?

Meanwhile Marbeck, Cecil's best intelligencer, is under a cloud, wrongly suspected of shady dealings with the Spanish. So when the son of his friend Lady Celia Scroop joins a fanatical Puritan sect, he's glad to leave London to try and find the wayward youth. But events move fast and Marbeck finds himself in a maelstrom: forced to confront plots from two directions, that threaten not only the peace of the nation but the very fabric of England itself...

MARBECK AND THE KING-IN-WAITING

John Pilkington

Severn House Large Print
London & New York

This first large print edition published 2014
in Great Britain and the USA by
SEVERN HOUSE PUBLISHERS LTD of
19 Cedar Road, Sutton, Surrey, England, SM2 5DA.
First world regular print edition published 2013 by
Severn House Publishers Ltd., London and New York.

British Library Cataloguing in Publication Data

Pilkington, John, 1948 June 11- author.
  Marbeck and the king-in-waiting. -- Large print edition. --
(A Martin Marbeck mystery ; 2)
  1. Marbeck, Martin (Fictitious character)--Fiction.
  2. Great Britain--History--Elizabeth, 1558-1603--
  Fiction. 3. Great Britain--History--James I, 1603-1625--
  Fiction. 4. Great Britain--Kings and rulers--Succession--
  Fiction. 5. Spy stories. 6. Large type books.
  I. Title II. Series
  823.9'2-dc23

  ISBN-13: 9780727896827

Severn House Publishers support the Forest Stewardship Council™
[FSC™], the leading international forest certification organisation. All
our titles that are printed on FSC certified paper carry the FSC logo.

Printed and bound in Great Britain by
T J International, Padstow, Cornwall.

PROLOGUE

Augusto Spinola's house stood in Broad Street, a short walk from the Royal Exchange. From the outside it appeared a fairly modest dwelling, until the visitor passed through an iron gate, crossed a paved courtyard and entered what the owner called his *sala*. From there, and throughout the rest of the house, the opulence became breathtaking. Gilt mirrors, marble statues and rich hangings were everywhere, along with ornately carved furniture displaying the finest plate. At the rear of the house Spinola had caused a colonnade to be built, overlooking a well-tended garden where his children had played, and where his grandchildren might follow. Here, had it not been for the noise and bustle beyond the high walls, visitors could imagine themselves in some Italian villa instead of in the heart of London. The only thing which might spoil the effect was the cold, and on this particular day in March, the heavy rain that fell. Not that it troubled the three men who arrived discreetly at the house in late afternoon, to be conducted by a servant to Signor Spinola's private chamber.

Here, in a room without windows, the newcomers were greeted by the financier himself, wearing a black silk doublet, gold chain and immaculate ruff. Soon they were seated around a table covered with a Turkey carpet, being served with sugared sack in silver cups. By now the host's smile had given way to a shrewd, penetrating gaze. In silence he regarded his guests, until the last servant departed. Whereupon Sir Roland Meeres, the oldest man, spoke up.

'You know why we've come, Signor Spinola.'

'I do, Sir Roland.'

'Do you have tidings for us?'

'I?' The Italian raised his eyebrows. 'I was expecting you to bring news for me.'

'If ye mean have we fulfilled our part of the undertaking, sirrah, then ye may consider yerself assured of that,' the second man said, in a broad Scots accent. The only one who bore a high-sounding title – the Earl of Charnock – he was also the worst dressed of the three. He sniffed, rubbed his thick beard, and looked to Meeres to elaborate.

'There are troops in the Netherlands under Sir Henry Flood, who merely await the order,' Meeres put in. 'You may know that he succeeded Bostock as commander of that regiment ... loyal followers of the true faith.

They're eager to set their feet on English soil.'

'Indeed?' Spinola glanced at the third man, who had yet to speak, then eyed Meeres again. 'I confess I have heard otherwise: that the so-called English Regiment is merely a rabble of renegades and malcontents who follow the one who offers the fattest purse. The Spanish consider them more of a nuisance than anything else.'

The visitors bridled; or rather, Meeres and the Earl did. The other man coughed slightly, then said: 'Does that matter?'

They turned to him: William Drax, veteran soldier, who levelled his gaze at Spinola. 'When a surgeon must deal at speed with a patient who's gravely hurt, he cannot afford to fret about the quality of instruments at his disposal,' he went on. 'England is that patient, sir – her very soul in danger, if another Protestant succeeds to the throne. As he likely will – and sooner than you may think.'

'Then it's true that the Queen is dying?' Spinola said, after a moment. 'I only returned from the Continent two days ago, but I heard she was in better spirits, and responding well to the treatment of her physicians.'

Charnock gave a snort. 'Stuff and lies, put about by yon whoreson devil Robert Cecil!' he snapped. 'There are post-horses stationed at every stopping place from London to

7

Edinburgh, and messengers ready to ride the moment Elizabeth breathes her last. Why, there's an exodus already – men slipping away northwards by road and by sea, eager to be first to kneel before James Stuart and swear their loyalty. Then there'll be knighthoods flying about, like chaff in the wind.'

'That may be,' Meeres broke in, clearly finding the Scot's outburst distasteful. 'But let us not leap so far. It's plain the Queen lies sick at Richmond ... she's not been seen in public for over a week. Yet she may rally...'

'I think not – not this time.'

Drax was shaking his head. 'There's a black cloud hanging over that place that has naught to do with the weather. And why else would Cecil be bringing boats upriver, filled with troops? He plans for the worst, as well he might. None are admitted to the palace now without his approval. I fear time is short, sirs – hence, we must set things in motion.'

A silence fell. Augusto Spinola glanced at each man, before turning aside. On the table by his elbow was a small box, beautifully enamelled. Producing a key, he opened the casket and drew out a folded document.

'This is a bill of exchange,' he said. 'Issued by my associates in Florence ... it may be drawn on parties in London, or in Brussels, or Antwerp. The sum is equal, in approximate terms, to twenty thousand English crowns.'

There was a stir. The Earl, unable to conceal his glee, slapped a hand on the table. 'By heaven, Spinola, I was told if any man could do it, 'twas you!' he exclaimed. He turned to Meeres, who smiled; only Drax remained impassive.

'Another bill may follow in time,' Spinola added, unfolding the paper and spreading it out carefully. It was in Latin, covered with text in a neat Italianate hand. 'Though my friends would no doubt want proof that matters are proceeding apace before issuing it. Hence my earlier question, sirs: apart from the apparent readiness of troops in Holland, what further assurances can you give me?'

Eagerly now, Meeres leaned forward. 'Many,' he answered. 'Why, in every county, loyal believers stand ready. The Infanta's claim to the throne is their beacon of hope – they will flock to her banner the moment she lands on our shores. For almost forty-five years they have endured the Protestant yoke – but now that the end draws near, they strain like hounds at the leash. Let Cecil keep his troops cooped up in their rotting ships; it will avail him naught, the moment our forces appear. If you ask me the matter will be settled within days – and a Catholic monarch shall once again be crowned in Westminster. Then all those who've striven to bring it about shall reap their just rewards!'

'Amen, sir...' Visibly moved, Charnock gave a sigh. Drax showed no emotion, save a trace of irritation.

'Fine words, Sir Roland,' he murmured. 'Yet we cannot rely on mere goodwill. The Earl of Essex learned that lesson two years ago, and paid for it with his head.' He faced Spinola; a look of understanding passed between two realists. 'I'm raising a small troop in Kent,' he went on. 'Picked men, seasoned and well armed – some have served under me in the past. They'll provide the bridgehead, if you will: an escort for Isabella Clara, to see her safely ashore and guard her in those first, crucial hours. Once it's known that she marches on London, others, as Sir Roland says, will rally to her cause. But of course, some of the population are likely to resist. Hence I propose that the English Regiment land elsewhere – perhaps at Gravesend. Once the people of London learn that forces are approaching from two directions, they will panic. They haven't forgotten the Armadas ... it takes little to spread alarm.' He glanced at the Earl. 'Perhaps you can assist us there, my lord?'

'Well, I've not been idle,' Charnock retorted. 'I too have people ready. But as you know, my task lies north ... to prevent the Stuart bastard getting any further south than Berwick!' His lips curled in a sneer. 'It won't

10

be the first time the wretch has been taken prisoner – only this time shall be the last!'

There was a moment, before Spinola gave a nod. 'I liked your words, my lord,' he said gently. 'Particularly the mention of knighthoods ... The new Queen Isabella will no doubt wish to reward those who have helped bring about her succession. And should men of noble birth wish to put my own name forward...' He gave a thin smile. 'I believe I have dwelled in your country long enough to merit consideration ... would you not agree?'

Charnock opened his mouth, but again Meeres was quicker. 'You may have few doubts about that,' he said smoothly. 'I can already imagine an escutcheon bearing the arms of Sir Augusto Spinola ... and perhaps in time, men may have cause to address you too as *My Lord.*'

Spinola acknowledged the compliment graciously – whereupon, wearing a sardonic look, Drax broke in.

'Before we fall to rewarding ourselves with titles just yet,' he observed dryly, 'I believe there are details to discuss – shall we begin?'

His fellow conspirators sat up, their faces suddenly grave, which prompted a chuckle from Spinola. 'But first, let us drink to success,' he said. 'Or should I say victory – to His Holiness the Pope?'

Smiling, he lifted his chased silver cup; while outside, the rain fell in torrents.

11

ONE

Marbeck ducked under the dripping eaves, pushed open the door and stepped into the smoky interior of the Angel tavern in Mortlake village. He shook the rainwater from his hair, glanced round and quickly found the person he was looking for.

'I thought we said Sunday,' he murmured, taking a stool and seating himself. 'I spent much of yesterday waiting for you...'

'Your pardon,' John Chyme said quickly. 'I couldn't leave the palace. You cannot know what it's like there, just now.'

'I can guess,' Marbeck replied. He looked up as the drawer arrived to ask his pleasure. Having called for the best ale he turned to Chyme, who put a hand over his own mug and shook his head. 'I cannot stay,' he said.

'Very well...' Marbeck waited for the tapster to depart, then eyed his informant: young and handsome, and somewhat well dressed for a riverside tavern like the Angel. Under his keen gaze Chyme hesitated, then said: 'It's worse than I thought.'

Marbeck raised an eyebrow.

'I'm not certain, but I think someone's trying to smear your name – to paint you in the darkest of colours.' The young gentleman, who was in the Earl of Nottingham's service but also served, without His Lordship's knowledge, as a sometime intelligencer for the Crown, gave a sigh.

'It's no secret you've made enemies, Marbeck,' he went on. 'Perhaps one who has the ear of Master Secretary himself is taking the opportunity to wield the knife, to your detriment.'

'It may be so,' Marbeck allowed. The drawer having arrived, he took his mug and drank. He set it down and gazed through the latticed window at the Thames swirling by, murky and swollen with the rains. It had been a grim winter.

'What news of the Queen?' he asked abruptly.

Chyme shrugged. 'None are admitted to her rooms, save her ladies and her closest councillors. The archbishop will come again soon, they say. Physicians go in and out, but there's little change.'

'Has anyone dared to put a forecast on it?'

The other shook his head. 'It could be days, or weeks. But death comes – most are resigned to it. I hear she merely lies on a pile of cushions, and will not eat or drink. It's as if she has lost her desire to live...' Suddenly there was a catch in Chyme's voice. 'That

13

great heart, sunk to this,' he muttered. 'I was at Whitehall for the Christmas Revels – she laughed and danced like a maid. Now see what change has come.'

He looked up, and with an effort mastered himself. 'This will avail us naught,' he said. 'And you have troubles of your own...' But Marbeck put a hand on his arm.

'Elizabeth's in her seventieth year,' he said. 'Yet her chaplains pray and her Council hope for miracles, as they have always done. Why, when she was almost fifty they still tried to arrange a marriage for her, as if she could have borne an heir at that age. Hope may often drive reason from the field.'

A frown creased Chyme's delicate features. 'None dare talk of the succession yet – indeed, it seems it's forbidden even to think of it – but the Papists' hopes remain high. Master Secretary has put all our people on the alert...' He looked embarrassed. 'That is, I meant to say—' but he broke off as Marbeck laughed.

'All the intelligencers – except me,' he said. 'But what you've told me may point at the reason. It also explains why my messages to Sir Robert have gone unanswered. He's keeping me at arm's length ... perhaps he even has me watched.' He levelled a gaze at Chyme, who gave a start.

'Surely you don't think that I—'

'Of course not.' Marbeck shook his head.

14

'There are few I trust; Gifford, and the God-fearing Prout of course. But rest assured, you too are among them.'

The young man sighed and took a drink. 'I fear I can be of little help to you now,' he said.

'Have you spoken with Cecil yourself?'

'Barely a word. He's preoccupied and says little ... but he watches everyone, as keenly as one of his own hawks. Unease fills the palace. Robert Carey, my lord's nephew, waits to take word to the King of Scots – if he is named successor of course, as we expect.'

Chyme fell silent, and for a while Marbeck almost forgot his presence. He thought of Derbyshire, where he had spent a tiresome few months passing himself off as a lutenist in the household of Bess of Hardwick, the Countess of Shrewsbury. Since that formidable woman's granddaughter, Lady Arbella Stuart, was next in line to the English throne after her cousin the King of Scotland, attention had naturally focused on the twenty-seven-year-old spinster. But Arbella, wayward and fanciful, was unlikely to pose a threat to the country's stability, Marbeck had decided. Even if she were used by others more determined than she, and married off to a Papist as some wished, he had still dismissed the notion. Any threat to the Crown would come from elsewhere, he was certain.

15

He had sent in his report on his return to London, but was struck by the way everything had changed, once the Queen had moved upriver to Richmond Palace. Not only had Marbeck since failed to get an audience with Sir Robert Cecil: Master Secretary had ignored his every approach. Which his best intelligencer found somewhat alarming...

'I must leave you now.'

He looked up to see Chyme draining his mug. Having set it down he got to his feet, adding: 'I cannot promise to discover more. But if you wish me to try...'

'I thank you, John,' Marbeck said quietly.

The young man nodded, walked to the doorway and stepped out into the rain. Marbeck watched him go, then waited a few minutes before rising and making his own way out. He had some thinking to do, but hadn't time for a long walk by the river, which he would have preferred. Standing under the Angel's sagging eaves, he resigned himself to returning to his current place of residence, the house of Sir Thomas Croft in Barnes.

It was only a short distance, though Marbeck wished it were longer; he was in no hurry to get back. Not only was he bored with Sir Thomas: he had begun to dread the attentions of his wife, Lady Margery. Two more nights at most, he thought, and he would seek somewhere else to stay. By then he would have decided what to do about his present predicament: whether to try sending one more message to Sir Robert, or to take himself away from the south-east. The Queen's demise, it appeared, would come soon enough ... though it also seemed clear that whatever followed, Marbeck would be unable to play any real part in it. That was what hurt most: ingratitude, hostility, even contempt, he had endured before and could again. But to be shut out by his spymaster without a word – not merely as if he were no longer trusted, but as if he no longer mattered ... it was hard to bear.

Suppressing the thought, he set his face to the driving rain and began to walk down-river, along the path towards the hamlet of Barnes. But when he entered the broad hall-way of Croft House, he found himself confronted by someone who, more than anyone he knew, made him feel quite defenceless.

'Richard Strang! I waited all morning, yet you didn't come!'

Lady Alice Croft, ten years old but with the will of someone twice her age, stood by the stairwell scowling at him. Her flame-colour-ed hair was elaborately dressed, she wore her best kirtle, and in one hand was the lute which Marbeck was attempting to teach her to play. Her puny chest heaving with indig-nation, she brandished the instrument like a weapon.

'My lesson was for ten of the clock!' Alice fumed. 'And I was eager to show you the scale of G, which I have practised in my chamber ever since breakfast!'

Dripping with rainwater, Marbeck put on a contrite look and made his bow. 'I beg your pardon, my lady,' he said. 'I was detained on some trivial business ... but we'll work now, if you will. I'm keen to see the fruits of your labours—'

'That sounds like mere soft soap, sir!' The child wore a prim expression, exactly like the one seen often on the face of her mother. But while Marbeck had realized some time ago that Lady Margery Croft's pious ways were but a mask for her true nature, her daughter had not yet learned such duplicity. Marbeck liked her for it; and now, he was ashamed.

'I swear it is not soft soap,' he said. 'And I'll make up for my failure in any way I can. Shall we to your lesson, or—'

'Well ... if you're truly sorry, perhaps we might.' Lady Alice's anger never lasted long. Under his new alias, Richard Strang, Marbeck had been engaged to tutor the girl a fortnight ago, on the strength of a forged recommendation. It enabled him to be close to Richmond Palace during the crisis, yet far enough away to escape notice. Though he was fast becoming something of a fixture at

Croft House, he knew, which made him uncomfortable. He smiled at his pupil, and gestured to the stairway.

'Then let's to the music room, my lady,' he said brightly. 'You may prepare yourself, while I fetch my own lute from my chamber.'

'Oh ... but you're soaked to the skin!' Alice broke in, having only just noticed.

'I will change my attire, too,' Marbeck told her. 'Then I will be ready, and eager to see how you've mastered the difficult scale of G.'

At that the child nodded and turned to go upstairs, whereupon Marbeck's smile faded. Leaving Lady Alice's company, he knew, would be his one regret.

At supper he was subdued, his mind busy, though he made an effort to converse. The Croft household was large, and bluff Sir Thomas made a point of advertising his goodwill to all, regardless of their station. Thus the more important servants ate in the hall with the family, Marbeck among them. He sat at the end of the top table with the murmur of voices about him, trying to ignore the looks aimed at him by Lady Margery. Having finished a dish of raisin pudding, he was on the point of excusing himself when the lady leaned forward, turned and called to him across people who sat between them.

'Master Strang, Lady Alice tells me you

were absent this morning, and so missed her lesson.'

Forcing a smile, Marbeck faced her. 'Indeed, madam, it was remiss of me,' he said. 'Yet Lady Alice and I resumed our studies as soon as I returned. She has forgiven me – and as always, she makes excellent progress.'

But tonight the lady of the house was not to be placated. Fixing Marbeck with a brazen stare, she said: 'My daughter may have forgiven you, but I haven't. I wonder what took you away – in the direction of Mortlake, was it not?'

Heads turned in Marbeck's direction, among them that of the steward, who was seated on Lady Margery's left. On her right, her husband was in conversation and unaware of their discourse. But at once Marbeck saw it: the steward, an officious man, had made no secret of his dislike for him from their first meeting. It was he, of course, who had learned where Marbeck had gone that morning. Silently he cursed the man, as he cursed himself for his carelessness.

'So it was, my lady, and thence to Richmond,' he admitted. 'I'll confess the reason: it was to get news of the Queen. But there was such a press of folk about the palace I could not get near, and came away having heard naught but gossip.'

'Then your journey was not only undertaken without thought for your duties, it was

20

also fruitless,' the steward said, with a smirk at his mistress. 'And I wonder that any man would wish to go out in this rain ... do you tire of us so soon?'

Marbeck met the man's gaze. 'Far from it,' he replied. 'Tutoring Lady Alice is a pleasure...'

'I am glad to hear that.' Lady Margery watched him, willing him to keep his eyes on hers. Coolly she half-turned to her steward, who took the hint and quickly gave his attention to his supper. Sighing inwardly, Marbeck waited.

'Our son Thomas reaches his ninth birthday soon,' the lady continued. 'I had a mind that he might take lessons upon the lute. Lady Alice, perhaps, should learn the virginals instead. That is more becoming to a young lady – would you not agree?'

For a moment Marbeck was lost for words. The thought of young Thomas becoming his pupil in place of Lady Alice filled him with alarm; the boy was as unpleasant as any he'd had the misfortune to meet. But the notion crystallized his resolve: he would go, and soon. He inclined his head to Lady Margery.

'As you wish, madam.'

'Good...' The lady kept her eyes on his. 'It will mean engaging another tutor, but I believe Sir Thomas will be agreeable.' She paused, and delivered the killing blow. 'And of course, Master Strang, your duties will then be somewhat lighter, since the boy has other lessons to fill his waking hours. I will have to think of other ways to keep you occupied.'

At that Marbeck had to make an effort not to wince. The look in Lady Margery's eye might have been enough, had he not received earlier hints of her intentions too: in particular the time, but a few days back, when she had stopped him in a corridor and made it plain that she would come to his chamber one night, and expect certain services of him. The memory evoked dismay, if not dread. With an effort he smiled again.

'Your ladyship is kind.'

The steward gave a snort, and stabbed at his pudding.

Later that night, Marbeck decided to take a risk and absent himself from Croft House for a second time. The rain had finally ceased, and though the roads were muddy he had thought of taking his horse out of the stables the next morning. Lady Alice's lesson was not until the afternoon. But he was restless, and would not wait for the morrow. He resolved therefore to walk downriver to Putney, take the ferry across the Thames and make his way to the house of Lady Celia Scroop in Chelsea.

Relations between Marbeck and Lady Scroop, widowed for more than two years now, had grown somewhat strained of late. Since the death of her husband in the Low Countries, a change had come over the woman. Though somewhat relieved by his death (had she not secretly wished for it?) she had become withdrawn, even towards Marbeck. Indeed, she had appeared almost to discourage his visits, rare though they were; his sorties as a Crown intelligencer often took him far afield. On returning from Derbyshire he had sent a message, however, and was relieved to receive a reply bidding him come to her soon. Now, he thought, was as good a time as any. In the light of this evening's conversation, he had resolved not to remain under the Crofts' roof a moment longer than necessary. So while most of the household were preparing to retire for the night, he slipped out through a side door and left by the stable yard. Within the hour he had crossed the river on the last ferry, and a short while later arrived at the door of Scroop House, where as always he was admitted.

Lady Celia was up, of course. Her habits, forged during the long years of her late husband's absences, had not changed. She often sat with her waiting-woman until the small hours, even until dawn. Marbeck found her in a small but comfortable chamber with a good fire burning, and made his bow. But as he straightened up, he received a shock.

In a matter of months, he saw, his lover and friend had aged. Not only had the spark in her eye dimmed: her face was drawn, even gaunt. More, the smile with which she usually greeted him was absent. Instead she nodded and remained seated, while her woman rose and, having thrown a brief look at Marbeck, left the room without a word.

'I ask your pardon for not coming sooner,' was all he could say.

She did not reply, merely beckoned him forward. He took the seat left by her servant, but first he bent forward and kissed her on the lips. To his relief she returned the kiss, then gestured to a jug that stood on the small table between them. Marbeck poured wine into two cups, but Lady Celia waved hers away.

'I have drunk enough today,' she said. 'But take what you will.'

He took a sip, searching for the words. But before he could speak, she forestalled him.

'There's a message for you. A boy brought it, then hurried away. I've kept it a week.'

He frowned. 'Here? But from who—'

'I know not,' she broke in. 'Perhaps someone who knew where you would be, sooner or later. As they knew to trust me to deliver it, with my usual discretion.'

Suddenly his mind was racing. Had there been word from Cecil after all – was he fretting over nothing? A week ... his frown deepened. He had already informed Master Secretary of his whereabouts by then; why send word here, instead of to Croft House?

'Where is it?' he asked.

'In my chamber, under lock and key.'

He met her gaze in silence. His affection for her was as great as ever, but it was now mingled with pity. What had happened to her? He longed to ask questions, but felt he must tread carefully.

'Shall I wait here while you fetch it?

At that she smiled, though somewhat wanly. 'Why this sudden delicacy? In times past you'd have had your hands on my person by now.'

'Your person?' Marbeck managed a smile of his own. 'Now who's being delicate?'

As quickly as it had appeared, her own smile faded. 'I've things to tell you,' she said after a moment. Somewhat relieved, he gave a nod. At the same moment he noticed a thin streak of silver in her hair, caught by the candlelight.

'It's my son Henry,' Lady Celia went on. 'He's eighteen now, as you know. He failed to come home from Oxford at Christmas time. Now I hear troubling things about him...' She looked away briefly, then met his eye again.

'You are the only man I can turn to, Marbeck. Indeed, I think you are the only one who might help me.'

TWO

Their coupling that night surprised Marbeck. He had expected Celia to be unwilling, wanting merely to talk. Instead, when they went to her bed she quickly became passionate, as if, now that she had confessed herself in need of his help, she could be as free with him as they had once been. It brought joy and relief, but it left him uneasy. When they were spent, lying in their sweat between her fine sheets, he turned to look at her. And almost at once she began to speak.

'I've had correspondence with the dean of Henry's college,' she said. 'Exeter, that is.' She lay on her back, gazing up at the canopy of the great bed. 'It seems he's been absent without permission, many times, and the college is displeased. They talk of refusing him his bachelor's degree. Worse, he appears to have got into company I dislike.'

At last Marbeck started to form a picture; his own student days were not so distant, after all. 'It's common enough for young men to run wild, both at Oxford and Cambridge,' he said. 'Why should Henry be any

26

different?'

'You don't understand,' Celia answered. 'If it were mere youthful behaviour on his part, I would welcome it. It's rather...' She hesitated. 'This company he keeps – I speak of their religion.'

'You mean Papists? That too is not unknown. He's exploring other ways of thinking ... or it may be a form of rebellion on his part.'

'It's not even that. If Henry had become attracted to the Church of Rome, I would at least try to comprehend it, and to dispute with him. Even his father, at one time, claimed to understand why some are drawn to their liturgy...' She turned on her side, and faced him. 'It seems he's become close with a Puritan sect ... Precisians, of the harshest kind. The sort who demand reform of the Church, who think wearing vestments is a sin, and that all books are frivolous save the Geneva Bible.'

It was a surprise. Though it had been some years since Marbeck had set eyes on Henry Scroop, he remembered him as a lively youth, who enjoyed the company of his friends. Yet people changed, once away from home...

'That too may be naught but experiment on his part,' he said after a moment. 'He could alter his views in a trice...'

'Their leader is Isaac Gow.'

At mention of that name, he fell silent. Gow was a notorious Puritan agitator. Sir Robert Cecil had had him watched many times, something of which Gow was not only aware, but deemed a badge of merit. Half a century ago, under the bloody rule of Queen Mary, he was the kind of man who would have gone willingly to the Smithfield fires, shouting defiance to Popery with his last breath. To him and others like him even the regime of Elizabeth was one of decadence, if not wickedness. Marbeck found himself frowning.

'What would you like me to do?' he enquired.

'Confront Henry,' was her reply. 'He has no father now to talk sense into him ... not that he was ever here to do so. His uncles are no use ... they shun me, since their brother's death. Some people believe I willed it – even that I arranged it.'

They gazed at each other. In this very bed, Celia had once confided to Marbeck that she wished her husband would never return from the war in the Netherlands.

'Sir Richard died in battle at Breda, along with many of his troop,' he said. 'How can anyone deny that?'

'Yet they know what sort of man he was, and how I grew to despise him. My children know it, too.'

He considered. 'Do you think the boy

would listen to me?'

'I don't know that he will, Marbeck,' she answered with a sigh. 'But you can at least *ferret about* – is that not the phrase you use? Find out why Gow is in Oxford, and how far Henry has become embroiled with him and his followers. Unless...' She put on a questioning look, to which Marbeck shook his head.

'I'm not busy at present.'

Celia showed surprise. 'Even now, when we hear naught but tales of the Queen's decline, and what may follow? I thought every servant of the state was at Richmond.'

'Let's say I'm being held in reserve.'

She hesitated, then: 'I've little right to ask your help. Save for enjoyment of my body, which is freely given, you—'

'And the loans of money you've made me over the years, not to mention the trust we've always placed in each other,' Marbeck broke in. 'In short, you have every right to ask. And I'll do whatever's in my power – do you doubt that?'

Her gaze softened. 'I do not...' Suddenly, she gave a start. 'The message – I'd almost forgotten.' She saw his expression, and put on a wry look. 'But you, of course, had not.'

'I thought we would get to it in good time,' he answered.

She lifted the coverlet and rose naked, her body shining in the light of the candles. Marbeck watched her go to the table where her tortoiseshell casket stood, unlock it and take out a paper. She returned and handed it to him.

'Shall I look away while you read it?' she asked.

He didn't answer. As Celia got back into bed he sat up, peering at the seal, which bore no device. The handwriting was familiar, however. Bringing the letter nearer the light, he read the name: it was addressed to John Sands – his usual alias. And then, even before he tore it open, he knew who the sender was.

This is in haste, before I go to Flushing. By the time you read it you may be in fear, and you are right to be. I know little, except that someone's denounced you to our crookback master for a servant of Spain. And since Roberto is dizzy with looking every way at once, his vision grows blurred. My advice: leave London and go north while you can. James Stuart will be king within the month, and if you get to him before others do you may yet save your neck. God speed!

It was signed with a name Marbeck knew was false: Edward Porter. But had he been in any doubt, two tiny initials were squeezed inside the loop of the letter P: *J.G.* His friend and fellow intelligencer, Joseph Gifford.

He lowered the paper, and saw Celia resting on her elbow watching him. 'Troubling news,' she observed. When he made no reply she added: 'You know now who it is from?'

Absently, he nodded.

'So ... you are called to duty after all.' Her tone was suddenly dry. 'My difficulties can wait ... how paltry they must seem, compared with the affairs of state that bind you...'

But he turned quickly to her. 'You're wrong. I must leave, and soon ... but I see no reason why Oxford should not be my first destination.'

She sat up abruptly. 'You will seek out Henry?'

'Of course. I'll do what I can, and write to you.'

She gave a long sigh. 'Then you carry my hopes,' she said. 'And my heart too, for what it's worth.'

'It's worth much,' he replied. And he would have said more, but her hands were about his face, pulling him towards hers.

In the grey light of a cold dawn, Marbeck took the first ferry across the Thames at Putney and walked briskly upriver to Barnes. He had made his plans, and would lose no time in implementing them. Within the hour he hoped to be on the road to Beaconsfield, which led thence to High Wycombe and on to Oxford.

Now that he had a purpose he felt relieved, despite the grim warning contained in Gifford's letter. The man had penned it a week ago; what surprised Marbeck now was the fact that, assuming its contents were correct, he himself was still at large and not languishing in a cell somewhere. Master Secretary Cecil had not merely been keeping him at arm's length, he realized: he was suspicious of him, and may indeed have had him watched. It galled Marbeck that, as a loyal intelligencer, he should be doubted so swiftly. Moreover, it threw suspicion on those he had been in contact with of late: John Chyme, and the people at Croft House ... He drew a breath, and dismissed such thoughts. His task was to gather his belongings and get Cobb out of the stable before anyone noticed.

The household was astir, a thin line of smoke already rising from the kitchen chimney. Skirting the main buildings he passed through a wicket gate, crossed the vegetable garden and entered by the back door. Some of the wenches were about, but none paid him much attention; a man of his age and station coming in at such an hour, looking somewhat sheepish, was not unknown. He went through to the hallway, ascended the stairs and gained his small chamber, where he quickly set about making up his pack. His lute he thought of leaving behind, then decided against it; the role of Richard Strang, jobbing musician and tutor, might yet come in useful. Having taken a last look round, he left the room. The upper house was silent, the family still abed. But as he gained the stair-head there was a creak, and a voice stopped him in his tracks.

'Master Strang ... where are you going?'

He turned, to see a barefoot Lady Alice standing by the doorway to her chamber. She was in her shift, hair unbound. Her face was puffy from sleep, but her eyes were wide.

'Your pardon, my lady...' Marbeck threw her a smile. 'I'm called away on urgent business ... a family matter.'

'You mean you're leaving?'

He nodded. 'I wish I could stay for your lesson, but I cannot.'

Her face fell, and for a moment he thought she would fly into one of her famous rages. But instead, she said: 'You will return, won't you?'

He hesitated. 'If I can ... one day.'

'When?'

'I know not.'

They eyed each other, then she gave a sigh. 'My father says the Queen may die soon, and everything will be different.'

'Likely it will, my lady,' Marbeck said.

He turned away from her and hurried downstairs. A quarter of an hour later he was leading Cobb out by the stable gate. Having tightened the horse's girth and checked that his belongings were tied securely, he placed foot in stirrup and heaved himself into the saddle. Then he was trotting along the path, while grey clouds scudded overhead. He did not look back.

The day was breezy, but as yet there was no further rain. It was approximately ten miles to Uxbridge, where Marbeck made his first halt. Having watered and fed Cobb he was soon back in the saddle, and despite the muddy roads made good pace, reaching Beaconsfield by midday. In the afternoon he passed through High Wycombe without halting, spurring his mount against the fading light. But the horse ran well, eager for exercise after being stabled for too long. To his relief, as darkness fell, he saw the lights of Oxford ahead. He had covered sixty miles.

The old city was quiet. Though Hilary term would draw to a close soon, he knew, and students would be restless in anticipation of the holidays. He neared the walls, half-expecting the gates to be shut. But the curfew was not yet in place, and Cobb's hooves were soon clattering on cobbles as they entered St Aldates, with Christ Church on the right.

Exeter College was to the north of the city, but Marbeck did not go there. Instead he found an inn and saw to the horse's stabling. Then, having left his belongings, he set out on foot for a house close to Jesus College, whose whereabouts he had learned from

Lady Celia. Here, she'd told him, Henry spent much of his time instead of in the shared chambers at his own college. Soon, in a narrow and gloomy street, he halted by a low door and knocked. After some delay, it was opened by a tousle-headed young man with a wispy beard.

'I seek Master Henry Scroop,' Marbeck said. 'Is he here?'

The young student was holding a small lantern, which he now raised. He blinked, then shook his head.

'Do you mind if I make certain?' Marbeck persisted, placing a hand firmly against the door.

The other drew back. 'There's no need,' he replied. 'Henry's gone from here – left more than a fortnight ago.'

'You mean he's at his college?'

'No – I mean he's left Oxford.'

Marbeck's eyes narrowed. 'Why would he do that?'

'Well, who are you, sir?' the other wanted to know. 'Are you a kinsman of Henry's, or...'

'A family friend,' Marbeck told him. 'And you – are you a friend of his? May I know your name?'

'Thomas Garrod,' came the reply. 'Yes, I'm a friend ... or rather, I used to be.'

'Indeed?' Marbeck gazed at Thomas Garrod until he flinched. 'How so?'

'Let's say that Henry has cast off his old acquaintances, in favour of other company.'

'A rumour tells that he now follows Isaac Gow, and those of his persuasion,' Marbeck said. But at that, unease showed in the young man's eyes.

'I care not for rumour,' he said.

'But you too, Master Garrod, are concerned for Henry's welfare, I think.' Marbeck lowered his voice. 'As are we all – in particular his mother, Lady Scroop. He is in his final year, yet he risks losing everything he has worked for. I wish to find the lad and talk with him – nothing more.'

Garrod hesitated. 'Then I fear you may be too late, sir,' he said finally. 'The last speech I had with Henry was weeks ago. He was withdrawn, even hostile. He bade me wake up to what England is, and what it will soon become ... then, he's been wont to say such things for some time.' The young scholar gave a sigh. 'There's no disputing with him any more. He's a cauldron of anger ... has been ever since his father died. What will become of him, I fear to think.'

Marbeck considered. 'Do you have any idea where he's gone?'

The other gave a nod. 'Emmanuel College, or so I understand ... Is that not the cradle of such philosophy as his?'

'You mean he's in Cambridge?' Marbeck showed surprise.

36

'Where he'll no doubt find others of similar mind,' Garrod answered in a dry voice. He stepped back and lowered the lantern. But before he could disappear, Marbeck stayed him.

'Wait – answer me this,' he said. 'Did Henry go to Cambridge to follow Gow?'

The young man gave a shrug. 'Gow has a house there, I hear ... Cambridge, or somewhere nearby. He preaches sometimes...' He sighed again. 'You may find Henry, sir, yet I doubt it will avail you much. His mind has become closed to all but the most dogmatic of Precisian views. A creed of the most rigid kind ... and against such blind certainty, even the gods of ancient times were powerless.'

Then he was gone, closing the door.

Through near-deserted streets, Marbeck retraced his steps back to the inn. He had no choice now, he felt, but to ride to England's other seat of learning: Cambridge, where he had once been a somewhat unruly student of St John's. He had not been there in more than ten years; nevertheless, he was resolved. And at least his whereabouts would be unknown to anyone, save a dour Oxford student. None could have followed him here, he felt certain, if he had indeed been under surveillance at Barnes. So with resignation he went to his chamber and slept, rising to another morning with the cloud lying as grey and thick as a horse-blanket.

* * *

Within the hour he had breakfasted and was leaving Oxford, taking the road east towards Aylesbury. From there, he faced another fifty-mile ride to Cambridge. Then, for Lady Celia's sake if no other, he would seek out Henry Scroop and try to reason with him.

Just now, however, it looked like a somewhat difficult task.

THREE

Cambridge, his *alma mater*; a place Marbeck knew as well as his boyhood home, and better than he did London. With mixed feelings he rose the next morning in a hired chamber at the Roebuck Inn, close to Pembroke Hall. His own college, St John's, was at the other end of the town, but he had no wish to be there. Some of his old friends might remain, as fellows or tutors. If recognized he would no longer be Richard Strang, or even John Sands: he would be Marbeck. And the tale he told his family in far-off Lancashire – his invented position, in a minor court role to do with arranging pageants – might ring somewhat hollow here. So, feeling somewhat conspicuous, he breakfasted and prepared to go forth, to discover if he could find the whereabouts of Isaac Gow.

The place to start was Emmanuel College, which as Thomas Garrod had said was a centre of Puritan thought, founded for the training of preaching ministers. Emmanuel was on the edge of the city, almost in the fields, and only a short walk from Pembroke Hall. Soberly dressed in a black cloak, and minus his sword, which he had left at the inn, Marbeck fell into intelligencer's habits. Walking a roundabout route, he turned in by Corpus Christi and skirted St Andrew's, to approach from the direction of the town. Finally he arrived at the college and made his way to the porter's lodge where, with luck, he might engage in some gossip. But in that matter he was disappointed: the porter was a taciturn fellow, who barely responded to his casual questions. So in the manner of a sightseer he strolled down a side street beside the college, which gave on to its gardens and orchard. Here his luck improved when a grizzled gardener in fustian, pushing a wheelbarrow close to the low fence, stopped to look at him.

'The entrance is round there, master,' he announced, pointing with his chin. 'You must knock and wait.'

'I thank you,' Marbeck said. 'I'm a stranger here. Yet I wasn't seeking admittance, so much as news.'

The other set his barrow down. 'News of what?'

Marbeck paused, uncertain whether or not this man would be sympathetic to his enquiry. It was hard to know nowadays where some people stood. The gardener might be a Puritan himself, or an unreformed Papist, or one who trod the broad path between as most tried to do. He decided to take a risk.

'There's a preaching man ... one of severe habits, who dwells somewhere about the town, or so I've heard,' he began. 'I've come a long way to see him ... his name is Gow. Do you know him?'

The gardener regarded him for a moment. Finally he pushed back his battered straw hat and gave a sigh.

'I know *of* him. But you won't find him in Cambridge ... not here at Emmanuel, or even at Sidney Sussex.' He named the other Puritan college, founded only a few years back and already known as a hotbed of dissent.

'That's a pity.' Marbeck put on a disappointed look. 'As I said, I've come far...' He watched the older man, and now detected a look of disapproval. Thinking fast, he added: 'I'm here on behalf of my father. It's my younger brother ... the boy's gone off with this Gow, and we're at our wits' end wondering what's become of him. I wish to find him, and see he's in no harm...'

'Harm, you say?' the gardener echoed, growing animated. 'Well, he may indeed come to it if he takes up with a man like Gow. Even Emmanuel is too tame for such as he. He came back from exile, in Germany or some such place, burning like a firedrake – like most of his kind. I will name them:

separatists. He's been travelling the country. But he has a lair hereabouts, so I heard ... too close, I might add.'

'Where is that, master?' Marbeck asked. 'Where should I go?'

'I wouldn't, if I were you,' the other grunted. 'But if you must it's a farm you seek, or it used to be. It lies south-east, by Gogmagog Hill ... have you heard of that?'

'I'm unsure,' Marbeck lied. 'But I will find it ... is there more you can tell me?'

The old man shrugged. 'Go swearing death to the Antichrist,' he said dryly. 'Or go with your ears stopped up ... Gow is a man filled with rage. Then, mayhap you've heard that already.' Signalling the end of the conversation, he picked up his barrow. With a word of thanks, Marbeck took leave of him and walked back to St Andrews Street.

Outside the church he stopped to think. He knew the chalk downs of Gogmagog well enough: students were forbidden to go there, on penalty of a fine. It was a strange place, where old ruins could be seen and where legends abounded. But it wasn't far: three or four miles. And it ought not to be difficult, Marbeck thought, to discover this farm where Isaac Gow dwelled. Here at last he might find Henry Scroop, and keep his promise to Celia.

In better spirits, he returned to the Roebuck and collected his sword. A short while later he was riding out of Cambridge by Grantchester, taking the road that led towards the hamlet of Cherry Hinton. After a while he veered southwards, where a range of hills appeared above the flat terrain. The Winterbury Hills, they had once been called. But to the folk of this region they were known as Gogmagog, named somehow after the giant of Albion. Soon the ground rose under Cobb's hooves, and the meadow grass grew longer. There were gulleys lined with trees, and here and there a glimpse of a hut or cottage. Finally, emerging on a slope dotted with sheep, Marbeck slowed down to take his bearings. There was a fold of withies at the far end of the field, and signs of movement; it was lambing time, of course. Walking his mount slowly so as not to scatter the flock, he found a shepherd at work. Fortunately the man was cordial enough, if phlegmatic. Yes, he knew the farm where Isaac Gow lived ... the owner had died leaving it in a poor condition, and Gow had taken it at a low rent. There were several people living there, the shepherd thought. It was no more than a mile further, close to the big hill where the giants slept.

Marbeck nodded his thanks, shook Cobb's reins and urged the horse onward. A short time later, having followed a rough track uphill, downhill and up again, he emerged from a copse and halted. He was looking across a shallow valley, at a collection of thatched buildings that seemed to huddle together for comfort. Smoke rose from a chimney, and there were what looked like mules penned beside the house. Slowly he rode down the track, allowing anyone inside full view of him. Finally he drew rein before the doorway, where he waited.

He waited, but nobody came out. The mules gazed at him over their fence, lost interest and moved off. Smoke continued to curl from the chimney, but there was no sound ... until Marbeck turned to a dilapidated barn that stood close by. He listened, and at last understood. There were voices in unison, all of which seemed to be male. Soon the murmuring stopped, and the same voices rose in song. A service was in progress.

He dismounted, released Cobb's reins and allowed him to walk away and graze. Then he stationed himself before the barn entrance, where he would be seen by those emerging. Here he waited a further few minutes, until the hymn had ceased and another prayer had been said, or so he imagined. Finally the door swung open and several figures garbed in black came out. The moment they saw him, they stopped dead.

'Good morning, sirs,' Marbeck said in a clear voice. 'Have I come to the right place? I seek Isaac Gow.'

There was a silence, while others emerged from their makeshift chapel. Soon nine or ten unsmiling men stood before Marbeck in a body. He glanced briefly at each, then his pulse quickened: on the edge of the group was the unmistakable figure of Henry Scroop; the young man and his mother were very alike. But there was no sign of recognition on Henry's part. Coolly, he stared at Marbeck as the rest of them did.

'Why do you seek our brother?' someone asked finally.

The speaker was a crabbed, white-haired man. 'In truth, it's not Master Gow himself I seek,' Marbeck answered. 'I came to find a friend ... a student who should be at his studies.' Deliberately he looked at Henry. 'Master Scroop, is it not?'

At once the boy stiffened, and a wary look came over his youthful features. 'Who has sent you?' he demanded.

'Lady Celia asked me to come,' Marbeck told him. 'She is most concerned about you ... as are all your family.'

There was a stir among the group, and heads turned towards Henry. 'I know you,' he said, frowning. 'I know him,' he repeated, turning to his fellows. 'His name's John Sands. He's a servant of the Crown – one of the Great Whore's lackeys.'

A sound went up: a murmur, almost of outrage. As if by instinct the members of the sect moved closer together.

'This boy is one of us,' the white-haired man snapped, glaring at Marbeck. 'He has abandoned foolish and idolatrous study to join the faithful. Whatever be your mission here, John Sands, it has failed. You should go.'

But to the consternation of them all, Marbeck took a pace forward. 'In my own time, sir,' he said calmly. 'First, I would speak alone with this young man...' He threw a stern look at Henry. 'He is a student of Exeter College, Oxford, and is here without permission. He's on the brink of forfeiting his degree, and his mother is distressed that he appears to have forsaken her and all his family...'

'And if he will not leave – what then?'

The voice came sharp as a whipcrack, and it came from the rear of the group. At once they parted, to reveal someone who had apparently been standing by the barn door, hidden from Marbeck's view. As he looked, the man came forward swiftly, to halt a few yards away. There could be no mistake: he was face to face with Isaac Gow.

His first thought was that the man was the image of the Scottish Puritan, John Knox: once a scourge of the established Church, dead these thirty years but never forgotten. Marbeck recalled the portrait – Gow wore his grey beard long, as Knox had done.

Moreover there was the same dour face that never cracked a smile; the fervid look of the zealot who is a stranger to doubt. And to cap it all, this man was also a Scot. Raising a finger, he pointed it at Marbeck as if to condemn him.

'I heard your name once, in London,' he said fiercely. 'Ye serve the she-wolf at Whitehall ... fashioning pageants and other frippery. She is a queen born of a harlot, and the harlot's fornicating husband-king! We are engaged in God's service, sir, and will not be challenged by such as ye! Go hence and beg forgiveness for your sins – leave the brethren to their work!'

The other men murmured their approval. But when Marbeck looked at Henry Scroop, the youth avoided his gaze. He frowned – was there conflict in his mind? Drawing a breath, he eyed Gow again. 'If the boy is unwilling to come with me, then I will leave,' he said. 'But I'll speak with him first, and hear it from his own lips.' He placed a hand lightly on his sword-hilt. 'Or do you keep him here against his will?'

Dark looks appeared, but none fiercer than that of Gow, whose face was as thunder. 'How dare you fling accusations against those of sanctified cause!' he cried. 'We account unto the Saints, and thence to the one true God – you and your like have no dominion here!'

47

'That's odd,' Marbeck observed. 'I've heard Papists use those same words.'

At that there was a collective gasp. 'He has the Mark of the Beast upon him,' one man said angrily. 'The children of perdition are filled with pride ... send him hence!' And he would have advanced on Marbeck, had not an unexpected voice risen.

'Wait – I'll speak with him.'

A hush followed, as all eyes turned to Henry Scroop, pale-faced but still hostile. 'That is, if our pastor will allow it,' he added.

Isaac Gow turned to him. 'You should not have discourse with this man,' he said severely. 'He will tempt ye with foul devices, using your family as a lever to prise ye from us.'

'But in that he will not succeed,' Henry replied. 'I have made my choice: I remain with you.'

There was a moment, before finally Gow gave a nod. 'I stand here,' he said, placing a protective hand on Henry's shoulder. 'Call upon me, if you wish.' With that he moved aside, throwing a look at Marbeck.

The others stood and watched as Henry walked over to him. Wordlessly the two moved away, walking beside the paddock fence. After a while the youth would have halted, but Marbeck led him further until they were out of earshot. Then he turned abruptly, and startled Henry as he had intended to do.

'Your mother is ill with worry,' he said. 'She's had no news of you in months, save that Exeter College may refuse you your bachelor's. Is that what you want?'

The boy swallowed, but stood his ground. 'It's of no importance,' he said. 'I've found a cause – a true purpose. This country's steeped in wickedness. I saw it at Oxford, where men flatter and vie for preferment, and debate only trivia ... but a better day is coming. Our pastor Isaac works tirelessly towards that day.'

'Does he?' Marbeck eyed him. 'What does he propose to do?'

'What does it matter to you?' Henry retorted. 'You're a man of no religion, I think. You merely wait upon the Queen – one of her army of flatterers...' He hesitated, and a look of suspicion appeared. 'And what, now, are you to my mother?'

'I'm her friend,' Marbeck said. 'I knew your father too ... he would be distressed to see what you have—'

'You lie!' Henry broke in, reddening quickly. 'If you truly knew my father, you would know his reputation: that of a lecher and a drunkard. He was a varlet, who deserved to perish as he did in the Flanders bog! I always thought—'

But he broke off then, as if he had said too much. He looked towards the farmhouse,

49

where Gow and others stood watching them. Marbeck glanced at Gow too, and back at Henry ... and in a moment he saw it. The boy was angry, of course: but from grieving, for the father he had rarely seen. And in Isaac Gow, he had found one who would stand in his place: one who seemed to be everything his own father was not. He waited, until Henry turned to him again.

'That may be,' Marbeck said, not unkindly. 'Yet it's a rare father that doesn't wish a good life for his son – especially one as clever as you. What of your future? How will you spend your days, if you forsake the university? Meanwhile Lady Scroop frets at Chelsea, losing her appetite as well as her sleep—'

'Enough!' Henry threw up a hand as if to ward off such thoughts. 'You speak to me as a child,' he said, with some bitterness. 'But I'm almost nineteen ... do you think I didn't hear rumours, when I was last at Chelsea? Servants' gossip, behind half-closed doors, but its import was clear. You visited late at night, while my father was at war ... you pretended legal business, yet you are no lawyer. I ask again – what are you to my mother?'

Marbeck hesitated. 'I'm her lover,' he said after a moment. 'And I would do anything in my power to help her, as I would you...' But he too fell silent, regretting his words. Suddenly, Henry looked close to tears.

50

'I knew it!' he shouted. 'You prey upon her – you're a vile sinner, like most of the population of this cess-pit! Pastor Isaac saw through you at once. You'll perish in the fires prepared for you – for you are too late to join the appointed brethren. You're no friend to me, and you're not wanted here!'

Cursing silently, Marbeck opened his mouth, but it was too late. The boy was backing away, and at the sound of his raised voice the others of the sect had started forward. Marbeck saw Gow advancing, striding through the grass like an angry lion.

'Henry, wait...' He moved towards the youth, who veered away. Then the others drew close, surrounding him like a bodyguard. At their head Isaac Gow stopped, and proceeded to direct his wrath against Marbeck.

'I know ye, fellow!' he roared, raising his fist. 'Ye were sent here to snoop – to beguile us with feigned concern for this boy, who is tender and in need of protection. Men of evil purpose always come in disguise, like the minions of Satan himself. Ye seek to entice him away – but I forbid it. Leave us, and do not return!'

The others gathered round, and in their faces Marbeck saw only fear and hatred. He looked at Henry, and saw a similar expression; but at least, he thought he understood the boy's emotions. Then there were hoofbeats: someone was leading Cobb up. Swiftly, Marbeck stepped forward and snatched the reins from the man's hand.

'Have a care, sir – he is particular who handles him,' he said softly. Startled, the man fell back, whereupon Marbeck mounted. Turning the horse in a rapid half-circle, he gazed down at Gow and his followers, knowing further words were useless. His last look was directed at Henry Scroop, but the boy had turned his back and was walking towards the house.

With a sigh, he shook the reins and rode away.

At the Roebuck, having stabled Cobb he went to the taproom and ordered mulled ale flavoured with spices. There was a good fire, and he sat down before it to drive the chill from his bones. On his way back to Cambridge the rain had started up again; now it fell in sheets, splashing against the windows.

Grimly he gazed into the flames. His mission to rescue Henry Scroop from the clutches of a crazed Precisian having stalled, he was at a loss. He could write to Lady Celia, but there was no way to embroider the news. Thereafter, his choices were few. *Go north*, Gifford had advised, meaning to Scotland and the court of James Stuart: the man most people supposed to be England's King-in-Waiting. He pondered the notion, not liking the prospect of several days' ride to an uncertain welcome. But it was true that others had gone already ... He breathed a sigh. Elizabeth's long reign would soon be over, and much would be swept aside with it. What the coming years would bring, nobody knew.

He finished his drink, left the taproom and walked up the stairs. He would pen the letter, then leave Cambridge. Though it would appear as if he had given up too easily, he thought ... should he make one further attempt to talk to Henry? The prospects of success looked bleak. With such thoughts in mind, he threw open the door to his chamber – and stopped in mid-stride. A swordpoint had appeared, its point directly above his heart.

'Well now,' someone purred. 'So it is you, after all ... grown somewhat careless, have you not?'

FOUR

Marbeck stared at the diminutive, ferret-faced man who stood before him wearing a sly grin; then recognition dawned.

'Poyns...' He breathed out in relief. 'What in God's name are you doing here?'

'Do you mean in your chamber, or in Cambridge?' Lowering his sword, Edward Poyns took a step back and looked Marbeck up and down. 'The first is easily answered: I saw you in the street. You looked somewhat fierce, so I kept my distance. Later you made for the Roebuck...' He shrugged. 'As for my presence in this town, that's a longer tale.' He raised an eyebrow. 'Can we talk over dinner? I'm rather hungry.'

His spirits rising, Marbeck took a long look at his fellow intelligencer, a man he had not seen in years. A lapsed Catholic and a quick-witted shape-shifter, Poyns could pass himself off as knight or beggar. Even Sir Robert Cecil had been known to express grudging admiration for him.

'It's no weather for venturing out.' Marbeck nodded to the window. 'Will the Roebuck's fare do? I could have a roast fowl sent up...'

'And a jug of something?' Poyns's grin widened. Having laid aside his rapier, he sat down on the window seat.

'So ... who do I address just now?' he enquired. 'John Sands, or Thomas Wilders perhaps?' He used the alias Marbeck sometimes employed on the Continent.

'I've put them aside,' Marbeck told him. 'Lately I've been Strang, a music-maker...' He indicated his lute, which stood in a corner. 'You're looking at a man without purpose – or even position. Have you not heard?'

Poyns shook his head. 'I've been buried alive for the past two months,' he said, his smile fading. 'I've seen no one ... that's why I'm in Cambridge, and mighty glad of it. I came down yesterday, from the Isle of Ely. Master Secretary, in his wisdom, saw fit to send me to Wisbech Castle. In short, Marbeck, you're the first man I've conversed with in what seems like an age who isn't a rabid Jesuit.'

His tone was dry, and Marbeck saw the strain about the man's eyes. Wisbech Castle, the remote holding-prison for militant Catholics and captured Jesuit priests, was a difficult posting. 'Few have infiltrated that place and kept their cover,' he said after a moment. 'But if any man could achieve

55

such, it's you.'

'I don't know that I achieved anything,' Poyns said. 'I sat through masses, heard debates, saw the anger of those who yearn for the return of their faith ... and in the end I caught a whiff of conspiracy. It's probably naught, yet it was enough, I thought, to give myself an excuse to leave ... but see, I prate too much. I'm eager for news – have you tidings of the Queen?'

'First let me go downstairs and bespeak our dinner,' Marbeck said. 'Then we'll prate all afternoon if you like ... unless you're in haste to travel on?'

For answer Poyns made a bow. 'You're the host, sir, and I'm your honoured guest.'

The dinner – a roast pullet with sauce, and cheese tarts – was more than adequate. So was the wine, and soon the two had done justice to both. They pushed aside the table the inn servants had brought, and Poyns raised his cup.

'To Sir Robert Cecil, known as *the Toad*. May he enjoy the favour of England's new monarch, as he did that of the old – when the day comes, of course.'

Marbeck drank with him and set his wine down. Having passed on such news as he carried, there was little to add. They had talked at length throughout the meal: of the Queen's decline at Richmond, and of the anticipation that kept all England on tenterhooks, and all Scotland too. Now, when Poyns pressed him, Marbeck told his own tale of what had befallen him these past weeks. He trusted the man enough to know that he was not a party to any suspicions he might be under. By the time he was done, his fellow intelligencer looked grave.

'I'd ask if you suspected anyone,' he said. 'One who holds a grudge, perhaps ... but for you and I, the question's foolish. There are men in half a dozen English counties – in Ireland too, for that matter – who'd stab me in the lights without a second thought.'

'I can't deny it either,' Marbeck replied. 'I'm only glad Gifford kept his ear to the ground at Richmond ... though I suspect it matters little in the long run. Our new King James – if indeed he becomes such – may have other plans for us. I hear he's no liking for espionage ... prefers diplomacy and negotiation.'

'And boys to women, from what I hear,' Poyns said, eying him over his cup. 'It will be a very different sort of court.'

'Yet there may be less war-mongering in the Council,' Marbeck said, 'now that the Irish struggle's over. They say James favours an early peace with Spain. And since that nation's all but bankrupt, I suspect Philip will have little objection to a treaty.'

'True enough.' Poyns glanced out of the window, then turned to Marbeck again.

'You'll have heard the whispers, that the Scottish Queen is secretly a Papist?' he asked, in a different tone.

Seeing his expression, Marbeck frowned. 'There were rumours she converted in secret, back in 1600,' he answered. 'Though James is a Protestant down to his boots...'

'Yet he's been seen with certain Scottish nobles who are of the other persuasion,' Poyns countered. 'And rumour also speaks of a softening on his part towards English Catholics...'

He trailed off. Marbeck paused, then said: 'This whiff of a conspiracy you detected, at Wisbech...'

'Indeed.' The other nodded. 'I heard talk of the Spanish Infanta – the fair lady of the Low Countries, and her Austrian husband. She does have a claim to the throne, you know.'

'Twelfth in line, through her father?' Marbeck looked sceptical. 'Not another threat of Spanish invasion – that's preposterous.'

'Unless someone were to finance it,' Poyns said. 'Someone with deep coffers – and a vested interest, of course.'

'That would be hazardous, not to say fool-hardy,' Marbeck objected. 'More immediate is the claim of Arbella Stuart, who has a stronger case. Yet having met the maid, I believe the chances of her becoming Queen are even less likely. Besides, do you truly think Elizabeth would name anyone else but her cousin James? Only weeks ago she was overheard saying who should succeed her but another monarch – meaning a king.'

'Well, I'm in agreement there,' Poyns replied. 'But thwarted hopes will always drive some to desperation ... you've said yourself Cecil fears an uprising, bringing soldiers into London...'

'He's merely planning for any eventuality,' Marbeck put in. 'You know him as well as I.'

Though conceding that with a nod, Poyns persisted. 'I told you I've been closeted among the Papists. There's an undercurrent at Wisbech – and not merely the usual kind, of fantasy and hope woven into whole cloth. Some mutter of foreign gold. I overheard no names, save one: the Earl of Charnock. Do you know him?'

Marbeck thought, but found no memory of the man. 'There's been talk of such plots before,' he said. 'A flotilla from the Spanish Netherlands, a landing in Kent or Essex ... Our people always found them to be without substance.'

'What if the Papists had support from within?' Poyns demanded. 'Small groups awaiting the command, who would band together the moment Elizabeth dies ... before James Stuart could even come south to claim his throne?'

At that Marbeck frowned again. 'Now you

contradict yourself. A moment ago you spoke of James showing signs of Papist sympathies, in which case—'

'Ah – now I've a confession to make,' Poyns interrupted, with one of his grins. 'I don't believe a word of that.'

In spite of himself, Marbeck managed a smile of his own. 'Then lay your thoughts bare, won't you?' he said. 'You may as well ... what powers do I have now, to act upon intelligence?'

'King James a Protestant down to his boots – was that your phrase?' Poyns resumed. 'Or down to his hose perhaps, which he seldom changes, I hear. The man smells bad, but we'll let that pass. No, Queen Anne's no Catholic convert – I'd wager sovereigns on it. Moreover, the two of them want a sweeter life in England than they've had in their cold little country, as well as a better future for their children. James is a wily monarch – cleverer than many realize. He's using the Papists, wooing them with promises in return for their support. He'll cast them aside once he's crowned – you may wager upon it.'

The man fell silent, and after pondering his words, Marbeck nodded. 'That sounds likely,' he agreed. 'And hence those at Wisbech are merely clutching straws.'

'Perhaps.' Poyns drained his cup and set it down. 'Yet there are some who'll see Elizabeth's death as an opportunity. And in the matter of religion, her attempts to tread the middle way made bitter enemies ... both Papists and Puritans.'

'Odd you should mention them,' Marbeck said. He gave Poyns a brief summary of his recent sojourn to Gogmagog, which unsettled the man somewhat.

'Isaac Gow is one I would fear, more than the Jesuits,' he murmured. 'They are prepared to die for their beliefs – one may even admire them for it. Yet they serve the Pope and their faith, and don't seek martyrdom for themselves. Whereas Gow...' He shook his head. 'What truly drives that man, I do not know. Some say he should be in Bedlam.'

'I think he's as sane as you or I,' Marbeck countered. 'And cleverer than most. His followers adore him – they're like a family, and he the father.' He frowned. 'Small wonder an unhappy young man like the one I went to find should seek solace in the fellow's company.'

'But what do they do here, skulking in the hills?' Poyns wondered. 'Gow was in London last year, spouting to any who would listen. He likes an audience – even craves it.'

Having no answer Marbeck remained silent, whereupon the other let out a long yawn. 'Your pardon, my friend ... I've had little sleep. I should find a chamber of my own.'

'There's no need.' Marbeck stretched himself, then stood up; he needed to walk. Glancing through the window, he was relieved to see that the rain had eased off. 'Take my bed,' he went on. 'I'll return at suppertime ... if you're asleep, I won't disturb you.'

'Then you have my heartfelt thanks.' Poyns rose too, and eyed the narrow bed gratefully. 'But if you hear any news – from Richmond I mean – you must awaken me.'

With a nod, Marbeck picked up his cloak and sword and went out. Within minutes he was walking the bank of the River Cam, pondering their conversation. It had thrown certain matters into sharp relief, one of them being the uncertain future they and other intelligencers faced. For almost fifteen years – since his recruitment at the age of eighteen in the Armada year, when Sir Francis Walsingham ran the network with ruthless efficiency – Marbeck had known no other life than serving the Crown. If that came to an end, what would he do: return to Lancashire, and live the dull life of a second son on his family's sleepy estate? The notion was as wearying as it was absurd.

He halted, gazing across the swollen stream. It was mid-afternoon, and a pair of poor scholars in threadbare gowns were walking the opposite bank, heads down in conversation. He watched them for a while, memories of his own student days welling up. Even back then, he had known he would not return home ... London beckoned, as it always would. But with Elizabeth gone, and a very different monarch in place...

Restlessly he turned away, and started for the town. Just now such speculation was pointless. He would walk off his energies, and if he were recognized, what did it matter? He would smile and bluff, as he had learned to do long ago. But as he walked – by Queens' College, then King's, then Trinity – another matter came to mind: that of Henry Scroop.

Now, he berated himself for abandoning the boy. For Celia's sake he would return to Gogmagog and try again – try harder. And having formed that resolve, he picked up his pace. Soon he had walked the length of the old city, not once but twice, threading his way through the crowds in streets and market. Finally, as twilight gathered, he arrived back at the Roebuck. Ascending to his chamber he found Poyns snoring loudly, and left him. Later he returned to the room, stretched out on the floor and wrapped himself in his cloak with a spare shirt for a pillow. As sleeping-places went he had known worse, he thought, as he drifted off into sleep ... only to wake the following morning with a start.

He sat up, looked at the bed and saw it was empty. He had slept late. Stiffly he rose, and padded to the window. The town was astir. He glanced up at grey skies; somewhere a bell was clanging. From downstairs came loud voices ... Frowning, he went to the door and opened it, just as feet pounded on the stairs. Poyns appeared, fully dressed and flushed with excitement – and at once, Marbeck knew what had happened.

'The Queen...?' He stepped aside as his fellow intelligencer hurried into the room. With a nod, Poyns delivered the news.

'She died this morning, between two and three of the clock. Already Robert Carey's riding north – he passed through St Neots a short while ago, and the word flies on the wind!'

He paused, breathless, while Marbeck stared. 'And James?'

'He is named successor after all. Elizabeth couldn't speak by the end, but she made signs. Carey carries the ring they forced from her finger, by which James will know it's true. He's already been proclaimed in London: James the First, King of England, France and Ireland.'

They were both silent. It was Thursday, the twenty-fourth of March: the last day of the reign of Elizabeth, and the first of James. It was also the eve of Lady Day – the start of the new year. The import was lost on neither of them.

'Well, it may be early but I think I need a

drink of something strong,' Poyns said at last. 'Will you come down?'

'I will,' Marbeck said.

From outside, there came the sound of cheering. Poyns went to the window and looked out. 'Fools,' he muttered. 'What do they think, that their lives will suddenly change for the better? There's another poor harvest likely to come – can the King of Scots banish the rain? Or fill our treasury's empty coffers, for that matter?' He turned to Marbeck. 'Even if, as some say, he consorts with witches,' he added with a wry look.

'And others say he thinks them charlatans,' Marbeck replied. 'You and I, however, will have to deal with base metal.'

'Indeed we shall,' Poyns said.

Sitting on the rumpled bed, Marbeck pulled on his shoes. While he did so his fellow wandered to the corner, picked up the lute and plucked a string or two.

'A fine instrument,' he said. 'Italian, is it not?'

'It is. The back is hardwood: cherry and rosewood. The face is of spruce...' Marbeck threw him a wry look. 'I suppose if nothing else, I may continue as a troubadour.'

Poyns put the instrument down. 'I'll go south, to London, I think ... though I confess I'm in no hurry. What about you?'

'I may go north,' Marbeck said. 'But first, I mean to pay Isaac Gow and his disciples another visit.'

At that, the other brightened. 'Well then, why not let me come along too?'

FIVE

They did not leave Cambridge until the afternoon, having stayed to hear the news that came in on horseback throughout the day, not all of it reliable. One report spoke of the Queen's corpse being abandoned in the presence chamber at Richmond Palace; another that people had flocked to touch it, even to tear clothing from it. Marbeck discounted such tales, knowing that Cecil and the other councillors would have moved swiftly to maintain order. Further reports appeared to have more substance. Elizabeth's body was to be taken downriver to Whitehall, and plans laid for a state funeral. Meanwhile London would prepare to receive the King, when he eventually made his progress south from Edinburgh. The Queen's kinsman Robert Carey had indeed set forth for the Scottish capital, using a relay of post-horses, and was expected to arrive soon. But for the moment, it seemed as if the whole of the nation was in a kind of limbo. The childless Elizabeth was dead, after a reign so long that few could remember any other. There was a new king, but he was far away and not yet crowned ... hence in the eyes of some, there was not even a government.

'And a vacuum like this yearns to be filled,' Edward Poyns murmured. 'This may prove to be England's most dangerous time ... even graver than the year of the Armada.'

He and Marbeck were leading their horses through the crowded street, where people had gathered since morning. As the day wore on a festival mood had arisen: bonfires were being readied, while bells seemed to be ringing out to no particular purpose. Some people were drunk, cavorting like children given an unexpected holiday. Students were about in large numbers, spilling in and out of taverns. Through it all the two intelligencers – Marbeck leading Cobb, Poyns a hired mount – moved slowly, catching bits of gossip as they went, none of it newsworthy. Finally they gained the edge of the town, mounted, and rode out as Marbeck had done the day before, towards Gogmagog.

They said little during the ride. Poyns had no other motive than curiosity, but Marbeck's purpose was plain: this time he intended to be much firmer with young Henry Scroop. He rode swiftly, letting Cobb have his head, while Poyns on his piebald jennet struggled to keep up. Finally, having followed the same track as before, they descended the valley to the old farmstead. But even as they approached Marbeck sensed that something had changed – and soon the matter became clear: the place was deserted. He knew it when he saw the empty paddock where the mules had been penned, and the absence of smoke from the chimney. In silence, he reined in before the house.

'What, have they flown the coop?' Riding up beside him, Poyns halted and looked about. 'Perhaps you scared them away.'

'I doubt that,' Marbeck said.

He glanced towards the barn: the door was open, swaying in the breeze. From the house there was no sound. After a moment he dismounted and walked to the door, found it unlocked and entered. He wandered from room to room, but there was nothing to see. Even the furniture, sparse as it was, looked forlorn. It was as if no one had lived here.

'They've been burning papers – only this morning, I'd say.'

He returned to the main room, to find Poyns kneeling by the fireplace where there was a pile of ashes. Nearby stood a basket of newly cut firewood.

'Left in a hurry, is how it looks to me,' he added, looking up. 'And I think your visit occasioned it.'

'I can't see why,' Marbeck replied. 'They have broken no laws that I know of. They consider themselves devout men...'

'Unless there's something they wish to keep secret,' the other interrupted. When Marbeck frowned, he added: 'You may accuse me of seeing a conspiracy behind every bush, if you will. But something smells wrong here.' He stood up, dusting off his hands. 'I've seen Gow preach, Marbeck. There's no fathoming a man such as he. He'd cut off his own hand to prove a point.'

Marbeck thought for a moment. 'I've a mind to pick up his trail and go after him,' he said finally. 'Whatever Gow intends, Henry Scroop shouldn't be a party to it. His mother would never forgive me if I let him get into trouble.'

'You and she are close, I take it,' Poyns observed, and received a nod in return. 'Well, I fear we must part company. I'd best go to London, see if I yet have a place in Master Secretary's service...' He glanced through a window. 'But the day draws in. I'll pass another night in Cambridge, then leave tomorrow. You?'

'I'll do the same,' Marbeck answered. 'But first I'll poke about, see if I can find anything. Shall we share a supper?'

With a nod Poyns walked to the door. Marbeck heard him ride away. Then, after a last look round the empty house, he went outside and took up Cobb's reins. Once in the saddle, he began to make a slow sweep about the farm, looking for signs of Gow's departure. The meadow grass was flattened in places, but that meant little. He made a wider sweep, and finally his efforts were rewarded. The valley lay on a rough north–south axis, and at its northern end he found what he sought: mule droppings, quite fresh, along with hoof-marks. Leaving the valley, he followed the trail as well as he could in the fading light, and found that it bent north-west, away from the hills. It suggested that Gow and his company meant to pass Cambridge to the north, perhaps crossing the river at a village higher up. In that direction lay Huntingdon, which stood on the Old North Road, the ancient highway from London to York and beyond: Gateshead, Berwick-on-Tweed, and the Scottish border.

In the gathering gloom he made his plans. There was no sense going to London; Master Secretary had shunned him, and in any case would be so occupied that Marbeck would be the least of his concerns. Whereas at Huntingdon, in the days to come, he might get news from messengers riding up and down the highway. Perhaps it would be best to head then for Scotland, as Gifford had advised. But he still wanted to find Gow and his followers, and speak once more with Henry. Having settled on his course, he rode back to Cambridge.

At supper he and Poyns ate in silence. They sat in the crowded parlour of the Roebuck, among loud-talking townsfolk. On all sides there was only one topic for gossip: the death of the Queen, and the coming of a new king. Having finished their meal, the two intelligencers spoke low.

'I've heard further news,' Poyns began. 'All eyes look north, as we'd expect. They say James will confirm members of the Privy Council in their present posts – in other words, just now Cecil reigns as if he were in the monarch's place.'

'Hasn't he always done?' Marbeck observed wryly.

'In recent years, perhaps,' Poyns allowed. 'But in James Stuart, he'll find someone less amenable than Elizabeth. They say he means to bring a great party of Scots south with him. He's laid his plans well, in expectation of succession – almost as if he were certain of it.'

'It was always believed he and Cecil were corresponding in secret,' Marbeck said. 'Indeed, our master's too shrewd not to have smoothed the way. He looks to his own future as much as to England's.'

'Then perhaps we should do the same,' Poyns murmured.

'Which means?'

'That, having mulled it over, I may not go to London after all. I think it wise to get to James before Master Secretary does. Cecil's a poor horseman ... he'd hate the thought of a long ride. Whereas you and I have a head start.'

Marbeck eyed him. 'I'd thought of going to Huntingdon,' he said. 'It straddles the north road ... and I think Gow's gone in that direction.'

'Why? To await the new King, and preach at him?' Poyns put on a sardonic look. 'Yet on reflection, going there might be a better course. Indeed, if you decide to continue as a musician, perhaps I'll join you.'

'You?' Marbeck raised an eyebrow. 'I didn't know you played an instrument.'

'I don't,' Poyns replied. 'But I have a fair singing voice – will that serve?'

So it was decided quickly. The following morning the two intelligencers left Cambridge, taking the road north-west and crossing the county border into Huntingdonshire. The distance to Huntingdon was a little over fifteen miles, and though the way was still muddy their journey was done by midday. With the church bells clanging, they rode through Godmanchester and crossed the Great Ouse by the stone bridge, entering the county town whose streets were as busy as those of Cambridge. Both men had passed through Huntingdon before, and soon got their bearings. While Poyns went to hire a room at the George Inn, Marbeck chose to look round. Taking leave of his fellow he rode upriver a short distance, at last finding himself at the great house of Hinchingbrooke, where he halted.

He could not help but admire it. Hinchingbrooke, a country mansion, looked even grander than when he had last seen it. It belonged to the wealthy Cromwell family; Queen Elizabeth had stayed here on one of her progresses, the guest of Sir Henry Cromwell. He gazed at the house, with its fine stonework and tall windows, standing in its own park. It struck him that here was a likely place for King James to stay on his eventual procession south. Indeed, all along the North Road and close to it, he guessed prominent noblemen would be readying their homes in hopes of a royal visit. Offering hospitality to the monarch and his train, though a costly business, could lead to preferment, even titles; and by all accounts the Scottish King was generous with gifts that cost him nothing to bestow. Musing on that, Marbeck turned Cobb about and made his way back to the town. Having seen the horse stabled, he entered the George and discovered Poyns in the taproom nursing a mug.

'The chamber's adequate,' he said as Marbeck approached. 'We're lucky to get it – the place is almost full. Sit – I have further news.'

With a glance round at the drinkers, Marbeck found a stool. But as he sat down, he remembered. 'I forgot to pen a letter to Lady Scroop. I must do it today—'

'I wouldn't, just yet,' Poyns interrupted. 'This news I spoke of concerns our friend Gow.' When Marbeck looked sharply at him, he added: 'There's a lad works here, who's a ready informant. He's heard talk, he says, that Isaac Gow will preach in secret to any who will hear him, this very night. The location is a wood outside the town.'

'He got here quickly,' Marbeck observed, in some surprise.

'So it would appear. My young friend does not know where Gow and his followers lodge – they're not in any of the inns, needless to say. But he's preached here before, it seems, and it will likely be at the same spot. Hence...'

'Hence, I'll have a chance to speak with Henry again,' Marbeck finished.

'I thought it would content you,' Poyns said. 'Though I won't accompany you to hear Gow prate – he makes my hackles rise.' He tipped his mug, peering into it. 'Ah, I seem to be empty...'

With a sigh, Marbeck looked round for the drawer.

But that evening, having been about the town through the afternoon, he returned to their hired chamber disappointed, to find Poyns sprawled on one of the beds.

'Gow's nowhere to be found,' he said, sinking on to the other bed. 'Your informant may not be so reliable after all. Nobody I spoke to knew of any meeting in a wood.' He sighed. 'Tomorrow I'll venture further afield, find out what I can...'

But his only reply was a grunt; Poyns was asleep.

Saturday, the last one of March, dawned grey once again. Marbeck rose early leaving his friend abed, and after a breakfast of bread and porridge ventured out to the stables. Having saddled Cobb he rode from the town, across the bridge into Godmanchester. Then on an impulse, he decided to continue south towards St Neots.

Two days ago Robert Carey had raced northwards along this highway, carrying news of the Queen's death. With luck the man might reach Edinburgh in another day, and take word to James Stuart at the palace of Holyrood. Thinking over the events, Marbeck couldn't avoid a sense of foreboding. If there were indeed people who sought to forestall the accession of the King of Scots, now was their hour. He was pondering the matter as he approached the tiny hamlet of Offord, perhaps four miles from Huntingdon. There was a horse-trough by the roadside, so he dismounted to let Cobb drink ... then he glanced across the broad river, and gave a start.

In a meadow beside a copse, a dozen mules stood in a huddle.

Instinctively Marbeck turned his back and moved behind the horse. Beyond the small herd he had glimpsed a tent, and figures moving. He seemed to have stumbled upon Gow's party, but for the moment he was unsure what to do. The notion of confronting Henry Scroop here and now seemed unwise – but he could at least keep the group under surveillance. Raising his head above Cobb's saddle, he gazed across the river again. There was no mistake: they were the same men he had seen at Gogmagog. He saw no sign of Henry, but had no doubt he was there. So, the horse having drunk his fill, he took up the reins, mounted quickly and rode back to Huntingdon.

A long day of waiting followed, and by the time evening drew in he was tense. During the day Poyns too had ventured out to gather news. Being unknown to Gow and his company, he had even ridden down to Offord and, finding them encamped where Marbeck had told him, made bold to observe them. From local villagers he had learned that Gow would preach this night near Godmanchester, so that townspeople from Huntingdon could easily attend. There was a wood to the west; people should look for torches that would light the way.

'Have you formed a strategy?' he asked

Marbeck. They were in their chamber after supper.

'Several,' Marbeck replied, 'all of which I've since discounted. I'll see how the land lies, and pick my moment.'

'And if young Master Scroop won't listen to you, what do you intend? Dragging him away by force?'

'I'll tell his mother I've done all that's in my power.'

'Well then, perhaps you require help,' the other said after a moment. When Marbeck looked up, he added: 'I'll eschew my distaste and accompany you. I'm a traveller passing through here, merely one of the curious.'

'There's no need for you to come,' Marbeck said.

'Yet I will,' came the reply. 'Having endured the dogma of dyed-in-the-wool Papists at Wisbech, hearing those who dwell at the other end of the scale might be something of a relief.'

So as dusk fell the two of them left the inn, walked through Huntingdon and crossed into Godmanchester. Here they found people making their way upriver, straggling in twos and threes. In a few minutes they were crossing a waterlogged meadow towards a dense wood – and soon, a single flame glowed ahead. It turned out to be a torch fixed to a post, beside a rough track. Several cloaked and hatted figures, both

78

men and women, were heading into the trees. Marbeck and Poyns, also cloaked, without swords but with hidden poniards, followed until another torch appeared. Finally they emerged in a clearing where a small crowd was gathering. There was a fire blazing, and beside it a stump on which, they assumed, Isaac Gow would stand to speak. For the moment he was not to be seen, though his followers were standing around. The talk was low and subdued.

Marbeck glanced about warily, keeping his distance from the fire. He wore his hat pulled low, fearing recognition after his confrontation with the company. Poyns however was at ease, wandering round with undisguised curiosity. He ignored Marbeck as if they were unacquainted. Meanwhile Marbeck worked his way across the clearing, keeping an eye out for Henry Scroop. At last he caught sight of him, standing near the fire with others of the company. In the glow, the boy's face appeared flushed with excitement. Then a hush fell as quite suddenly Gow appeared, striding purposefully as always, bareheaded and stern-faced. Quickly he mounted the tree-stump, placed feet firmly apart, and addressed his congregation.

'Brethren, I bid you welcome! In the name of the holy saints, peace to you all. And in anticipation of the rapture to come, I urge you to join the faithful in worship!'

There was a murmur, while the little crowd gathered about him. Marbeck stepped aside as people brushed past. Gow's own followers stood behind him in a tight body as if to defend him, but there was no threat. These soberly dressed townspeople, if not Puritans of the strictest kind, were at least a sympathetic audience. As they surged closer Marbeck peered over heads and saw Henry at Gow's side, face upturned eagerly ... then he stiffened, and whirled round.

There was a rustling in the trees behind him, which became running footsteps. Then came shouts, as several men crashed into the clearing wielding sticks – and in a moment, panic broke out. Cries and screams followed, as the crowd fell back in alarm. One of the interlopers charged past Marbeck, swinging a billet. Dropping to a crouch, Marbeck looked round for Poyns, but saw no sign of him. People were running in all directions ... he caught a glimpse of Gow, being hurried away by his followers. Then he too was running, towards the spot where he had last seen Henry Scroop ... until he tripped over something hard, and landed flat in the grass. Winded, he got to his knees, while figures moved crazily about him in the glow of the fire.

Then someone hit him, and the firelight became a galaxy of stars.

SIX

With confusion all about him, Marbeck struggled to clear his head. He had received a blow to the temple, but was not badly hurt. Looking round, he saw that the clearing was almost empty, the congregation having scattered into the wood. But there were shouts nearby, where several men were seemingly engaged in a scuffle. On his feet, he turned sharply as someone ran towards him, then saw it was Poyns.

'Are you hurt?'

'The boy...' Marbeck began.

'Forget him. Come away – quickly!'

He hesitated, but seeing no sign of Henry, moved off with his companion. Someone shouted after them, but they were soon in the trees and away from the firelight. Stumbling in the dark, they eventually saw a glow from a torch and headed towards it. Others were doing the same: they heard footfalls, and a woman weeping as she ran. Soon they were on the track leading out of the wood. A few minutes later, their shoes soaking wet from crossing the meadow, they reached the

Godmanchester bridge and halted.

'They were hired men,' Poyns said. 'Sent to break up the meeting...' He bent to regain his breath. 'They've taken Gow prisoner.'

'What of Henry – did you see him?' Marbeck asked.

The other shook his head. 'It was a melee. Some people got hurt, but most ran away. Gow might have done so too – his followers tried to resist, but they were scared off.'

They started walking, but as they crossed the bridge both slowed down. On the Huntingdon side there were torches, and several men standing to bar their way. At sight of them one called out.

'Come forward and show yourselves!'

Marbeck turned to Poyns. 'Can you sing *O Mistress Mine*?' he asked.

'Are you in jest?' Poyns retorted. But seeing Marbeck's expression, he gave a nod. They walked on until they found themselves facing three or four townsmen in plain garb, who looked ill at ease.

'State your names and your business.' The leader, a morose fellow, held a stave which he levelled at Marbeck.

'Richard Strang, player upon the lute,' Marbeck said. 'This is my friend ... Wisbech. We're entertainers—'

'Do you trifle with me?' The constable glowered at him. 'You've been at the meeting in the woods – you went to hear the separatist devil Gow.'

'We did,' Marbeck admitted. 'But out of curiosity ... it was an idle notion, nothing more. I thought to make a ballad of it. Let me assure you, we're not of his persuasion.'

The men exchanged glances, but their spokesman remained sceptical. 'Entertainers, you say?' He surveyed them in the torchlight. 'Where do ye lodge?'

'At the George,' Poyns replied, before Marbeck could. 'If you search our chamber you'll find my friend's lute. He's a fine player ... favoured by many of the gentry.'

'Then what do ye here, in Huntingdon?'

'I thought to call at Hinchingbrooke,' Marbeck said, silencing Poyns with a glance. 'I would present myself to Sir Henry Cromwell – he's sheriff of this county, is he not?'

At that the other men shifted their feet. 'He was,' the leader answered. 'Not any longer...' He hesitated. 'See now, I've a mind to let you go, if you're what you claim to be,' he said finally. 'Even though I—'

But he broke off as, without warning, Marbeck launched into the opening of *O Mistress Mine*. It was Feste's song from the play of *Twelfth Night*, which he had seen only the year before, at the Globe Theatre in South-wark.

O Mistress Mine, where are you roaming? he sang. *Oh stay and hear, your true love's coming* ... Whereupon Poyns joined in, in a

83

passable tenor:
That can sing both high and low,
Trip no further, pretty sweeting;
Journeys end in lovers meeting,
Every wise man's son doth know...
'Enough!'

They stopped, eyes on the constable, who looked embarrassed. His fellows, however, seemed to have enjoyed the recital. 'Let 'em pass,' one said. 'They're harmless.'

After a moment the other gave a nod. But as he moved aside, Poyns, having recovered his wits, seized the opportunity.

'That prating fellow, Gow,' he said, jerking his thumb back in the direction they had come. 'I heard he's taken prisoner – what'll become of him?'

'He'll go to the lock-up, what do you think?' the constable retorted. 'But then, it's not my warrant...' He broke off, looking past them: other people had appeared on the bridge. Without waiting Marbeck tapped Poyns on the arm and moved off.

A short while later the two of them were back in the George's taproom, where Poyns lost no time in calling for strong sack. 'It's a good thing you chose that theatre ditty,' he muttered, as they warmed themselves by the fire. 'It's one of the few songs I know.'

But Marbeck wasn't listening. Once again, he had failed with Henry Scroop. Now the boy might be anywhere, fleeing with other members of Gow's company. Though at least, he thought, if their leader was in custody he would no longer have a hold over him ... He sighed. What could he do now, search the entire county? He glanced up as Poyns nudged him, and accepted a cup.

'You remember what I said, back at that farmhouse in the hills?' his fellow said. 'That something didn't smell right?'

After a moment Marbeck nodded.

'Well, it still doesn't.' Poyns took a drink, then put his cup on the floor. 'I've rarely heard of a gathering being broken up in that way,' he went on. 'Gow may be a fanatic, but what's his offence? Why is he arrested – and on whose orders?'

'Perhaps the town fathers are edgy,' Marbeck said. 'All along the route from Edinburgh to London, it'll be the same. If word were to reach the King that they couldn't keep order in their parishes, when he travels south...'

'But that may not be for weeks,' Poyns objected. 'Though I can understand they won't want men like Gow waylaying James, presenting petitions and the like...' He broke off, pondering the matter.

'I mean to find out where they've taken Gow,' Marbeck said. 'I'll go and see him, ask him where Henry might have gone.'

Poyns frowned. 'You'll get nothing out of that man – he'd ward you off as if you were

85

Beelzebub himself.'

'Nevertheless, I must try.'

'And what if you do find the boy? Do you still have a mind to drag him back to Oxford, or to his mother?'

'Oxford,' Marbeck said. 'Before it's too late.'

'Well, tomorrow's the Sabbath...' Poyns stretched out his legs towards the fire. 'I suppose I could attend a church, tune my ears to any gossip. If there's a gaol...'

'I'll find it,' Marbeck finished.

The next morning brought disappointment, however. There was a small lock-up in Huntingdon, but Gow wasn't there. Nor, it seemed, did anyone know what had become of him. There was talk of a gathering of Separatists being disrupted, but little beyond that. The town was quiet, its people spending Sunday in their usual manner. So in early afternoon Marbeck walked alone across the bridge into Godmanchester again, to take a look round the village. And here, in a tavern near St Mary's church, he made a discovery. The Puritan Isaac Gow, it seemed, was being held in the magistrate's house on the road to St Neots, close to where Gow had originally made his encampment. He overheard this from two men talking idly by the doorway, quaffing ale between sentences. He had been about to make his way out, but stopped to speak with them.

'I too heard the man was arrested last night, masters,' he said in a casual tone. 'But why is he held there, instead of in the constable's charge?'

The men eyed him, saw he was a stranger and hesitated. 'Mayhap because he's a troublemaker,' one said finally. 'And we've no gaol here.'

'Is the house at Offord?' Marbeck enquired.

'Close by...' The man's eyes narrowed. 'Why do you ask?'

'Merely curious ... I have friends thereabouts.'

'Indeed?' The other peered at him over his mug. 'Best tell 'em to keep clear of the Lambert house, then. Gow's voice is as the serpent's, that draws folk to their doom.'

With a nod, Marbeck clapped him on the shoulder and left.

Back at the George Inn, he found Poyns absent. So without delay he buckled on his sword, went to the stable, saddled Cobb and rode out again. Within the half-hour he was approaching the hamlet of Offord, stopping by the water-trough as he had done the day before. But now there were neither mules nor tent in the meadow across the river. Pressing onwards down the highway, he drew rein at a cottage where an old man was at work in the garden. On enquiry he learned that the Lambert dwelling was south of the village, set back from the road. So after a ride of only a few minutes more, he found himself before a large, well-built house, protected by a stout fence and gate.

During his ride he had considered several cover stories, but none seemed satisfactory. Now, thinking fast, he decided on a bold approach. If Gow was being held here, he would need a strong excuse for visiting him. Having dismounted, he approached the gate and was about to lift the latch when some-one hailed him.

'Stop there ... what's your business?'

Looking towards the house, Marbeck saw the front door was open. Down the garden pathway, walking smartly, came a tall man in russet clothes. As he drew near, Marbeck saw that he too wore a sword.

'Master Lambert?' He raised his eyebrows.

'Who are you, sir?' The man looked him up and down, quickly assessing his status.

'John Sands,' Marbeck answered. 'Servant of Sir Robert Cecil. I would like to see your prisoner, if I may.'

The man blinked. 'What prisoner?'

'The separatist, Isaac Gow. I hear you're holding him. My master's had the man watched in recent times. I was one of those ordered to observe him.'

'Indeed?' The tall man eyed him. 'Then perhaps you didn't observe him closely enough. And who told you he's here?'

'It's common knowledge, in Godmanchester and Huntingdon,' Marbeck told him, giving his voice an edge. 'If you wish for discretion, perhaps you too have been somewhat lax. The meeting last night turned into a riot, from what I heard.'

The other bristled. 'What proof have I that you're Cecil's man?' he demanded. 'I haven't heard of you...'

'Nor I of you,' Marbeck said. 'I would ask on what charge you imprison Gow – and indeed, on what authority.'

'I've not admitted to holding anyone,' the other threw back. 'And I dislike your tone, Sands.'

A moment followed, before Marbeck decided to bluff. 'Very well,' he snapped. 'I'll return to London this very day, and go to Richmond where Master Secretary awaits my report. I fear it will be somewhat short, and lack the details I hoped to obtain from questioning Gow. Yet I'll not fail to describe the manner in which I was treated by you.'

With that he turned and walked to where Cobb stood, taking his time. But as he caught up the reins, he was called back. 'Come inside,' the householder said shortly. 'But I still require proof of your station.'

Calmly Marbeck drew Cobb to the fence, and gave the reins a few turns about it.

Once inside the house, he found that the

man had company. Two other men, who had apparently witnessed their exchange through a window, watched him as he entered a large, well-furnished room. Noting that these two were also armed, he turned to the one who had escorted him.

'I asked if you were Lambert,' he said, and received a curt nod.

'Daniel Lambert, gentleman and loyal servant of the King. Now, Master Sands – give me proof that you're Cecil's man.'

'His clerk, Weeks,' Marbeck said after a moment. 'He fell sick at Christmas ... another deputized for him at Whitehall. In the matter of private disbursements, that is. His name is Williamson.'

At that the other two men stiffened, and one of them took a step forward. Marbeck looked into a heavily bearded face.

'Sands?' The man wore a basket-hilt sword like Marbeck's, on which he had casually placed a hand. 'I know that name...' He frowned. 'Would you care to expose your right arm?'

Marbeck hesitated. Then he unbuttoned his doublet, took it off and rolled back his shirt sleeve to reveal the livid scar: the powder burn he had received in Flanders three years before, which had faded but would never heal.

'You got that wound escaping the Spanish, did you not?' the other went on. 'Yet your companion was not so lucky, I heard ... what was his name?'

'Moore.' Marbeck met his eye, as if daring him to continue. But instead the man nodded. 'He's who he says he is,' he said to Lambert, who let out an audible sigh of relief.

'Then it's likely you work to the same ends,' he murmured.

'Indeed?' Marbeck glanced from him to the other, before rolling his sleeve down again. All the men had relaxed somewhat. As he put his doublet back on, he took a longer look at each. The third was a subordinate, here to serve and keep his mouth closed. While the leader, he now saw, was not Lambert but the one who had recognized him for what he was: a Crown intelligencer.

'May I know your name?' he enquired.

'Rowan,' came the reply. A smile followed, to show that it was no more his real name than John Sands was Marbeck's.

'Well, Master Rowan...' As he buttoned his coat, Marbeck raised his brows. 'Is Isaac Gow here, or not? And if he is, may I speak with him?'

But it was some time before his request was granted, and by then he had learned several things. One was that Gow was indeed here under guard, and one of his companions with him. Another was that Rowan had orders to take him to London, where the man would be held at the King's pleasure. They would have left today, it transpired, had Gow not been slightly hurt in the fracas in the wood, and allowed a day in which to rest. And now Marbeck understood the words of the constable on the bridge the previous night. Those who broke up the meeting in the wood, he realized, were bullies hired by Rowan. It was he who carried the Council's warrant, about which he would say little. But in the end he gave Marbeck to understand that Gow was suspected of plotting against the Crown. And whether the man truly posed a threat or not, at this time no chances could be taken. Malcontents of every stamp and stripe, it seemed, were being rounded up and confined until the new King took the throne and made known his wishes.

'Well, now I understand,' Marbeck said. A somewhat guarded conversation had taken place around a table in the parlour. But he was relieved to find that Rowan knew nothing of his being under suspicion by Sir Robert Cecil. 'And I'll not trespass on your warrant,' he added. He hesitated, then decided that in the matter of Henry Scroop, telling the truth was best. Briefly he outlined his difficulty, describing Henry as a foolish and impressionable youth, the son of a friend who had come under Gow's influence. He wished to discover where the boy might have gone, and nothing more. In the matter of Gow's activities beyond preaching and stirring up dissent, he had no knowledge. So having made his case, he fell silent.

'There will be no coercion,' Rowan said finally. 'And I too must be present when you question him.' When Marbeck nodded, he added: 'The man's wild with talk of the day of wrath, and God's judgment on us all. Yet I think he lies as brazenly as any clapper-dudgeon.'

He glanced at Lambert, who said: 'I've no desire to hear what the fellow has to say – I merely wish to be rid of him.' He eyed Marbeck. 'My father was magistrate here before me. It's not the first time this house has held felons – even murderers. But Gow would try the patience of a saint.'

'I've observed that, Master Lambert,' Marbeck said. 'At my one meeting with him and his flock, I was told I bore the Mark of the Beast. Yet I would try him once more.'

'Then so be it,' Rowan said. He nodded towards the doorway. 'We have him in a bed-chamber – shall we go up?'

Marbeck drew a breath, and got to his feet.

SEVEN

The room was small, furnished only with straw pallets and stools. After Rowan had unlocked the door, he and Marbeck entered to find Gow and his companion seated by a window, Bibles in hand. At once Marbeck recognized the white-haired elder he had spoken with, at the farm by Gogmagog. The man gave a start as they came in: he was dishevelled, though unhurt. Gow had a bruise on one cheek and a bandage on his right hand. He remained seated, staring defiantly at the newcomers ... then recognition dawned.

'You!' He pointed at Marbeck. 'What treachery is this? You came before, bent on taking our brother from us...' His gaze flew to Rowan, who stood by the door. 'I'll not have discourse with this man!' he snapped. 'Remove him – he's steeped in wickedness...'

'Be silent,' Rowan ordered. 'It's not your place to say who comes and who goes. There are questions to be put, and it will go ill with you if you refuse to answer.'

'Go ill with me?' Gow glared at them both.

'You should fall on your knees, and prepare for the tumult to come! You hold me captive without cause ... you are as the—'

'Cease your ranting,' Rowan said irritably. Marbeck, familiar enough with such situations, remained calm. He found a stool and placed it deliberately in front of Gow.

'Where would Henry Scroop go now?' he asked, sitting close enough to make the man flinch. 'I wish to help him, and return him to his college or his family. Otherwise he will end up a fugitive. Is that what you wish?'

But Gow was recovering quickly. 'You dare to question me?' he retorted. 'You are an enemy to the faithful – I saw it when you came to Gogmagog. There's a pit prepared for you, where untold torments await! The boy saw through your wickedness – you came to corrupt an innocent youth, who has chosen the path of righteousness!'

'The matter is,' Marbeck said as if he hadn't heard, 'if I don't find him, others might. And they're likely to be far less gentle. I ask again, what do you wish?'

'By all that's holy, what devilry he spouts.'

It was Gow's companion who had spoken. Marbeck looked, and saw fear in his eyes. He glanced briefly at Rowan.

'Perhaps you should come down and take some air,' Rowan said to the older man. 'We'll leave my friend and your master...'

'No – I will not go!' the other cried. 'You

95

seek to divide us...' But he broke off as Gow laid a hand on his arm.

'Peace, Silas,' he murmured. 'They shall not part us, nor will they prevail in their cruelty.'

'I use no cruelty,' Marbeck told him. 'If you refuse to help me, I'll merely continue searching for Henry until I find him. I made a promise to his family.'

The old man lowered his eyes, clutching his Bible to his chest. But Gow threw a look of contempt at Marbeck.

'I will *not* aid you,' he said, making it plain that was his final word. From the doorway Marbeck heard Rowan sigh, but kept his eyes on Gow.

'In which case,' he replied, 'I will swear out a warrant for the arrest of all your followers still at large on a charge of sedition – or perhaps treason. The punishment is death.'

It was a bluff, and almost at once he thought better of it. He sensed Rowan's disapproval, as the man shifted his feet. But watching Gow, he saw a look of dismay flicker across his features. It was soon replaced, however, by one of rage.

'You pagan devil!' Suddenly the man leaped to his feet, startling everyone. 'You dare speak of treason? I'm a man of God, who walks a straight path!' He lifted the Bible in his bandaged hand, as if it were a weapon. 'You serve the forces of Antichrist –

the scarlet Elizabeth, who gives way to the bastard James Stuart, born of a Papist whore! Yet your days are numbered in the book of reckoning – and yours too!' He turned on Rowan, his hand shaking. 'You may do what you will – burn me or break me, you cannot prevail. Matters are in motion, as unstoppable as a tide – the tide of God's wrath!'

All at once, Gow was almost frothing. His companion plucked at his sleeve, but he shook him off. His anger, once roused, was unquenchable. Marbeck saw it, and tried at once to turn it to his use.

'Matters in motion?' he echoed, raising his brows. 'What might they be?' But there was a footfall, and Rowan came up beside him. Glancing round, Marbeck read the man's expression: these were things for him to uncover, once Gow was taken to London. Meanwhile, the man ranted on.

'You'll learn nothing here!' he cried. 'Torment is naught to us, in light of the rapture to come! Even the boy has his task appointed ... He is as the holy lamb, and will find bliss when his mission is fulfilled! Praise him, and all who serve. While you...' He pointed at each of them. 'Your time draws short. Take heed, and beg mercy of your maker. He may forgive – I do not! This land – my country – is become a fount of evil that must be cleansed! Death awaits your new master, by means none will foresee...'

Then to the surprise of all Gow gave a great gasp, bent double and fell into a fit of violent coughing. His face was dark, and sweat stood on his brow. He sank back on to his stool, even as his companion jumped up. The fit continued, Gow taking wheezing breaths between coughs, until slowly it began to subside.

With a muttered curse, Rowan went to a pitcher that stood by the wall and carried it over, along with a wooden cup. He poured water and held it out, whereupon Silas put it to Gow's lips. He drank, then waved it away.

'Why don't you leave us?' the old man said, turning to Rowan. 'Can't you see what you do – what this man suffers?'

A moment followed, in which Marbeck and Rowan exchanged glances. Then with a sigh Marbeck stood up. 'Your pardon,' he said. 'You should—'

'Go!' Silas glared at them both. 'We'll tell you nothing. We cannot in any case, for we've no knowledge of where our brethren have fled. But be assured their faith is unbroken, as is their resolve. And I know the boy will stay true. Do what you will – you have failed, as your King will fail. A thunderbolt comes, and there will be no means of escaping it!'

With that he turned his back and, pulling a kerchief from his clothing, proceeded to mop Gow's face. The two of them spoke low, as if they were alone. Rowan was already leaving, and the look on his face spoke clearly enough.

But as he went out Marbeck took a backward glance, and stiffened. Gow, his chest heaving, was looking steadily at him over his companion's shoulder. There was an odd light in his eyes, but his expression did not suggest madness; it was more like one of triumph.

In the afternoon, Poyns having returned to the inn, the two intelligencers talked in their chamber. Marbeck told his tale, which his companion heard with growing unease.

'There's some scheme afoot,' he said finally. 'I knew it ... Gow's mad enough for anything, and his fellows are bewitched by him.' He thought for a moment. 'You need to find that boy and get him away from them, or it'll end badly.'

Marbeck said nothing. What had begun as a promise to Celia to speak with her wayward son, he thought, had turned into something more serious. On his ride back to Huntingdon he had turned the matter over, and disliked what he saw. Poyns's instincts, it seemed, had been right all along.

'If those Precisians have hatched a plot, whether it be directed at the King or not, Gow will confess to it in the Marshalsea,'

Marbeck said finally. 'Even he couldn't stand up to questioning at the hands of an interrogator like Sangers...' He grimaced. 'I should be there too, if only for Henry's sake.' He looked at Poyns, who was pacing the room. 'Yet I'm out in the cold, as far as Master Secretary's concerned. How am I to move? Going to Scotland's out of the question now...'

'Is it?' Poyns broke in. 'Might it not be better for you to go there at once, and warn the King of a plot against his life? Even if it proved groundless, you could be rewarded for your service. In any case it's no idle fancy – think how many were directed at Elizabeth during her reign. She could have been murdered several times over...'

'I remember,' Marbeck said. 'But what evidence would I carry? We know nothing of when and where, or how it might be played out ... there's naught but our suspicions, and Gow's ranting.'

'The boy ... it may be mere fancy on my part, but hear me,' Poyns said. 'What if Gow means to use him – make him his instrument? It's not unknown for plotters to employ an innocent dupe ... sacrificing him like—'

'A lamb?' Marbeck gave a start. 'Gow talked of his *mission*...'

'We've heard of such practices,' Poyns went on. 'A fair youth may easily draw close to the

King, on pretence of making a speech or presenting a gift...' He frowned. 'And if Gow has it in his head that James leans towards the Papists, he may be desperate enough to attempt the worst.'

'Indeed, it fits,' Marbeck agreed with a sigh. 'Henry's green as a young shoot; loyal, dependable...'

'And *ex*pendable,' Poyns finished. He went to the window and sat, gazing out at the street below.

'I have only one course open,' Marbeck said finally. 'Riding to Scotland offers too many uncertainties. Time may pass before I even see the King – if I'm allowed near him at all. For all I know, Cecil's suspicions may have run ahead of me – I may not be believed. Besides, what could I offer but hearsay and speculation? Meanwhile Gow's followers are free to continue with their plans, at least until their master buckles under questioning. I must try to discover whatever he spills.'

He looked at his fellow, who stared back. 'I hope you're not asking me to be your ears in the Marshalsea,' Poyns said. 'This is Rowan's warrant ... he won't want me poking in.'

'I ask no such thing,' Marbeck said. 'But do you know Rowan? I never saw him before.'

'I do not. No doubt he uses other names...' Poyns shrugged. 'Master Secretary has always kept his intelligencers apart. The less we know of each other's activities, the better. Meanwhile the Toad sits upon his stool in the Strand, and keeps everything hidden beneath it.'

'Well, I've made my resolve,' Marbeck told him. 'For better or worse I ride for London tomorrow ... what of you?'

'I'll linger another day,' Poyns answered. 'Then I'll follow, and deliver my report. It's best we remain at a distance ... but if you find yourself in need, I'll speak for you. Whatever our master may think, I believe you're loyal.'

Marbeck threw him a grateful nod, then rose and began packing his belongings.

Three days later he was installed at the Boar's Head Inn, outside the city walls by Whitechapel.

The Boar's Head – a large, rowdy inn that doubled as a theatre for the Earl of Derby's players – was not one of his regular haunts. Hence, for a time at least, he was confident he could remain unrecognized. He kept the persona of Richard Strang, a musician who had come to the capital on hearing of the Queen's death. The King of Scots, it was known, enjoyed music and plays as much as Elizabeth had, and a lutenist would not be alone in seeking opportunities.

After settling in he ventured into the city,

and found it peaceful enough. The Queen's body, he learned, was lying in state at White-hall, having been brought downriver by night on a torchlit barge. The funeral would not be for some weeks, by which time the new King should have arrived. Gossip was rife on the subject of James's impending journey. It was known that Robert Carey had reached Holyrood Palace on the Satur-day night, less than three days after Eliza-beth's death: a remarkable ride that had ex-hausted the man. Now, news flew back and forth between Edinburgh and London by the day. A large number of Scottish nobles was expected to come south, the prospect of which was causing unease among the Coun-cil. Queen Anne, however, was pregnant and unable to travel. It was believed that James would make a leisurely progress through his new kingdom, stopping to meet prominent citizens and noblemen along the route. To Marbeck's ears, he sounded like a man who intended to enjoy every moment of his jour-ney.

Having judged the mood, he made a deci-sion. Early on the Wednesday evening he left the inn and walked through the city's east gate into Aldgate Street, to the church of St Andrew Undershaft. Here he watched the small congregation arriving, until at last the man he sought appeared in a doublet and old-fashioned breeches of sombre grey.

Whereupon Marbeck stood in his way, causing him to stop dead.

'Prout...' He nodded a greeting. 'Forgive my abruptness, but this was one place I knew you'd be.'

Nicholas Prout, former intelligencer and Crown messenger, gazed at him in surprise, then in consternation. 'Marbeck...' He gave a sigh. 'What in the name of heaven do you want?'

'To talk to you. There's no one else I trust enough...'

'No – save your sugared words.' Prout waved a hand. 'Your name's besmirched, do you not know it? I've heard tales...'

'No doubt – and I would like to know who spread them,' Marbeck replied. 'But answer me this: do you, in your heart, suspect me of treachery?'

The other eyed him, but made no answer.

'You've known me since I entered the Queen's service – a cocky youth who thought he knew everything,' Marbeck persisted. 'I've heard I'm denounced as a traitor. But you know me – as you know such accusations may often be made against men like me. So I ask again – do you think the charges valid, or false? Please answer me.'

A moment followed. People brushed by them, one or two greeting Prout as they went. The man's gaze strayed to the church entrance, then back to Marbeck. Finally he drew a breath and shook his grey head.

'I think them false,' he murmured. 'Indeed, I believe in his heart Master Secretary does too.'

Marbeck showed his surprise. 'I thought he had me watched,' he said. 'Even followed...' But Prout silenced him with a look of impatience.

'I won't speak with you – not here,' he said. 'If you wish, we may meet tomorrow. Though it may be to little purpose.'

'I do wish,' Marbeck answered. 'I lodge at the Boar's Head without Aldgate. But I'll attend you where you choose.'

'The Boar's Head must serve,' Prout said, with some distaste. 'I'll come tomorrow at noon.' And with that he moved off to the church. Marbeck watched him go in, then with relief turned round and walked out of the city.

Their meeting, however, started badly. The following day was wet, and Prout was late. When he arrived, hatted against the drizzle, he found Marbeck waiting, looking uneasy. His reason was that the Earl of Derby's men had arrived to hold a rehearsal on the open stage in the inn-yard. But because of the weather they had called a halt and were milling about, sheltering under the galleries and fortifying themselves with bottled ale. The strait-laced Prout, as pious a man as Marbeck knew, regarded them frostily.

'Do you have a chamber to yourself?' he asked.

'I do,' Marbeck said. 'But being short of money, I had to make concessions. I must vacate it at times. It's ... a delicate business.'

'You mean it's used by whores?' Prout snorted. 'Then where will we go?'

Marbeck looked about. He knew Prout disliked inns, indeed seldom drank anything stronger than watered ale. Then his gaze lifted towards the galleries, where spectators paid extra to sit. Eyeing the messenger, he received a nod. So the two of them climbed a staircase and sat down in the best seats, overlooking the empty stage. It was likely, Marbeck mused, that this was the only time Prout had entered a theatre.

'I'm obliged to you for coming,' he began, then stopped short as the other raised a hand.

'I cannot stay,' Prout said, pulling his hat low against the drizzle. 'But if we're trusting one another, Marbeck, you should know that Master Secretary has no knowledge of our meeting. As far as is known you left Croft House in a hurry – to the displeasure of Sir Thomas and his wife, I hear – and rode off to none knew where.' He paused. 'Does anyone else know you've returned?'

'Edward Poyns,' Marbeck answered. 'I met him in Cambridge, where he'd come from the fen country.'

At that Prout frowned. 'Did he speak of his mission?'

'He did. We talked a good deal ... he's one other, at least, who places his trust in me.'

They eyed each other, then Prout looked away. Marbeck sensed that the man was troubled, engaged in some debate within himself. Keeping expression from his face he waited, until the other turned to him again.

'Master Secretary is as taut as a wand,' he murmured. 'I never knew him so on edge ... he is terse with everyone. He sees treason behind every greeting. He keeps to Burleigh House like a fox gone to earth.'

Marbeck made no reply; he could imagine it well enough.

'Meanwhile, reports whirl about us like leaves in the autumn,' Prout went on. 'The Council meet and argue, part and whisper, then meet again, their faces full of suspicion. While England lies open to a gale, from any direction...' He sighed. 'I do not welcome the coming of the King of Scots. I've heard little that's good about the man. He will drive the people of this country apart, as the Queen tried to draw them together.'

Raising his brows, Marbeck let him know that he understood, even shared the sentiment. Never, he thought, had Prout been so open with him before. And like Lady Celia, he too seemed to have aged a good deal in a few short months.

'So when intelligence arrives, as it has of late, tainted with prejudice, even panic,' he continued, 'it's doubly hard to sift grain from chaff. Especially when some seek to report what they think our master wishes to hear. And, I've heard it said, our new King is a man's man, and not subject to the whims and caprices of the woman who ruled us until a week ago.' He lowered his gaze. 'You follow me, I think.'

'Perhaps I do,' Marbeck said, after a pause.

'Hence at times like these, loyal men may need to step back, and act as their consciences dictate. Would you not agree?'

'I suppose I would.'

Prout said nothing further. A moment went by, and an unspoken current of thought passed between them.

'Well then, I'm glad I sought you out,' Marbeck said at last. 'And how might I serve Master Secretary, without him knowing of it?'

EIGHT

That evening, in the parlour of the Boar's Head, Marbeck ate the best supper he'd had in days. He did so because Nicholas Prout had given him a small sum and bade him spend it as his needs dictated. Afterwards he returned to his chamber and waited until twilight, before buckling on sword and poniard and leaving the inn. Aldgate was still open, and he was soon passing along Fenchurch Street before turning down Mincing Lane, towards the church of St Dunstan's in the East.

As he walked the wet streets he ran over his conversation with Prout, as he had done all afternoon. Suddenly, from being almost an outcast he found himself an intelligencer again – though one without the authority of his spymaster Sir Robert Cecil. It was a role he had neither sought nor imagined, but his talk with the messenger had made something clear: just now, there were matters that must take priority. The loyal Prout, for better or worse, was calling upon men he could rely upon, without Master Secretary's knowledge. Cecil was cold and distant, pre-occupied with the King's accession; but a small circle of intelligencers, working in secret, might act independently of him. The notion excited Marbeck, though it also made him uncomfortable. Somewhat warily he halted, as Prout had instructed him, outside a small house opposite the church, on the bend of St Dunstan's Hill. The street was quiet, the place in darkness. He glanced about, then knocked in a prearranged pattern. Soon the door opened to reveal a middle-aged woman in workaday garb, who smiled in greeting.

'Master Sands?'

He was admitted, and followed her down a passage to a half-open door. But when he entered the candlelit room, he stopped in surprise. Three men rose from a table. One was Prout, another was a stranger with the look of an old soldier, but the third was a handsome young man in good clothes, wearing a wry smile: John Chyme, his informant of a fortnight ago, when the Queen was dying at Richmond. There was a brief silence, before Prout spoke.

'Here is the last of our party. He uses the name Sands, though some of us know him by another...' He turned to Chyme, who gave a nod.

'I'm glad to see you well.'

'And I you, John...' Marbeck's eyes strayed

to the other man.

'He is Llewellyn, whose house this is,' Prout went on. 'Or rather it's that of his sister, who admitted you. He will not speak, because he cannot.'

By way of explanation, Llewellyn opened his mouth. Marbeck looked, and understood. At some time in the past this man's tongue had been cut out: a harsh punishment.

'Shall we sit?' Prout looked somewhat embarrassed; he was unused to playing host. As they sat down the woman, who had disappeared after showing Marbeck in, re-entered bearing a tray with cups of wine and a dish of sweetmeats. She set it on the table, then departed again. As she went she laid a hand on Llewellyn's shoulder.

'These people have my trust,' Prout said, his eyes on Marbeck. 'Llewellyn served in France and the Low Countries – he has knowledge that's of value to us. As do you all,' he added, with a glance at Chyme. 'Along with your courage. For what I will ask you, is of grave import...' He hesitated, then: 'To come quickly to the nub of the matter, there's a scheme being set forth, that threatens England's very heart. Confronting it may tax you to your limits – even to loss of life. Hence, before we proceed, I offer you the chance to go now and take no further part. And this gathering, you will understand, never took place.'

A silence followed. Chyme merely lowered his eyes, while Marbeck glanced at the others. He saw the tension in Prout, but he sensed determination too. While Llewellyn ... he met the man's gaze, and saw plain courage; the kind that only those who have faced death and defied it would understand.

'I congratulate you, Prout,' he said at last. 'This company you have assembled may accomplish much – and I'm eager to hear more. As are we all, I think?'

Another moment passed; then Llewellyn smiled, and began passing round the cups.

The conversation that followed was long. And by the end of it, the plot Prout had spoken of filled the minds of all. It alarmed both Marbeck and John Chyme, as it had the others. The matter had come to Prout's notice via a written report from Llewellyn that, poorly spelled as it was, spoke eloquently enough. It lay before them now on the table. The man had penned it on his return from Holland after a hard campaign, and passed it to Prout as the only man he knew who might act upon it. For its implications were as momentous as could be: a scheme was in train to seize the English throne, before James Stuart was crowned King. Prout laid it forth to the intelligencers, though details were frustratingly scant. But when the name of the Earl of Charnock was mentioned, Marbeck looked up sharply.

'Poyns heard him spoken of, among the Papists at Wisbech Castle,' he said. 'He should have made report of it by now to Cecil...' But he broke off as Prout shook his head.

'Intelligencers' reports go through a new clerk just now,' he said. 'He will show it to me first, before it reaches Master Secretary. Indeed, it may not do so ... not yet, anyway.' He gave a shrug. 'Things get lost or misplaced, at times ... you understand.'

Marbeck and Chyme exchanged glances, and the latter showed his surprise. 'I never knew you to take such risks before, Prout,' he said.

'I've not found myself in this position before,' the messenger admitted. To Marbeck he said: 'Will you tell us the gist of what Poyns told you?'

He did so, though there was little to add. When he finished Prout was fingering Llewellyn's letter, squinting at the man's fearful scrawl.

'The Earl of Charnock's a hothead,' he said, laying it down again. 'An old-style Papist, who's never forgiven his countrymen for hounding the Queen of Scots. He and a few others like him burn for revenge as much as for a restoration of their faith ... and now, I believe they see their chance. The last

I heard the man was in Scotland, but I cannot be sure.'

Llewellyn made a sound in his throat, and pointed to the paper. When Prout held it out he jabbed at a passage with his forefinger.

'My friend here often passes for a deaf mute,' Prout said. 'Hence at times, he over-hears matters that men would otherwise forbear to speak of.' He looked at Marbeck, then at Chyme. 'He heard private talk in Holland of the English Regiment ... that rabble of traitors who fight for Spain against our own troops. They're abuzz with new purpose – they talk of going home, even of claiming their birthright. I think we can guess what that means: a full-blown Papist rising at last. And to my mind, we may guess at the woman they propose as England's new Queen.'

'The Spanish Infanta,' Marbeck said at once. When the others turned to him he added: 'I was contemptuous of the notion, when Poyns spoke of it in Cambridge. Even when he voiced the suspicion that someone might finance such a scheme. Yet from what Llewellyn has heard, I may have dismissed it too readily...' He frowned. 'Perhaps someone needs to go to Holland and infiltrate the traitors' regiment; someone with knowledge of the country.'

He fell silent, for he was the obvious per-son for such a mission. Both he and Prout knew it, though the thought of returning to that war-torn land filled Marbeck with dismay. But instead Prout shook his head.

'That should not be necessary.'

The intelligencers eyed him, sensing further revelations. Llewellyn was nodding, and again he pointed to the report.

'There's a name here that's not unfamiliar to me,' Prout added, after a moment. 'Mayhap you know it – William Drax?'

Marbeck raised his brows. 'Drax ... the one they used to call the Basilisk?'

'I've heard of the man,' Chyme said with a frown. 'As wily a rogue as ever drew sword. He was once tried as a traitor, but walked free.'

'That he did,' Prout agreed. 'It was said he had help from important men ... nobles for whom he'd done private service. He's a man for hire, without scruples.' He paused, then added: 'And he's here, raising an army in Kent.'

There was a sudden silence.

'A small army perhaps,' Prout went on. 'Billeted in villages and outlying farms, so as not to arouse too much attention. Well armed and well fed, and within a short march of Dover...' He gave a shrug. 'Do I need to say more?'

Chyme was aghast. 'But surely Master Secretary is aware of these activities, right under his nose? He could not – he *would* not, ignore

115

such reports...'

'Providing they've reached him,' Marbeck broke in. A picture was forming that troubled him. 'If this army you speak of is well organized enough to maintain secrecy – and moreover, to have intelligence of its own...'

'Indeed,' Prout nodded. 'It's the reason we're here.'

Each man was silent, as the import of his words sank in. Suddenly it seemed that England was indeed in peril – not merely from without, but from within too. Marbeck threw a look of approval at Llewellyn. 'Our nation might have cause to be grateful to you one day, my friend,' he said quietly.

Llewellyn made more signs, the meaning of which was unclear. But Prout nodded and said: 'There's a mission for you, Marbeck – not in the Low Countries, but a mere sixty miles away: to attach yourself to Drax's force. Llewellyn can offer his services as a mercenary soldier for hire, pretending only greed as his motive. But if he were accompanied by one who could move among officers as well as men...' He trailed off, whereupon Marbeck gave a nod.

'Then what part do I play?' Chyme spoke sharply. 'I'm as eager to know what Drax and his rabble are up to as you are—'

'I know.' Prout turned to him. 'But I need a courtier. One who may mingle with the Council, as I cannot. One who will—'

'Hang about Whitehall with the gossips?' Chyme retorted. 'The notion appals me. My lord has no need of me just now – I may as well ride north towards Scotland, to fawn upon our new King as others do. Indeed,' he added, as a thought struck him, 'could I not take word to him of this treason, so he may send troops to meet it?'

'He has none to speak of,' Prout countered. 'The Scottish King's no military man. He's spent the pension Elizabeth allowed him on his court, and his pleasures. Besides he's yet in Edinburgh, and will not ride south for days. When he does set forth it will be a slow journey. I doubt he'll arrive before the Queen's funeral is over, by which time—'

'It may be too late,' Marbeck finished. But he sympathized with Chyme; the young man was loyal and eager to serve. To Prout he said: 'There's merit in what John says. We have troops here in London, do we not, for this very eventuality? They could move down to Kent – Drax's army would scatter.'

'That's what I fear Master Secretary will say, once he learns of it,' Prout replied with some impatience. 'But that may be what they want him to do. Once our troops are drawn away from London a landing may take place elsewhere, at any of half a dozen ports. Drax and whoever he's bound up with – even Charnock, perhaps – will have made plans

117

for any counter-move. We've no time to explore all possibilities – my way is the only one, I'm sure of it.'

'But what way is that?' Marbeck asked. 'After Llewellyn and I have joined the rebels in Kent, how do you expect us to thwart them? Two of us against an army...' But he broke off. A grim smile had appeared on Prout's face.

'The money,' he said phlegmatically.

Marbeck frowned. 'You mean locate the source of their funds, and stop it?'

The messenger nodded. 'Once Drax's troops find out they're not getting paid, they'll down weapons and desert within the hour. And if word got to the English Regiment, the same would happen there.'

He glanced at Chyme, who also saw the logic. Indeed, it was so simple any man could have guessed it.

'It's the only way,' Prout said again. 'The same purse, I believe, provides for both the English Regiment and the raising of Drax's force: their aim to restore this country to the Catholic faith.'

'Well – one thing you may wager on: the source of this mysterious wealth isn't Spain,' Marbeck said after a moment. 'The country's broken, ravaged with plague and tired of war. King Philip looks to make peace with James. Nor will ducats be flowing out of Rome ... Pope Clement is as cautious as he's

118

parsimonious. We must look closer to home.'

'My thoughts too,' Prout said. 'There are several rich men I might suspect, but I have no proof. This scheme has been in the planning for months, I fear – perhaps longer. It's a pity Master Secretary did not weave the shreds of intelligence together sooner, meagre as they were.'

Nobody spoke for a while. Then, taking the opportunity, Marbeck at last aired the other matter that weighed upon him. 'We may face a Papist rising,' he said. 'And I'll do my part in contending it. But though I've no wish to add to your troubles, Prout, I fear I must. For it's just possible that England faces another threat – from the opposite direction.'

At once all eyes were on him. 'What do you mean?' Prout asked sharply. Whereupon Marbeck drew a breath, and gave a quick account of his activities since leaving for Oxford, just two days before the Queen's death. He said little about Celia, leaving the other men to draw their own conclusions. But when he spoke of interrogating Isaac Gow in Daniel Lambert's house at Offord, Prout sprang up.

'Why did you not speak of this sooner?' he demanded.

'I would have,' Marbeck said, in some surprise. 'Yet since the matter you've set before us is so grave—'

'But I could have told you more,' Prout interrupted, in some agitation. 'Isaac Gow has not been brought to London for interrogation. He never got here – he escaped!'

'Escaped?' Marbeck echoed. 'How? He was under armed guard – besides, he's a sick man...'

'Is he?' Prout grimaced. 'According to the account I've seen, he feigned a coughing fit at a roadside inn near Hitchin, then disappeared through a back door. Some of his followers must have dogged the party – they had mounts waiting, and made their escape. It was near dark – by the time the escort had chased after them, they'd got clear away.'

'Then what of Rowan?' Marbeck asked, with growing unease. 'He seemed to know his business...'

'Rowan's in disgrace,' Prout snapped. 'He sent in a report two days ago, then disappeared. I believe he's gone looking for Gow in an attempt to make amends. But for the present, you may assume your Puritan friend is still at large...' He frowned at Marbeck. 'Is that the real reason you returned to London? To hear Gow's confession, so you could hurry off again to rescue this foolish boy Scroop – the son of your paramour?'

There was silence, before Marbeck too got to his feet. 'And if it was, will you condemn me for it?' he demanded. 'I had little else to occupy me just then, being shut out of Master Secretary's service – or have you forgotten?'

They eyed each other: the pious Crown servant, and the intelligencer whose behaviour had always been a source of friction between them. Then Llewellyn gave a grunt, causing them both to look his way. The man raised both hands, urging calm: this was his home, he seemed to say, and he wished no imbroglio. Whereupon Prout gave a sigh, and sat down heavily.

'By all that's holy,' he muttered.

After a moment Marbeck too sat. 'If our positions had been reversed, Prout,' he said, 'I don't believe you would have acted differently.' When the other made no answer, he looked across the table. 'I ask your pardon, Llewellyn.'

The man nodded, but suddenly John Chyme spoke up. '*Now* there's something I can do,' he said. When the others turned, he added: 'You must go to Kent, Marbeck. I'll admit I'm not suited to such a mission, whereas you and Llewellyn may achieve much. But if there's indeed a crack-brained plot being hatched by Gow and his flock, I may make progress among them. The man doesn't know me, but I've known enough people of his ilk. I'll find them, see if I can attach myself to their little band.' He grinned, apparently warming to his idea. 'As soon as I hear a whisper about Henry

Scroop, I'll be on his neck. If necessary I'll return him to Oxford tied across my saddle. As a Magdalene man, I've small patience with students of Exeter.'

Having said his piece, Chyme sat back and took a gulp of wine. The others eyed him, then Llewellyn too broke into a smile. Prout looked glum, but Marbeck breathed a sigh.

'Once again, John, you have my thanks,' he said. 'And if you can succeed where I failed, you will earn my gratitude, and that of the boy's mother, for all eternity.'

Embarrassed, the young man dismissed the compliment. But when he looked at Prout his face fell somewhat. Marbeck too eyed him, expecting some further rebuke. But finally the messenger sighed, and managed a nod.

'So be it,' he said tiredly. 'Chyme may ride north and mingle with Precisians, while you two...' He looked from Marbeck to Llewellyn. 'You should go into Kent, and swear loyalty to the Infanta. That way the threat to England from two poles of hatred may at least be exposed, if not broken...' He shook his head. 'Great heaven, what times are these? I can only pray that one day, if it pleases God to let him live to be crowned, King James will learn what was done. Meanwhile I will attend Master Secretary, and sift reports, and wait.' Then to the surprise of the other men, Prout looked round with an expression that was unlike him.

'You go with my blessing, and my desire to see you all alive to witness that day,' he added quietly. 'I speak of the coronation: the end of the dynasty that's ruled England for over a century, and the start of another.'

With that he too drank, and pledged God speed to them all.

Two days later, on another grey morning, Marbeck led Cobb across London Bridge, then waited in Long Southwark until Llewellyn appeared leading an old chestnut warhorse. The two men shook hands, climbed into their saddles and urged their mounts southwards, away from the smoke and haze of London. Soon they were at Blackheath, turning towards Dartford: the first stage in their journey into rural Kent.

Llewellyn wore a battered helmet and a battle-scarred coat; fixed to his saddle were a sword and a Spanish caliver in a closed scabbard. Marbeck wore a padded doublet and tooled leather jerkin, along with his basket-hilt rapier. He also had a pistol, and certain other weapons that looked nothing of the sort: a tailor's bodkin in his pocket, and a lute string sewn into his waistband.

NINE

The main camp of Drax's small army, according to the scant intelligence Prout had pieced together, was said to be near the hamlet of Ewell, on the river Dour a few miles above Dover. This, however, turned out to be untrue. On arriving there that evening after their day-long ride, Marbeck and Llewellyn found only half a dozen men warming themselves round a fire, who claimed to be local villagers. Their leader was suspicious, although one look at Llewellyn was enough to convince anyone that he was an old soldier. Marbeck however, was obliged to work harder. He was Jack Duggan, he said, who had served in Ireland with Henry Bagenal. In fact he'd been a horseman at the Battle of the Yellow Ford, when that commander had lost his life. Now that the war was ended, he found himself at a loose end. But he'd heard from an old compatriot that officers were in need here, and that the pay was good. Would the corporal ... he was a corporal, was he not? Would he send them on to the commander?

Fortunately it worked. After some further questioning, Marbeck's performance convinced the man he was a mercenary, as hard-nosed as they came. The two of them should ride on, they were told, to the ruined abbey of St Radigund, on a hill three miles west of Dover. They should seek out a lieutenant named Follett, who could answer their questions. But it grew dark – did they wish to rest for the night? Marbeck declined, saying they would travel in what twilight remained. Without further delay he and Llewellyn rode to a ford in the river, and having crossed over, soon found St Radigund's. Leading their tired horses, the two of them approached the old abbey, its jagged ruins showing stark against the sky. Here they were challenged by a sentry, sword in hand. Once Marbeck had made his explanations, however, they were directed to a camp on the fringe of a nearby wood, where they would find the lieutenant. So at last they reached a cooking fire, with perhaps a dozen men seated around it. As they emerged from the gloom some got to their feet, whereupon Marbeck raised a hand.

'We seek Lieutenant Follett. Is he here?'

A man stepped into the firelight. 'He is ... Who are you?'

'Two gamesters, looking for a game,' Marbeck answered. 'We heard there might be one here ... Are we welcome?'

There was silence as Follett came forward. He was young and belligerent, wearing a good corselet and sword. Indeed all the men, Marbeck saw, were well fitted out; it was no rag-tag company. At his side, Llewellyn regarded them without expression. His and Marbeck's eyes met briefly, but when they faced the lieutenant again his words came as a disappointment.

'You were misinformed,' he said, looking Marbeck up and down. 'I'm holding a muster here, gathering levies for the King. I'm not recruiting strangers.'

'No?' Marbeck looked sceptical. 'You've no need of veterans, then?'

The young man paused, gazing at each of them. Finally he pointed at Llewellyn. 'Where did you serve?'

'Garth can neither hear nor speak,' Marbeck said, using Llewellyn's assumed name. 'He has no tongue, and was deafened by cannon-fire. He served in the Low Countries under Bostock.'

One or two men stirred at mention of the former leader of the renegade regiment. But Follett kept his eyes on Llewellyn, who met the gaze unflinchingly. Finally he looked to Marbeck.

'I was in Ireland,' Marbeck said. 'One of the lucky ones, who came through Yellow Ford alive...' But he broke off when the other turned and spoke over his shoulder.

126

'Robbins – over here.'

Another man, who had remained seated, got up and came to stand at the lieutenant's side. 'You were in Ireland,' Follett snapped. 'Why don't you ask him a few questions?'

Robbins, a fighting man down to his boots, gave a nod. 'So you were at Yellow Ford,' he said to Marbeck. 'That would be September, 1598...'

'August,' Marbeck corrected. 'The fourteenth, to be exact.' He gave the man a hard stare, and waited.

'Who was your commander?'

'Bagenal, of course,' Marbeck answered tartly. 'I was an officer of horse ... and I'd watch your tongue if I were you, fellow.' The soldier stiffened, but with a nod Follett bade him continue.

'So ... were you close to Bagenal when he fell?' he asked.

'Too close,' Marbeck replied. 'I saw him shot through the head. He was too far forward – he would never heed advice.'

'And who took command after that?'

'Thomas Maria Wingfield ... not that it did much good.' Marbeck gave a snort. 'And before you ask, in the rout that followed I changed sides, as others did. Thereafter I fought for the rebels under Red Hugh O'-Donnell.' Deliberately he faced Follett, who looked surprised. 'There now, Lieutenant,' he added. 'I've given you reason to have me arrested and hanged as a traitor, if you wish. My name's Duggan – do you require any further testimony from me?'

All eyes were upon him. Taken aback, Robbins lowered his gaze, but the lieutenant was frowning. 'Who told you where to come?' he asked.

'A compatriot,' Marbeck said. 'I'll not give his name. But he spoke of good pay and victuals, for men who were prepared to earn them. Men who asked no questions, but looked to a new future – perhaps not a Scottish one. Do I hit the target?'

Another silence followed, though it was short-lived. Follett dismissed Robbins, who rejoined his comrades. When he eyed Marbeck again, he wore a different expression.

'You may rest here tonight,' he said finally. 'Eat, and see your horses fed. Tomorrow I'll send you to the colonel, who will question you further. If you are who you claim to be, he might find a place for you. But if you are not...' He paused for emphasis. 'If you are not he will know, and the consequences will be grave. Do you follow?'

Instead of answering, Marbeck turned to Llewellyn and made signs, to which the old soldier nodded. The first part was over: they were all but accepted. The meeting with the colonel, however, promised a more stringent test, and Marbeck knew he must convince. Facing the young officer again, he expressed agreement. The other men relaxed, turned away and began talking. One came forward to show the newcomers where to take their horses. But as he led Cobb away, Marbeck's thoughts already raced towards the morrow. He had a good idea of the name of Follett's colonel; he could only hope that the man did not know who he was.

The next day was the Sabbath, which Marbeck had almost forgotten. Hence his surprise, when he awoke under canvas to the sound of men singing. The words of the hymn were familiar, and he sat up to listen. It struck him as odd that this mercenary army should bother to hold a service. But rebels or not, they were Englishmen, as far as he had observed; and old habits died hard. He stretched and looked round. He was in a circular tent, patched but serviceable. There were several pallets, spread out on ground still damp from the rains. All were empty save the one beside him, where Llewellyn dozed. After waking him he dressed quickly and went outside – only to stop in his tracks.

Two soldiers with calivers stood facing him. As he stared, a sergeant appeared with a sword, which he levelled at Marbeck.

'Up at last ... I was coming to get you,' he said. 'Bring your friend out – you're both to come with me.'

They went unarmed, having been obliged

to leave their weapons behind. Llewellyn was stolid, Marbeck tense but composed. In the morning light, they saw that the camp was small: no more than eight or nine tents on the edge of the wood, half-hidden among the trees. They passed a fire where a steaming cauldron of porridge hung on chains. Men gazed at them; there was no sign of Follett. Finally they reached a larger tent, in front of which stood a folding table. As they appeared, a man seated behind it looked up. He was black-bearded and heavy-browed, wearing a Brigandine coat of steel plates riveted onto canvas. His eyes took in Llewellyn, then went to Marbeck. Suddenly, they were prisoners ... and in no doubt whom they faced: William Drax himself.

'So you're Duggan,' he said. 'Is it your real name?'

'It is now,' Marbeck said.

'Sir!' the sergeant snapped at him, from behind. 'You're addressing the colonel.'

A moment followed, then to Marbeck's surprise Drax waved the sergeant away. Along with his escort he departed, leaving the two intelligencers alone. Between them, Marbeck thought fleetingly, they could have seized the colonel and taken him hostage, or worse. He was short, with a head too large for his body. But his face was a hard mask, the eyes pitiless. Marbeck recalled the man's nickname: the Basilisk. He had faced brutal killers before, and saw that Drax had no use for mercy.

'I've heard your history from the lieutenant,' he said. His eyes went to Llewellyn. 'He is a deaf mute, then?'

'He understands some of what's said, if you face him,' Marbeck replied. 'He watches how your mouth moves.' He did not look at the old soldier; Llewellyn knew his part.

Drax spoke loudly. 'So you lost your tongue ... Can I see?'

Llewellyn stepped forward, bent and opened his mouth. With grunts and signs, he made it known that the punishment had been inflicted long ago, in prison. After a moment Drax nodded and gestured him aside. 'Whereas you, sir...' He eyed Marbeck. 'You served under Bagenal, or so you claim, when the fool lost his life. What were his losses that day, would you say?'

'Nine hundred dead,' Marbeck answered. 'Not that I stayed to count them – sir.'

'No – you were too busy saving your own neck,' the other said dryly. 'So after turning tail you fought under O'Donnell – is that so?'

Briefly, Marbeck nodded.

'What sort of commander was he?'

'Good. His men loved him – they'd have followed him through the gates of hell.'

'Well, many of them went there anyway, did they not?' Drax watched Marbeck closely. 'I mean three years later, at Kinsale – were you there?'

'I was not.' Marbeck remained calm, but in his mind he was sifting everything he knew about the Irish war. The man strove to trick him; his life, and that of Llewellyn, depended on the answers he gave.

'What a day that was, eh?' Suddenly Drax smiled, but his teeth showed. 'We paid the Irish back in 1601 ... lost three thousand, if they lost a man. A Christmas Day gift.'

'I believe our ... I mean the Irish losses were nearer twelve hundred,' Marbeck said mildly. 'On Christmas Eve that was, not Christmas Day. O'Donnell escaped to Spain afterwards. They treated him as a hero.'

'I know that,' Drax snapped, as if angered by his argument. 'He's still in exile, I suppose?'

'No, he returned to Ireland,' Marbeck told him. 'Died last year, and is buried at Simancas Castle.'

There was a moment, in which Llewellyn's stomach could be heard rumbling with hunger. Rigidly he stared ahead, whereupon as suddenly as it had appeared, Drax's anger vanished.

'Mayhap you did know him,' he said finally. 'A soldier never forgets a good leader, and even an illiterate rebel may command respect in the field. I'll admit he fought well for a man of his advanced years – wouldn't you?'

For a second, Marbeck was almost fooled: his instinct had been to agree, and bow his head in feigned remembrance. He had all but exhausted his knowledge of Hugh O'-Donnell, the clan leader – apart from one fact, which now saved him.

'Advanced years?' he echoed. 'You're mistaken, sir. He was little more than a boy: thrown into prison at fifteen, taking the battlefield as a youth. He was barely thirty when he died...'

He trailed off. Beside him Llewellyn stirred, as Drax stood up behind his table. He glanced at each of them, then to the relief of both said: 'If you join me, you'll sign a paper and swear allegiance.'

As one man, they nodded.

'Nor may you turn tail, if things go badly,' he added briskly. 'My officers have orders to shoot deserters...' He eyed Marbeck. 'You will do the same; in other words, you would be obliged to shoot your friend here – not to wound but to kill. Is that clear?'

'Of course,' Marbeck said. On impulse he added: 'I don't have friends. Garth's one who travelled with me ... nothing more. It's best he and I now part, and he's posted elsewhere.'

Drax seemed to approve. 'We'll find a place for him,' he said. 'You, Duggan, will remain here. You'll dine with the other officers tonight, and receive your orders. In

133

the meantime, you may both go and take breakfast.'

With that he sat down, drew a paper towards him and ignored them. In silence they turned to walk back towards the cooking fire, and the aroma of hot porridge.

And after that, the day went somewhat better. For later the same morning, while grooming Cobb, Marbeck made a discovery: in Drax's army, a soldier told him, the Sabbath was welcomed for other reasons than those of religion. It was also payday.

The paymaster was named Thomas Burridge. He was bald and moon-faced, with the look of a harassed clerk. He arrived with an armed guard at midday, and set up his station at the table outside Drax's tent. There the entire company assembled, numbering perhaps forty men. Others, Marbeck knew, were scattered about the area in smaller camps, but he asked no questions; for the present he would watch and listen. He stood aside as soldiers were called – by names that, he was certain, were all as false as his and Llewellyn's – to receive their pay from a small iron-bound chest. He soon discovered that the daily wage was one shilling and sixpence: a generous sum. What the officers received he could not guess.

The last soldier to be paid was Llewellyn, the newest recruit. Skilfully feigning deafness, he waited until he was waved forward. Men watched as he took the coins, then walked off without looking at Marbeck. Soon all the men dispersed leaving only the stout sergeant, Marbeck's escort from earlier, and the officers: Lieutenant Follett, a beanpole of a man known as Captain Feaver, and Drax himself. Then to his surprise Marbeck heard his own name called, so unhurriedly he walked over. The other leaders eyed him coolly, especially Drax. For a moment Marbeck feared the man was having second thoughts about hiring him, until he said: 'Your pay will come later, Duggan. You've yet to prove yourself to me.'

Concealing his relief, Marbeck gave a nod.

'So you're a seasoned horseman, sir...' Feaver peered down his long nose at him. 'We must decide how best to use you. You'll answer to me, by the way.'

Politely Marbeck acknowledged his place. Questions rose in his mind, but were held back. Follett was looking tense, he thought; perhaps relations among the commanders were less than cordial. The impression was reinforced when Drax suddenly turned on his heel, strode past the paymaster and entered his tent without a backward glance. Marbeck was about to move away, when Burridge spoke up from his table.

'Is there a dinner for me?' he asked in a high-pitched voice. 'I have a busy afternoon ahead.'

'Of course...' Feaver waved a hand vaguely. 'See the quartermaster.' He turned to go, but the paymaster stayed him.

'I require a bigger escort,' he went on, squinting through a pair of thick spectacles. 'I've come to dislike these woods ... two men hardly seems enough, in view of what I carry.' He tapped the pay chest, which was now locked.

In some irritation Feaver looked to Follett. 'You'll see to that, won't you?'

The lieutenant sighed, and waited for him to walk off. To Burridge he said: 'I'll have men waiting, after you've dined. Then you should make haste ... the paths are muddy.'

'I'm aware of that,' Burridge retorted. 'Yet I made good speed this morning from Dover...' but he broke off, as Follett threw him a warning look. Marbeck pretended not to notice, though he understood: he, of course, was not trusted. He wondered, in view of the purpose of this regiment, whether anyone here trusted his fellow. With a glance at the other men he walked away, thinking fast. Burridge had come up from Dover: that suggested the pay chest was not carried overland, as he had thought it might be, but arrived by ship. Head down, he strolled towards the commissary tent where men were assembling for their midday mess, then gave a start as someone blocked his way. It was Llewellyn.

'Have they put you in a file?' Marbeck asked, drawing close. The other jerked his head, towards a tent at the far end of the encampment. By now Marbeck had been told that he would share quarters with Captain Feaver; perhaps that worthy had been instructed to keep an eye on him.

'The money comes in through Dover.' Marbeck lowered his voice, and Llewellyn bent to listen. 'I'll try and find out where from.'

Llewellyn patted his jerkin. They had agreed on the journey that he would write down anything of importance on a scrap of paper, and leave it at an arranged spot; to this purpose he kept an inkhorn in his baggage. Marbeck nodded quickly.

'At the end of the picket rope, where the horses are tethered, is a log of beech,' he said. 'Hide any missive under it – I'll pass there every few hours.'

After signalling agreement, Llewellyn suddenly gripped his sleeve. Marbeck followed his gaze and stiffened: Drax had emerged from his tent, and was gazing across the camp towards them. Without a second thought, he acted.

'See – you must look to yourself now, Garth,' he said loudly. And with an angry movement, he tore his arm from Llewellyn's grip and faced him. 'I've helped you all I will

– follow orders, and leave me be!' And with that he stalked off.

Alone in the middle of the camp, he drew breath. Somehow he must discover the route by which Burridge arrived each week, before he travelled to the various billets to distribute money. And, he surmised, there were likely other payments made to the commanders, for perishables and equipment. He had already seen that the horses were well supplied with fodder, along with a farrier to look after them. He had also noted an old barn on the path that led to St Radigund, which seemed to be guarded day and night: likely a store for powder and arms. There was an unspoken sense of purpose in the company, if not of haste. How long they would remain here before being called upon to take part in the planned landing of the Spanish Infanta, he did not know.

But that very evening, at supper, he found out; and the news forced him into action.

TEN

The officers dined in some comfort, around a table under an awning, sheltered from the night breeze and waited on by Drax's own servants. The food was good: broth, fish brought fresh from the coast, and loin of pork. During the meal there was little conversation, but as soon as he had finished eating Drax turned his attention to Marbeck.

'You've pledged allegiance, Duggan,' he said, eyeing him from under his heavy brows. 'And you may now share our confidence. For you will be called upon sooner than you think.'

The others – Feaver and Follett – were silent. Marbeck inclined his head.

'Our total strength is two hundred,' Drax went on. 'Mostly pikemen, with forty harquebusiers – eight ranks of five. They're capable of maintaining continuous fire, rank by rank. Not that we expect to engage in a pitched battle – but I think you know that already.' He paused, then: 'Indeed, perhaps you should tell us what it is you think we're doing here.'

Inwardly Marbeck tensed. All three men were watching him: it was a further test. Unhurriedly he wiped his mouth with a napkin, then leaned forward.

'I believe you're preparing to welcome a certain noblewoman to our shores,' he said, speaking low. 'To provide an escort, and see her safely to London. Is that so?'

'If it is so, would you be content to see that lady become our Queen?' Drax asked at once.

Marbeck raised his brows. 'Quite content, sir. Especially as she has a rightful claim to the throne, as I understand it. And especially if – as I've been given to expect – the rewards for those who help bring about a coronation should prove generous.' He hesitated, then in an embarrassed tone added: 'Must I lay my cards before you? I have certain debts, which prove difficult to discharge. There's also a small manor in the north that would provide a good living for a man of modest needs like myself...'

He trailed off. A short silence followed, before Feaver gave a snort of laughter. The man had already drunk freely of the table wine, and now lifted his cup. 'Capital!' he said. 'And is the hunting good, on this small manor in the north?'

'I hear it's excellent,' Marbeck told him.

Drax shifted on his stool, but appeared

satisfied. He glanced at Follett, who said: 'All who do their part will be rewarded. But to begin with we face a storm – many of our countrymen may rise against us. Could you stand alongside Italians and Hollanders, even Spaniards, and fight loyal Englishmen to the death?'

'If they come against me, they must take the consequences,' Marbeck said coolly. 'I've fought foes of every stamp. And it's a matter of no import to me who wears the crown, so long as I may live in comfort befitting a gentleman.'

To that Follett said nothing, while Feaver seemed to be warming to his fellow officer. 'Capital,' he said again. But when he turned to Drax and saw him frown, he lowered his gaze.

'To return to matters in hand,' the colonel snapped, 'we have scant opportunity to exercise our forces here. Secrecy has been our watchword ... but then, the men we've recruited need little instruction. People hereabouts have been paid for their silence. Those who looked as if they might prove difficult...' He eyed Marbeck grimly. 'They're no longer a threat. The way is paved for us to march to the port and form a bridgehead when the lady's ship arrives. Thereafter we will deploy in a column – a protective force about her and her train – and make at once for London. Do you have questions?'

'I assume there are other forces arriving from elsewhere,' Marbeck said, after a moment. 'Will they rendezvous along the way, or advance separately upon the capital?'

'It behoves you not to know that,' Drax answered. 'You will be in the rearguard, to deal with any possible pursuit.'

'How many foot, and how many horse?' Marbeck threw back.

'Pikemen and harquebusiers on foot, officers and a few others horsed. A large number of mounts would have drawn attention.'

'Arms and armour...' Marbeck began, whereupon Feaver spoke up.

'There's a stout corselet and helm for every man. Swords where needed, round shields and plenty of powder and ball. Dog-lock carbines, and good store of wheel-lock pistols.'

Marbeck showed surprise; that much weaponry would have incurred considerable expense. 'You are well furnished, sir,' he said.

'Nothing's been left to chance,' Drax replied. 'I need not tell you that your life and mine, and that of every man in this undertaking, depend upon it.'

'The port...' Marbeck began, emboldened by being given more information than he had expected. 'Do we speak of Dover, or...'

'Does it matter?'

It was Follett, eyeing him keenly; the man was suspicious of him still. Marbeck shook his head. 'Of course not. When the order is given, whatever the destination I will be ready.'

The others said nothing further, and the discussion appeared to be over. Feaver drained his cup and spoke of going to his tent. Marbeck said he would take the air before retiring. But before he could rise, Drax held up a hand.

'The man you arrived with – Garth,' he said. 'Where did you find him?'

'An old comrade sent him to me, in London,' Marbeck answered in a casual tone. 'He was down on his luck ... I'm assured he's a bold fighter.' When Drax said nothing, he added: 'Will you post him to another camp, or...?'

'I think not.' The other fixed him with a cold stare. 'I think it best he remains here, where I can keep an eye on him. Do you object?'

'Object, sir – why should I?' Marbeck returned the man's gaze. 'If I were in your position, I would do the same.'

'Very well...' Drax looked round at the others. There was a moment, in which Marbeck sensed that a decision had been made; then abruptly the commander delivered his news.

'We leave here on the evening of the tenth of April.'

Marbeck's heart thudded. Glancing at

Feaver and Follett, he found both men eyeing him again. 'One week,' he said, with a nod. 'Then I seem to have arrived just in time.'

Whereupon he rose, and gave them good-night.

In the night, while Feaver snored nearby, he lay awake on his pallet and turned the matter about.

His choices were stark. He might desert, ride to London as fast as he could and sound the alarm, provided he could evade any pursuit. But that, he knew, would prevent neither the arrival of the Infanta Isabella nor her march upon the capital. And when the other force arrived from the Low Countries, England would be plunged at once into what could quickly become a civil war. The plan decided upon at Llewellyn's house – that of sabotaging Drax's army by removing their source of income – still seemed the best. But a week was an alarmingly short time.

He stretched out on his back, drew a long breath and examined the facts. During the afternoon he had done some rough mental arithmetic. Two hundred men at a shilling and a half per day, plus the higher pay the officers would receive, together with food, fodder and other disbursements, suggested a weekly expense of at least six hundred crowns merely to maintain the army. They had been here for weeks, hence thousands had already been spent. *Someone with deep coffers ...* Poyns's words came back to him. Whoever was financing the enterprise risked a good deal – but then the rewards, if the plan succeeded, would no doubt be great.

Now he thought of Burridge, coming up from Dover each Sunday with the pay chest. That afternoon he had watched the man depart, heading deeper into the wood with his escort. Marbeck had no knowledge of where the other camps were. He'd hoped that Llewellyn, if sent elsewhere, could learn the locations of some of them at least. But since he now knew the strength of the entire force, it mattered less. What did matter was that he found out where Burridge went on his return journey. The next payday was in a week's time – on the very day the army was supposed to leave. It had puzzled him briefly, but now it made sense: mercenary soldiers marched and fought better, not merely on full stomachs but with full purses too.

Now, he saw only one course of action. Somehow he must get to Dover before Sunday morning, and watch the harbour for Burridge's arrival. Then he would waylay the man and force him to reveal who had sent him. Before that, he could spread a rumour in the camp that the money had dried up – and perhaps that the forces from the Continent would not arrive. Burridge's non-appearance would confirm it, whereupon the army would surely refuse to march. That, at least, was his hope. He had some days in which to forge his strategy, while maintaining his persona of Duggan the mercenary. Provided his and Llewellyn's cover held firm, they might just succeed. At least, he thought grimly, no one could force Llewellyn to talk. With that he turned on his side and tried to sleep ... until a new thought struck him.

There were other means of sabotage. Without powder, for example, every harquebus, caliver and pistol was useless. Without their long shafts of ash-wood, so were the pikes. And since there were few weapons in the camp, the bulk of them had to be in the old barn near the abbey.

Despite the night chill, he found he was sweating; but as the idea took shape he grew calmer. He and Llewellyn must destroy the armoury, then ride to seize Burridge. The timing must work so that Drax was left stranded, with neither men nor arms. As his force melted away, the man would flee ... but that would be for others to deal with. Once Prout had apprised Sir Robert Cecil of the whole picture, Marbeck felt sure, the man would move quickly. As for the Infanta: when her ship reached Dover and no troops arrived to see her ashore, she would be confounded ... but that, too, was for others.

Marbeck forced himself to focus on his aims, and suddenly a feeling of elation came upon him.

Finding the source of this treachery, he realized, would be a satisfaction greater than any he had known – and despite the risks, he relished it. Then, if everything went to plan, perhaps when it was over Master Secretary would review his recent opinions of him. At that, a weariness settled upon him at last.

As he drifted into sleep he thought of Celia, and remembered that he had not written to her after all.

The week went by, at a snail's pace; and by the end of it Marbeck was heartily sick of the camp and everyone in it. But he had laid his plans, and was doing his best not to dwell on their slim chances of success.

On Saturday night, he and Llewellyn had agreed, they would leave their billets after dark and head for the armoury. Marbeck would approach the guards boldly on some pretext, then despatch one of them while Llewellyn emerged from cover to deal with the other. Their horses would already be saddled and tethered nearby. They would then break into the barn, open the powder kegs and lay a long fuse before riding off, so that by the time the place blew up they would be clear. Their final act would be to untie the other horses from the picket line and drive them into the forest, delaying any pursuit. That, of course, meant despatching more guards. Then it merely remained for them to get to Dover in the dark, locate Burridge and capture him. If he was accompanied by others, that might present further difficulties ... in fact, it had now become clear to Marbeck that the whole scheme was probably doomed.

On the Saturday morning he forced himself to face it, as he sat on a log gazing across the camp. All was prepared for tomorrow's march; packs made up, orders issued. He barely noticed when Captain Feaver arrived and sat down beside him.

'Scares you too, does it?' he enquired in a casual tone. 'Tomorrow, I mean. It scares me ... There, I've admitted it.'

After a moment Marbeck nodded. 'I'll wager there isn't a man here who doesn't feel the same.'

Feaver shrugged. 'I keep one thing in my mind, and one only: an escutcheon bearing my arms, together with all that goes with the title. Then Sir George Feaver will set about righting a few wrongs...' He looked away. 'Men will pay for what they did to me.'

Marbeck said nothing; not only was he uninterested in Feaver's tale, he was running over his plans for that night, from every angle. In the past few days he had received two hasty, misspelled messages from Llewellyn, wrapped in scraps of cloth and hidden in the agreed spot. They spoke of the fact that while he was now generally accepted and assigned to serve as a pikeman, Marbeck was still distrusted. Follett in particular was uneasy about him, and had promised Drax he would keep a watch. Drax was preoccupied; messengers arrived in the camp with increasing frequency, and the number of sentries was being doubled. It merely added to the risks the two intelligencers faced, this very night. For Marbeck, it couldn't come quickly enough.

'Do you take the late watch?' he asked Feaver. 'I mean to get as much sleep as I can.'

'No, Follett has it,' the captain muttered. 'But as for sleep, you're a lucky man if you get any.' He sighed, and got up. 'I've letters to pen ... just in case, you understand.' He met Marbeck's eye. 'Do you, er, have someone...?'

'Nobody,' Marbeck answered abruptly, and stood up too. 'My horse is my truest companion ... I'll go and see to him now.'

Turning from Feaver, he walked off into the trees. Soon he arrived at the picket where the horses were tethered, went to Cobb and found a brush with which to groom him. The animal greeted him with a jerk of his head. As Marbeck patted his neck he noted the guard, who was giving him a sidelong look.

'Will there be extra feed tomorrow?' he asked sternly. 'I want my mount to be at his best.'

'There will, sir,' the man answered. 'You should come around midday and take him. We've got to dismantle the picket. If you've any needs, you may tell the horse-master...'

'I have none,' Marbeck said shortly, and busied himself at his task. But as he worked he glanced about, considering his approach for later. The sentries had rigged up a small shelter nearby, where they usually sat to smoke their pipes. He would have to come up behind it, and use a billet to lay them both out; or if necessary, his poniard. His eyes strayed towards the camp: after pacing it for a week, he knew every tree, bush and tussock. His initial fear, he realized, was getting clear of his tent without waking Feaver. But the man was drinking more heavily as each day passed ... at supper tonight, Marbeck would keep his cup well filled.

A short while later he left Cobb and strolled through the camp. He saw Llewellyn, engaged with other men in carrying stores into the wood; anything that might slow the progress of the company was to be buried or hidden. Their eyes met, and the old soldier gave a nod. There was nothing further to do now but wait.

Supper that night, without the awning, was

a cold and tense affair. The officers sat in the wind, saying little. It was the last meal they would share here, though none referred to the fact. But as they finished, Drax demanded their attention.

'I have news,' he said. 'It seems James Stuart left Edinburgh four days ago, on his progress south. He's already reached Berwick.'

The others exchanged looks. 'It's to be expected,' Follett said. 'It'll take him another week to reach York...'

'Longer than that,' Feaver put in. 'Knowing what I do of the man, he'll be stopping off to hunt every day.'

'Nevertheless, we will make haste,' Drax said. 'Which is why I've decided to bring the march forward.'

Marbeck had been about to take a drink, but lowered his cup instead. Without expression he stared ahead, his pulse racing.

'That suits me well,' Feaver said. 'I've no desire to sit in this damned forest an hour longer than necessary.'

Drax glanced at Follett, who was nodding. 'The sooner we're at Folkestone the better,' he said. 'I'm concerned about getting to the harbour in good time.'

'Folkestone...?' The word was out before Marbeck could stop it. But when the others eyed him, he managed a shrug. 'I always thought we would march to Dover,' he

151

added. 'Since nobody told me otherwise ... Not that it matters.' He met Follett's gaze, whereupon the young lieutenant spoke sharply.

'With a castle sitting above the town, and a garrison inside it?' he snapped. 'That would be somewhat foolhardy, would it not?'

'I suppose it would,' Marbeck admitted, cursing inwardly. 'It's merely that Dover's near, while Folkestone is – what, six or seven miles away...'

'Nearer five,' Drax corrected. 'And as I told you on your first day here, Duggan, the way is paved. New orders have already gone out to the other camps, to muster here. Advance riders will mark our every step, while others will go into the town to guard the harbour. The moment the lady's ship is sighted, a beacon will be lit. You think I haven't planned for this moment?'

'Then ... we march tonight?'

Marbeck struggled to appear excited by the prospect; but in his mind, he saw his plans crumbling to dust. More, he read suspicion in the other men's faces, particularly Follett's. While making an announcement like this was not unlike Drax, he couldn't help feeling that he was the last to be told the details. But at the man's next words, it was all he could do not to sigh with relief.

'Of course not!' The commander threw him a scathing look. 'I mean we leave early in the morning, not the evening. My intelligence is that the ship will likely come in before midday. When it does, we will be ready.'

'Capital!' In some relief himself, Feaver seized his cup. 'Then the Queen-in-Waiting will be ashore, and our first part is done. It's on to Westminster, and to our destiny!'

He grinned, drank deeply, then raised the cup; and his look of satisfaction was such, even Drax cracked a smile. Follett drank too, and gave a nod of approval.

'Morning's best for a march,' he said. 'I'd no relish for kicking my heels all day – nor had the men. We can be in the port before noon, and post a watch on every road out.'

Forcing a smile, Marbeck too drank ... then it hit him.

'The paymaster,' he said, more sharply than he intended. 'He's supposed to come here tomorrow, isn't he?'

There was a moment's silence – but it was broken by Feaver giving a yelp of laughter. 'Good Christ, so that's why you're looking so glum!' he exclaimed. 'You haven't been paid yet, have you?' He turned to Drax. 'I pray you, sir, put our friend out of his misery. Tell him he'll get what's due to him – then he can stand us all a dinner in Folkestone!'

With a glassy look Marbeck turned to face Drax ... and for the second time, had to conceal his relief.

'There's no need to soil your breeches, Duggan,' the commander said dryly. 'Burridge will come. His orders are to journey on to Folkestone and meet us there, after he lands at Dover as usual. I cannot be certain the man isn't watched, hence all must appear normal...' He frowned at Marbeck. 'Indeed, I cannot be certain that any of us isn't watched,' he added. 'But you'll get your pay. Now, have you any other fears you wish to air, before the evening's over?'

But Marbeck shook his head, and in his relief allowed a genuine smile to appear. 'None, sir,' he replied. 'Now that I know, I'll get a good night's sleep...' He lifted his cup, and raised it. 'May I pledge success to our enterprise – and good health to England's new monarch.'

After a moment, the others too drank. Feaver drained his wine to the last drop, whereupon Marbeck seized his chance. Taking up a flagon, he refilled the man's cup to the brim.

But his mind raced ahead to the night and his plan to spoil Drax's entire enterprise with the help of just one man. Try as he might, he could not help thinking that it now looked like sheer madness.

ELEVEN

Marbeck stood by the path and waited for
Llewellyn.

He had heard the night-birds calling, and
knew his comrade would have done so too.
He squinted into the gloom: the clouds had
cleared, and there was a half-moon to see by.
Two hundred yards away, the dying embers
of the cook's fire still showed faintly. But
there were no stragglers this night; in readiness for the morrow, the camp slept. To his
relief, it had been easier to get away than he
had expected. Feaver lay like a dead man,
muttering in his sleep; no lights showed at
the other tents. The sentries were spread beyond the edges of the camp, and a man of
Marbeck's skills could avoid them. Stalking
the guards at the picket had been more difficult. The first one Marbeck had downed at
once, knocking him unconscious before he
hit the ground. The other had jumped up
and would have shouted, had he not seized
his throat. They had struggled, whereupon
Marbeck had used his lute-string. As he
throttled his victim, the man fell and thrash-

ed about before lying still. His fear was that the struggle had alarmed the horses; a dozen in number, they fretted at the picket-rope until Marbeck was able to calm them. He had then untied Cobb and led him through the trees. Llewellyn was to wait a little longer, to make sure all was quiet before he untethered his own mount.

Now at last he appeared: a bulky shape looming out of the dark. Marbeck gave a low whistle, and the old soldier came towards him leading his warhorse. He tied it to a sapling some yards away from the path, alongside Cobb.

'The other horses – are they at ease?' Marbeck asked. Llewellyn nodded, then pointed towards their destination ... and now Marbeck sensed his alarm.

'What's wrong?'

The old soldier held up two fingers, shook his head rapidly, then held up three and pointed again. His meaning was clear: there were not two guards at the armoury, but three.

'I'll take the first,' Marbeck said quickly. 'You round the barn and take another – with luck the third will be confused. Whichever of us is nearest must despatch him...' He gripped the other's shoulder. 'Ready?'

Llewellyn merely touched his arm, before hurrying off. Marbeck counted to ten, then started along the path that led to the ruined

156

abbey. Soon he saw a light ahead, with the outline of the barn beyond. Drawing a breath, he straightened himself, strode forward and was challenged at once.

'Who's there? Stand and be seen!'

He halted. The light came from an iron brazier, where the guards warmed themselves. Two came towards him: one was Robbins, the veteran of the Irish War Marbeck had encountered on his first arrival. The other man was somewhat nervous. They had tucked pistols into their belts, and wore swords.

'It's Duggan,' Marbeck said. 'I've new orders from the colonel...' He glanced round. 'Where's the other sentry?'

'At the rear, sir...' Robbins eyed him. 'What new orders are those?'

Marbeck fumbled in his doublet. 'They're written down,' he replied. 'Let's move into the light, shall we?'

He stepped towards the brazier, and the others followed. He fumbled again, produced a rolled paper tied with cord. He tugged at the knot and muttered a curse.

'Here, take it,' he said to Robbins. The man hesitated, then turned to his companion. 'You read better than I do,' he said. The other soldier nodded and took the paper. Both men bent to look at it ... whereupon Marbeck struck.

His fist shot out, cracking Robbins on the

jaw. As he reeled away, Marbeck was already drawing his dagger. A sharp thrust in the other soldier's side, and the man went rigid, his eyes bulging. But as he fell he gave an agonized cry – which was answered by a shout from some distance away. Marbeck, however, had no time to look round: Robbins had recovered in an instant and was bearing down upon him, drawing his sword.

'By the Christ ... the lieutenant was right about you!' he breathed. 'Drop your poniard!'

They faced each other. Marbeck wasn't wearing his sword: it would have hampered his movements, and was fixed to Cobb's saddle. Dropping to a crouch, he held the dagger forward. Where was Llewellyn? he wondered. Then came a shriek from behind the barn: the other sentry had been despatched.

'You've a simple choice, Robbins,' he said. 'Submit, and be tied and gagged. Resist, and we'll kill you.'

'We?' Robbins glared. 'You mean your tongueless friend? Where is the whoreson bastard – I'll spike the pair of you!'

'He's there,' Marbeck said. Calmly he straightened up, and pointed past the other's left shoulder.

But Robbins wouldn't turn. 'He may be,' he muttered. 'Yet I have you in my grasp ... and it'd be worth it, to take you down!' He let out an oath, and his sword arm flew up. Marbeck stiffened, preparing to dodge. His gaze was on Robbins ... then at the last moment, his eyes flicked to the man's left – whereupon he reacted as Marbeck had hoped. With a rapid movement he swept his weapon around, ducking as he did so, but met only thin air. Too late, he saw the trick: Llewellyn had come up on his right. There was a caliver in his hands, which he had taken from the other guard. As Robbins whirled about, Llewellyn struck him on the head with the butt; the thud was enough to make even Marbeck wince. Without a sound the man toppled over and lay still.

In grim satisfaction Marbeck eyed his companion. 'The other sentry?' he enquired, and for reply received a sharp gesture across the throat.

'The keys...' Marbeck looked towards the barn. 'There's a padlock...' Then he heard it. Llewellyn heard it too: running feet, coming from the direction of the camp. They both span round, whereupon a shout came out of the dark.

'Hold still! Any man that moves will be fired upon!' The voice was unmistakeable: that of Lieutenant Follett.

Llewellyn moved fast: bending double, he began searching Robbins by the brazier's light. Marbeck glanced, then saw the glint of a steel ring at the belt of the other soldier.

He squatted beside him, hearing the man groan: he was alive, but fading. As he wrenched the keys clear, he looked up to see Llewellyn busy with the carbine.

'Can you hold them off for a minute?'

For answer, Llewellyn dropped to one knee and raised the gun to his shoulder. There was a crackle as flint ignited match, a spurt of flame and then a roar. Twenty yards away he heard a cry of alarm, then silence.

'I'll get inside,' Marbeck breathed. His plans were collapsing, but he refused to think about it. In a moment he was at the barn door, fitting the key to a heavy padlock. It turned, and the shackle sprang free. Tearing it from the hasp, he seized the latch and swung the heavy door open; he was in.

For a moment he could see nothing. Then he saw a lantern by the doorway, found his tinder-box and struck a light. There was an eerie silence outside, which troubled him; he doubted Llewellyn had the means to reload the gun. Then the lantern's flame rose, and he almost gasped.

Against the rear wall, kegs of powder were stacked. Nearby were stout chests which would contain balls and fuses. By another wall lay long boxes: carbines and harque-buses. Shields were piled up, along with helmets, steel corselets and wrapped bundles which he guessed contained swords. Pikes by the dozen stood upright, their points reaching the apex of the roof...

A shot from outside, closer than he had expected, was quickly followed by another. Then came a hissing: Llewellyn had found a pail of water and was dousing the brazier. A third shot came, and a fourth; Marbeck heard a ball slam into the barn wall. Gritting his teeth, he went to work.

There were no tools to hand, so he used his poniard – but when he tried to open a keg, it snapped in two. Throwing it aside he took down a pike and, struggling to manoeuvre in the cramped space, attempted to break its twelve-foot shaft. The tough ash pole resisted, so he was forced to swing the weapon round so that one end was outside the door. Resting it on a box, he jumped on it and was rewarded with a loud crack. Then he was at the powder kegs again, forcing the pike's head into the nearest one. Soon he was able to prise the lid open, whereupon he tipped the keg over. Even as the contents spilled he was attacking another barrel – then at a sound from the door he whirled round, to see Llewellyn stagger in: and one look at him was enough.

'You're hit!' Dropping the pike, Marbeck started towards him – but the old soldier waved him back. Rasping sounds came from his throat; he wheezed and stumbled, but kept his balance.

'Get out – make for the trees!' Marbeck

hissed. 'They can't follow you in the dark. I'll set the fuse—' He broke off. Llewellyn was shaking his head vehemently. He still held the carbine, which he now dropped. In his other hand he clutched a pistol ... but as Marbeck glanced down, the weapon slipped from his hand. Its butt was covered with blood, glistening in the lantern light.

'Aah!' Struggling to make himself understood, Llewellyn struck Marbeck on the chest with his fist. He jerked his head towards the doorway, shook it, then nodded to the barrels of powder.

'Have you lost your senses?' Marbeck demanded. 'You couldn't hold a troop of boys at bay ... go while you can!'

But his answer was a shake of the head. With his unblooded hand Llewellyn shoved Marbeck away, towards the door.

'I won't.' Marbeck shook his head too. 'I won't leave. We may not be able to stop the paymaster, but we can blow this place to the heavens!' He indicated the barrel he had opened, from which powder ran on to the earth floor.

'Daah!' Llewellyn glared, his breath coming fast. He raised his hand as if to push Marbeck again, then thought better of it. Instead, moving clumsily, he went over to the powder kegs and dropped to one knee. Marbeck started after him – then stiffened: there was noise, alarmingly near. He peered out into the darkness, but saw nothing.

'The building is surrounded! Come out unarmed!'

Follett's voice came from some distance away, but his men were closer. Marbeck thought he heard voices: he had no idea how many were there, but all chance of surprise was gone. The whole camp would be awake ...With a curse, he turned to Llewellyn. The old soldier was seated on the floor, working at another keg. The lid split with a crack, whereupon he dropped the pike and struggled to his feet. Seizing the keg in both hands he scattered the contents over other barrels and onto boxes. When it was empty, he threw it aside and turned to Marbeck.

They eyed each other, and the moment seemed long. Words were useless: the look on Llewellyn's face was enough. With a final jerk of his head, he made it plain what must be done. Marbeck was unhurt and had a chance, albeit a very slim one, while Llewellyn was weakening fast. Blood soaked his sleeve and ran to the floor. It was needless for them both to die here: Marbeck knew it, even as his throat tightened in near despair. Once before, in a house in Flushing, he had escaped, leaving a friend to his doom; the face of Giles Moore rose before him now, yelling at him to go. Feebly, he shook his head. He made as if to walk towards Llewellyn, but his companion had already turned away. Instead of returning to the kegs, however, he caught the lantern by its handle. Then with a grim look at Marbeck, he lifted it.

Follett's voice rang out again. 'Last warning – then we storm the building!'

It was followed by a shout: Marbeck thought he recognized the sergeant's voice. For a second he hesitated – then all at once his instinct took over. A coldness welled up in his vitals; a feeling that on this occasion had almost failed him. Suddenly he was calm: he had things to do, things more important than his life or Llewellyn's. He gave his comrade a last look, saw him poised to throw the lantern.

'If I live, your sister shall know how you died,' he said.

Llewellyn nodded briefly, then turned away. Whereupon, using a move he had learned from his old mentor, the player Ballard, Marbeck dropped to the floor. Making himself into a ball, he rolled out through the barn doorway.

There was an immediate crash of carbine fire; he heard a ball whistle past, but did not attempt to get up. Instead he kept rolling, using his hands like paddles: past the rigid bodies of Robbins and his companion, past the steaming brazier. Shapes rose in the gloom, and another shot roared out. This one was closer: he felt a tug at his sleeve, but no impact. Shouts came and were answered, he was unsure from which direction. Like a snowball he kept rolling, through long grass, then bushes. Darkness enveloped him: he had lost his bearings, but kept moving. Brambles tore his arms and legs, and from somewhere a bird shrieked in alarm. Another shout: it sounded like *he comes your way!*, but he wasn't certain. *Not yet* he told himself, and kept going even though he was weakening. Then another shot, but it was far off: he heard no patter from the bullet. Finally, his breath coming in rasps, he stopped and lay motionless ... whereupon at last, Llewellyn blew up the barn.

The explosion shook Marbeck to the bones, and temporarily deafened him. From an unexpected direction – for he had rolled far from his intended route – there followed a great roar. Then the night sky blazed, noon-bright. Panting, sore in a dozen places, he got to his knees and stared at the sight: the building, barely thirty yards away, covered in flames. But half of it, he now saw, was gone: where the roof should have been was a gaping hole. Timbers cracked, while powder, ball and weapons were consumed in the inferno. Now there were screams: some of the soldiers had been close. Peering through undergrowth, Marbeck saw a terrible sight: a man engulfed from head to foot in flame, moving crazily. Figures danced against the light, lurching about in panic. There was a crash as more of the building collapsed ... more cries, more cracking of timbers ... then at last, somewhat shakily, he got to his feet. A swift look round, then he was running.

Away from the blazing barn he ran, until he regained the path some twenty yards away. Voices came towards him, and boots thudded: at once he ducked into the bushes, heard men running past. Shouts were everywhere: the camp was in uproar. He waited, then got up again and ran to untether Cobb – only to stop in dismay.

There was a whinny of fear, and a horse raced out of the trees towards him, reins and stirrups flying. Seeing him in its path it screamed again and swung aside – but with relief, he saw it wasn't Cobb. Frightened by the explosion, Llewellyn's mount had torn itself free. Marbeck caught a glimpse of the old soldier's pack and scabbard, before the horse galloped away.

Fearing the worst, he stumbled to the spot where he had tied Cobb, then halted. There was a neigh and a stamping of hooves, but nothing more. Then he was at his horse's side, murmuring soothing words. He fumbled for the tether, found it taut. In a trice he had loosed it, seized the pommel and launched himself into the saddle. Then he was riding, ducking branches that threatened to unseat him, guiding the animal by moonlight. Soon he eased Cobb into a trot, keeping the roar of flames and the distant shouts at his back. Finally he broke cover, found himself on a road, and drew rein. Swiftly he took his bearings: the moon was before him, the camp behind.

He was facing south. He even smelled the sea, two miles away. He took a great gout of fresh night air, then turned Cobb to his left: towards Dover.

TWELVE

In the dawn, Marbeck walked Cobb slowly through cobbled streets. Wisps of smoke rose as the town stirred into life. Dover Castle loomed in the distance, its flag flying from a turret. Bleary-eyed, grimy but uninjured, he stopped at a corner and dismounted. Then he was leading the horse by the reins towards the harbour. The sea lay before him, flat and pewter-grey.

He had spent the last few hours outside the town, watching the road from St Radigund's. But there was no pursuit, nor did he expect one. Part of his plan, at least, had succeeded. And even though the horses had not been driven from the camp, Marbeck couldn't imagine that finding him would be a priority for William Drax. What gripped his heart like a cold poultice was the memory of Llewellyn, lantern in hand, bidding him save himself. It would stay with him all his life.

By the sea wall he halted. Looking to the harbour at his right, he saw boats drawn up and figures moving; a fishing smack was about to set forth. Shielding his eyes, he peered out to sea, but saw no vessels. The sun was coming up, the sky almost cloudless; for once, there would be no rain. It now remained for him to find a base from which to work. He would take a room overlooking the harbour, though he did not intend to stay a night – in fact if matters went to plan, he would be gone by noon.

Within the hour he had made his preparations. Seated by a window on the upper floor of a waterfront inn, stripped to his shirt and hose, he ate hungrily from a bowl of hot porridge. Cobb was in the stable, feeding on oats. The place was busy enough for a traveller like Marbeck not to attract much attention. The room was small and unclean, but it had the view he wanted: from here he could see any ship that arrived. It had not taken him long to learn that the only vessel to dock in the past two days was a merchantman from Calais. But a small barque was expected today; that was the vessel Marbeck gambled on, which would bring Thomas Burridge along with his pay chest. Tired yet alert, he finished his breakfast and set himself to watch.

To his relief the wait was short. Having scanned the horizon for an hour or so, watching small craft and fishing boats come and go, he was rewarded at last by the sight of a larger ship coming up from the east. Entering Dover roads, the barque shortened sail and veered towards the harbour. Another half hour and she would dock; Marbeck kept his eyes on her as he dressed. Then, having buckled on his sword, he left the room as he had found it.

The quay was crowded, but that was to the good. Shoremen were making ready, eyeing the small vessel as she hove close. Carts had drawn up, horses stamping in the shafts. More people were gathering to greet passengers. Then quite soon the barque was there, and ropes were being thrown over the side. Figures crowded the small deck, sailors scurrying to their tasks. Finally a gangplank appeared, and the first arrival teetered along it, grasping a rope stay for balance.

From the edge of the little crowd, Marbeck looked over the ship. People on board were calling to those ashore, and being answered. Sails had been furled and more passengers appeared, of both sexes. He eased forward, hat pulled low against the morning sun. Soon he was close to the gangway, watching each person alight. None, however, looked like Thomas Burridge. The numbers thinned, and his unease grew. He saw an old man being helped ashore by a younger man and woman, and eyed them keenly ... the paymaster might well employ disguise. Casually, he turned to a seaman who stood near.

'Where does this vessel hail from?' he

asked.

'Why, from London, sir,' the man answered. 'Where else?'

Marbeck kept a straight face. 'You're certain of it?'

'Indeed, sir. She's but a coaster – sailed on Thursday, made Gravesend the same night. Do you await someone?'

Without answering Marbeck moved off. Suddenly things were becoming clearer. The paymaster didn't cross the Channel, but merely skirted the coast. Prout's suspicions were correct: the money came from London.

He moved nearer to the gangplank, then halted. Another couple were coming ashore, seemingly the last people to do so. For a moment despair threatened him: had there been some further change of plan, of which he was ignorant? Indeed, had Drax and the others lied? He watched as the two reached the quay. One was a young man, well dressed, a sword at his side. The other was a rotund woman in heavy skirts, face half-hidden under a broad-brimmed hat. She had no baggage, but the man carried a stout leather bag that looked heavy. As they came ashore, both glanced around. Then the woman's eyes met Marbeck's – and at the same moment, recognition dawned.

'Duggan? What in heaven's name...' From under the hat-brim, Burridge's moon face stared into Marbeck's. At once he stepped

171

forward; he was on.

'Our plans are altered,' he breathed, bending close. 'The colonel sent me ... we've no time to waste.'

'What ... is something amiss?' Burridge took a step back – but his escort stiffened, a hand flying to his sword-hilt.

'Who the devil are you?' he demanded.

'Captain Duggan, sent by Drax.' Marbeck's tone was urgent. 'Please, we cannot talk here...' He indicated the bag, which he knew held the pay chest. 'I mean, in view of what you carry.'

There was a moment, as the young man's eyes flicked to Burridge. But when the paymaster gave a nod, he spoke again.

'Have you brought horses?'

Marbeck nodded. 'They're in a stable. We should go there at once.' Thinking quickly, he added: 'I'm alone – there's been a difficulty, but it's in hand now.'

'Difficulty?' Burridge echoed. He was afraid, his eyes darting everywhere. 'You don't mean the landing...?'

'No.' Marbeck's reply was firm. 'All will proceed as intended. We're to journey to Folkestone together, and an escort will meet us on the road...' With a show of nervousness, he too looked about. 'Come – the place isn't far.'

The two eyed each other, Burridge very uneasy, the other man suspicious. But after a moment he signalled his assent, whereupon Marbeck turned and led the way through the press of chattering people. The walk from the sea strand to the town took minutes, but finally they were climbing uphill to the tavern. There was a narrow lane beside it, which led to the stable in the rear: Marbeck had surveyed it that morning in some haste, and decided on his action. He had expected a guard of at least two men, so the odds were somewhat improved.

Wordlessly the three of them turned into the alleyway, out of sight of the sea. The armed man was short of breath now, holding the heavy bag to his chest. Burridge was in the rear. The stable entrance opened ahead, to their left. To Marbeck's relief there was no one about, not even the ostler: he was unsure how he might manage witnesses. Slowing his pace, he entered the gloom of the stables, allowing the others to follow. Horses shifted in their stalls, among them Cobb, who jerked his head on recognizing his master. But Marbeck didn't look; he merely waited for the two men to get clear of the doorway – then he acted.

His turn was so sudden, Burridge's escort was caught off guard; by the time he had dropped the bag, which hit the floor with a thud, Marbeck was upon him. Two rapid blows to the stomach were followed by another to the jaw. With a grunt the man staggered, doubling over. But he fumbled for his sword-hilt, leaving Marbeck little choice. He had no dagger: it lay broken in two, in a burned-out barn by St Radigund's Abbey. Nor did he intend to engage in a fencing bout. What he did was snatch his opponent's own poniard from its elegantly tooled sheath, and stab him in the neck.

The fellow gasped, a fountain of blood spurting from the wound, but Marbeck didn't wait for him to fall. Instead he turned on Burridge, then saw at once that there was no threat: the man was rigid with terror. In a moment he was pinioned, arms held fast while Marbeck hissed into his ear.

'Pick up the bag, and walk outside with me. One squeak, and you'll die.' For emphasis he put the dagger's point to the man's side, pressing it through his thick skirts.

'No! God help me ... please...' Burridge choked on his own words. Trembling visibly, he looked down at his escort, who lay sprawled on the straw-covered floor in the throes of death. Then he raised his eyes to Marbeck's.

'Take the bag,' he stammered. 'It's yours ... I'll not follow, I swear! There's a fortune in there—'

But he broke off with a yelp, as Marbeck prodded him. 'Pick it up,' he repeated.

They walked out of the stable. There was no one about, so Marbeck ordered his prisoner to wait. Hurrying back inside, he loosed Cobb from his stall. The horse was still saddled, pack in place: his orders to the ostler had been clear on that point. It took but a moment to get the animal to the doorway, past the lifeless form of Burridge's escort. He delayed long enough to drag the body aside and cover it with straw. Then catching up the reins, he led Cobb outside ... to see Burridge, skirts flapping in ungainly fashion, running off up the lane.

With a muttered curse, Marbeck mounted and rode after him. In seconds he was alongside the man, who was puffing like an ageing hound, the bag clutched to his ample stomach.

'Stop,' Marbeck said.

Burridge stopped.

'Stand still, while I dismount.'

The paymaster stood, while Marbeck got down and faced him. With one eye on his quaking captive, he opened his saddle-pack and found a short rope. He took the bag from Burridge, passed the rope through its handles and tied it firmly to his saddle. 'Now we'll walk together,' he said. 'You'll come to no harm, provided you do as I order. Is that agreed?'

With a gulp, Burridge nodded. So the two set off, Marbeck leading Cobb, up the lane and into a wider one that led westwards. Then they were crossing the town, threading through streets that were suddenly busy. Church bells rang out – and at once the absence of the ostler was explained; Marbeck had forgotten it was Sunday.

'Where are you taking me?'

All at once Burridge had found his voice. Turning shakily to Marbeck he added: 'What use am I to you? I'm on foot – you can take the money. Surely you know what Drax will do when he finds out—'

'He has other matters to concern him just now,' Marbeck broke in. His eyes were on the castle to their right, and the road that skirted it, leading north.

'You don't understand!' The man wet his lips; sweat sheened his brow. 'There's too much at stake—'

'You mean the arrival of the Infanta?' Marbeck turned sharply, making him flinch. 'I think you'll find matters have gone somewhat awry, as far as that goes.'

'What do you mean?' Burridge stared, his eyes widening. 'Is robbery not your motive? In God's name, then what—'

But Marbeck raised a hand. 'Not yet,' he said. 'Wait until we're on the road.'

'Road to where? Burridge asked anxiously – then glancing ahead, he gulped again. 'You mean to Canterbury? But why—'

'I mean to London,' Marbeck said. 'We'll walk a little, then ride, taking turns in the saddle. If we can make thirty miles a day, that means under three days' travel. By then I'll have answered your questions, Master Burridge ... some of them, anyway. And you will have answered mine. But for now, keep your eyes on the road and your thoughts to yourself – agreed?'

They gained the outskirts, then walked for a half-hour until Dover was far behind. The day was fair, and larks sang in the meadows: it seemed as if spring had arrived with a rush. But Burridge, panting and sweating in his skirts, was utterly miserable. Often he glanced aside as if assessing his chances of escape, but each time he found Marbeck's eyes upon him; while one hand gripped Cobb's reins, the other hovered near his belt. Finally Burridge could stand it no longer. He halted, wiping his dripping brow with a sleeve. Marbeck stopped too, and saw that he was close to tears.

'I cannot travel like this!' the paymaster cried. 'I must rest ... I've just spent three days at sea, damn you!'

Instead of answering, Marbeck glanced up the road. There was no one in sight. Thus far they had encountered few travellers, though those who passed looked askance at the oddly matched couple. Seeing a clump of trees some way ahead, he pointed.

'We'll rest there, and you can drink.' He indicated his leather flask, tied to the saddle. 'Have you no other clothes?'

'Of course I have!' Burridge retorted. 'If you'd allowed me, I'd have taken these off – do you see?' With that he lifted up his skirts. Small wonder the man sweated so much, Marbeck thought: underneath gown and petticoats, he wore shirt and breeches.

'Come, then.' Marbeck gave Cobb's reins a gentle tug and started forward. 'That copse will shield you while you disrobe,' he added. 'But before we ride on, I have questions for you.'

With a groan, Burridge resumed walking. A few minutes later they were in the shade, Cobb cropping grass while Marbeck sat against a tree-trunk. But as the paymaster removed his woman's garb, he began to talk quickly.

'You cannot succeed in this,' he said. 'Even if you got me to London, it would do no good. Whatever your aims, you have diverted the regiment's pay chest...' He paused, then: 'Clearly that was your aim, rather than mere robbery. But if you think you've ruined Drax's plans, you don't know the man. Others are involved too...' He broke off, regretting his words. And seeing Marbeck's expression, his face fell.

'I don't doubt that,' Marbeck said grimly. 'And in a few days' time, you'll be telling what you know of them. More, even if you're merely the paymaster, your part in the scheme will not be overlooked. You'll hang –

but not before you've been racked until your arms are torn out.'

Burridge had removed his petticoats, and was standing in shirt and breeches. But as Marbeck's words struck home, his legs gave way. With a look of horror, he sank to the grass.

'No, I pray you...' He swallowed, and his hand went to his mouth. 'I'm but a hireling ... Duggan, please...'

'That's not my name,' Marbeck said shortly. 'It's Sands. And I work for the Crown – did I not say?'

The other stared, shaking his head in dismay.

'I work for the Crown,' Marbeck repeated, 'and soon your whole design will be laid bare. Whoever your masters are – Drax, the Earl of Charnock, I care not – they will fail. And when the new King comes, they'll pay for their treason.'

Burridge opened his mouth, then closed it. He was shaking, and tears rolled down his pudgy cheeks. 'What must I do?' he asked finally. 'Can I not tell you what I know here and now, and save you the effort of dragging me along?' With a sob, he lowered his head. 'My life's worth naught, whatever follows,' he wailed. 'Do you truly think you can get me to a prison? They have intelligence – they'll waylay us before we reach London. And whatever I say, they'll deem me a risk.

I'll die where I stand – as will you, and...'

But he broke off, as abruptly Marbeck got to his feet. 'Have you finished dressing?' he asked. 'If so, leave the woman's things here. You can ride first, while I walk. I'll bind your hands, leaving you enough leeway to hold the pommel. I will have the halter, so you won't be able to get clear.'

He looked down coldly at his prisoner; all discourse was over. After a moment Burridge got up unsteadily.

'I'd like to have my doublet,' he said feebly. 'It's in the bag.'

Marbeck went to Cobb, untied the bag and set it down. He unlaced it and rummaged inside, then pulled out a blue-grey coat. 'Good serge, and silk-lined,' he murmured. 'I'll wager your pay's somewhat more than a shilling a day.' He threw the garment unceremoniously at Burridge, then peered into the bag again.

'Well now...' Reaching inside, Marbeck drew out a wad of papers tied with white ribbon. He looked up at Burridge, whose face was now the same colour. 'Despatches, perhaps? Final instructions to Drax – or are they letters intended for her royal highness, the Infanta?'

Burridge looked away, shaking his head. Having noted with satisfaction the pay chest filling the bottom of the bag, Marbeck closed it, stood up and retied it to Cobb's

180

saddle. Then he turned, one hand on the pommel. 'Come here while I bind your wrists. Then place a foot in the stirrup, and let me hoist you up. I'll try not to let you fall.'

The paymaster hesitated. He no longer wept; his eyes scanned the landscape, but he knew he was no match for his captor. With a sigh, he came forward and held out his hands.

'I thought you had questions,' he asked, speaking so low that Marbeck had to cock an ear to hear him.

'I do,' he replied. 'But on reflection, we'll save them for tonight. We might even find an inn to rest in – though if you've any notions of getting away, I'd set them aside. I mean to drive you until you can barely stand up.'

Then without expression, he drew a stout cord from his pocket.

THIRTEEN

By nightfall they had reached Canterbury, and Marbeck was as good as his word. Though Burridge had ridden for as much of the way as his captor had, the man was exhausted. He limped badly, his shoes being unfit for walking any distance. Despite shedding his woman's clothing, he stank with sweat. Dirt streaked his breeches. As they approached the archway known as the Riding Gate, he stumbled to a halt. Marbeck sat in the saddle, scanning the walls of the old city.

'There's a place close by Greyfriars,' he said. 'We'll take the best room...' He looked down at his captive, who gazed up blearily. 'The reckoning can be paid out of that chest.'

He dismounted, and after removing Burridge's bonds, led Cobb through the gateway into bustling streets, the paymaster dragging behind. The inn was near, and they were soon installed. The landlord, used to dusty and weary travellers, barely looked at them as Marbeck detailed his needs: hot water and a good supper sent up. Once upstairs in a chamber overlooking St George's Gate, Burridge almost collapsed on the truckle-bed beside the four-poster. He looked like a man who would never rise again. Marbeck decided to let him sleep.

But later, when the paymaster had rested and eaten ravenously of a now-cold supper, he found himself seated against the wall of the room facing his captor. He was in shirt sleeves, grim-faced and sullen. Night had fallen, and Marbeck had lit candles.

'We'll have our discourse now,' he said. 'And if you harbour any notion of calling for help, I'd advise against it. I've told the inn-keeper you're my poor, distracted uncle. You've become unhinged after the death of your wife, and are in need of confinement. In short, I said I'm taking you to Bedlam.'

Burridge was aghast. 'By the heavens,' he muttered, 'what further torments have you in store?'

'We'll see,' Marbeck replied. 'For now you must spill your tale. Who instructs you, who provides the money, and so forth.' He glanced at the pay chest, which stood on the floor near the master bed. Having relieved Burridge of the key, he had looked inside and satisfied himself of its contents. The chest contained not merely angels, half-angels and silver coin but gold ducats too: intended, or so he guessed, for the Spanish Infanta's party. Fixing the paymaster with a cold eye, he waited. But when the man's answer came, it was an attempt at resistance.

'I won't talk to you,' he said bitterly. 'If I'm to die, then I'll make my testimony to the proper authorities. And I want a priest to hear my confession.'

'You don't understand,' Marbeck said. 'Just now, I am the authority. I serve the Council, who care not a fig how I obtain my intelligence.' He touched the dagger he had taken from Burridge's escort, which was now at his belt.

'Then God forgive you,' the other threw back. 'You're a knave – one who does their bloody work. What will you do, stab me as you did my companion?' Wincing at the memory, he looked away. 'You're naught but a murderer.'

Calmly Marbeck reached into his doublet and drew out a tailor's bodkin, letting it rest on his palm. 'Making a noise will avail you naught,' he said. 'You're a madman, remember? I'll say I had to restrain you when you tried to injure yourself.'

It was a bluff; he loathed the means by which the Crown's servants obtained confessions, though he had been obliged to witness them more often than he cared to remember. As for murder: he forced aside the image of Burridge's escort, back in the stable at Dover. Instead he thought of Llewellyn, wounded but defiant, blowing himself to pieces.

'Then damn you, Sands!' the paymaster exclaimed. 'And in any case you'll learn little – do you think they confide in me? You cannot prevail. A sum far greater than that' – he indicated the chest – 'can be raised within days. You're but a sprat in a lake full of pike!'

'I like the conceit,' Marbeck murmured. 'I wonder what it makes you ... a bloated newt, perhaps?'

The other was breathing hard, fear in his eyes. He wet his lips, then changed tack. 'Whatever your masters pay you, it's but chaff compared to that, isn't it?' He nodded towards the chest. 'Why don't you take it? This country's finished – can you not see? You could make a new life elsewhere...'

'Enough!' Marbeck snapped. 'I'll not debate my future with you. Start by telling me who commands you, and where you go to receive your orders. Quickly – my patience runs short.'

A moment passed. Burridge's eyes blazed, but his rage was short-lived. Marbeck had often watched men pass through such stages: anger, defiance and finally resignation. The paymaster had seen Marbeck fight, and knew his chances were nil. He sighed heavily and lowered his eyes.

'I only know Drax and his people,' he said in a sullen tone. 'The ones who hold the purse are...' He shrugged. 'There's no word for men like them. They live by money as others live by their toil. They buy and sell nothing, yet their fortunes multiply as if by sorcery.'

He looked up. 'I take my instruction from one man – I don't know his name. He meets me in a private room over a tavern, with armed men standing by, in near-darkness. I never see his face ... I bring the chest with me, and they fill it. They also give me letters to carry. I take ship at the Custom House in disguise, and my escort meets me. We skirt the coast to Dover ... if storms or winds delay the ship we put in, though I've seldom missed a Sunday. At the port Drax's soldiers meet us dressed as farm folk, with horses. After performing my duties to the regiment, I return and take ship again.' He gave another shrug. 'The rest is known to you.'

'You don't know this man's name?' Marbeck echoed.

Quickly Burridge shook his head. 'He found me ... I was secretary to Bartolomeo Renzi, in Gracious Street.'

Marbeck thought about that. All London knew of Renzi, a financier whose influence was felt in every corner of Europe. At last a picture was emerging.

'They must have a hold over you, Burridge,' he said after a moment. 'I wonder what it is? The promise of mere gold sits somewhat ill with you, I think. You haven't the courage to be a fully-fledged traitor, Papist or no.'

At that the man looked uncomfortable. 'You're mistaken. My agreement is purely financial...'

'I think there's more to it,' Marbeck told him.

'And I swear there isn't,' Burridge insisted, but his hands fluttered nervously. 'I'm but a secretary ... the man knew my station.' He raised his eyes, and an imploring look appeared. 'Ask no more – I'm small fry, in the scheme of things.'

'Yes, the scheme.' Marbeck eyed him coolly. 'To support an invasion that would topple England's rightful King, and replace him with a usurping Spaniard. A princess of Philip's lineage, the people we've been fighting for seventeen years...' He shook his head. 'That's treason, Burridge. I said you'll die a traitor's death – you know it's true.'

The paymaster swallowed. 'What will this avail you?' he asked anxiously. 'The regiment will already be in disarray. Without their pay the soldiers may mutiny – and what will follow I cannot imagine.'

'Without their pay, and without arms and powder, they'll certainly find it difficult,' Marbeck said dryly. 'Did I not mention that the armoury was blown up last night?' He eyed the other man grimly. 'A friend of mine

187

died carrying out that task. So I'm not inclined towards mercy just now, Burridge – do you follow me?'

Wide-eyed, the paymaster stared at him. 'You destroyed the armoury?' When Marbeck nodded, a sickly expression came over his face. 'Then the rising cannot take place...' He gazed downwards, as the import sank in. 'We are undone!'

'That's what I've been trying to explain to you,' Marbeck said patiently. 'So the best thing you can do now is tell me the name of the man who gives you your orders – for I think you know who he is.'

After a moment Burridge raised his eyes. His expression was bleak, but there was a glimmer of something else. 'Is it truly beyond hope, for you and I to strike some manner of bargain?' he asked finally.

Marbeck gave him a withering look. 'You have naught to stake,' he answered. 'And I hold the cards.'

'But...' The man's mind was working. 'What if I told you where I meet my superior? News may not have reached him yet...'

'You said they had good intelligence,' Marbeck countered.

'They do, but...' The paymaster was desperate now. 'He will expect me to return by Tuesday. The same night I go to the meeting-place and make my report. I may be able to bluff – tell him all has gone to plan, and any rumours to the contrary should be discounted. And more...'

Marbeck was nodding. 'Plausible,' he allowed. 'Though the risks are many. But if you were to give me the man's name...' He raised his eyebrows and waited.

Another moment passed. Burridge looked away: at the flickering candles, at the pay chest, and finally back to Marbeck. 'If I tell you, what will you do?' he asked finally. 'My life will likely be forfeit – do you understand? Mine, and perhaps that of my wife...' Suddenly, as on the journey, the man was in tears again. 'You may as well kill me here!'

But Marbeck merely waited; and at last, as he expected, Burridge gave way. 'See now ... I cannot be certain. But I believe he is Sir Roland Meeres.'

In spite of himself Marbeck was taken aback. 'Meeres – one of the Queen's councillors? I should say one of the King's councillors...' He frowned. 'I'd have thought he had too much to lose ... but now I think on it, it was always believed the man was a Papist in secret.'

He eyed Burridge, who merely hung his head; he had told all he could. For a moment Marbeck almost pitied him. 'You'd better rest,' he went on. 'I regret I must bind you again. Tomorrow...' He glanced at the pay chest, and a thought struck him. 'Tomorrow, why don't we both ride? We'll buy another horse – no, a mule. Then with luck we'll make London by nightfall. Does that not cheer you a little?'

There was no answer. Burridge had closed his eyes, and leaned against the wall as if he were asleep.

The next morning Marbeck was in better spirits. The paymaster, however, was in despair; even after they had been to a horse-courser and Marbeck had purchased a mule for him, along with a comfortable saddle. Thereafter they left Canterbury by St Dunstan's Street, and clattered onto the London road. Marbeck rode behind Burridge, whose hands were no longer tied. He knew that flight was impossible, the mule being no match for Cobb. They travelled in silence; not a word had passed between them since rising. The man seemed to have resigned himself to the journey, and was lost in his own thoughts. Marbeck however, used the time to think – and on this fair spring day, he found his hopes rising.

Two days earlier, things had looked very bleak indeed; now, armed as he was with intelligence, possibilities loomed. By the time they broke their journey at Gillingham, midway along the route, a strategy was taking shape. By evening, as they walked their tired mounts by Blackheath, it was almost complete.

'Do you visit the theatre, Burridge?' he asked, turning to his prisoner. When the other merely gave him a blank stare, he added: 'I've learned a great deal from watching players work. The nub of my question is: if your life depended on it, how well could you pretend?'

'If my life were truly at stake, I suppose I could do well enough,' the paymaster replied morosely. They were the first words he had spoken all day.

'Good...' Marbeck peered ahead. Already the spires of the city were rising in the distance.

'You mean to set a trap of some kind,' Burridge added, frowning. 'But if you require my help, I've decided to refuse you. There's nothing left for me, except for...'

'Your family,' Marbeck finished. 'Where do they reside?'

The other wouldn't answer.

'No matter...' Marbeck considered. He needed to find Nicholas Prout and acquaint him with everything that had occurred. One of them would also have to break the news of Llewellyn's death to his sister ... He sighed. Prout would have to go to Sir Robert Cecil, too.

'How many men-at-arms does Meeres bring, when you meet with him?' he asked. 'Assuming that it is him, of course.'

Burridge shrugged. 'Two or three...' Lifting

his head, he threw Marbeck a baleful look. 'You may plot all you like – I'll not play.'

'The matter is,' Marbeck said, 'once inside the Marshalsea you'll see things differently. There's an interrogator there who can make you tell everything you know. I only hope they don't insist on my watching it...' He gave a theatrical shudder.

With a curse Burridge turned away, tugging the reins of his plodding mule. Even the animal looked unhappy, Marbeck thought. 'But if you were to turn King's evidence,' he went on, 'perhaps an arrangement might be made. For your wife and children, I mean.'

His tone was casual, though he felt somewhat guilty; Sir Robert Cecil regarded pacts with traitors as invalid, and would break his word without a second thought. They walked on in silence, passing Deptford now. Lights showed in the distance; already the hum of the great city was rising. Southwark was not far. If Burridge refused to take part in the entrapment Marbeck had in mind, he would have no choice but to deliver him forthwith to the Marshalsea prison. However, though he knew the paymaster was sick with fear, he also knew that he was debating within himself. And despite his plight, Burridge was still holding something back. Marbeck sensed it, as he detected a final stir of hope within the man. All at once, he stopped.

'I have no children,' he said heavily. 'And I know you cannot offer me freedom. You would lie if you claimed that.'

Marbeck said nothing.

'My wife knows nothing of this,' the other went on, somewhat hurriedly. 'She thinks I travel on an errand each week, for Signor Renzi. She's a well-born woman, the daughter of a rich man. It's for her, I...' He trailed off; but for Marbeck, it was as if a curtain had been drawn aside.

'So that's it!' he exclaimed. 'Poor fellow. Then, you're not the first man to take a wife he cannot keep in the manner she expects. It's not Meeres or Drax who have a hold over you, is it? They knew your weakness, and how to buy you. But it's not them you risk everything for – it's your spouse.' He gazed at the man, whose expression was enough. He refused to meet Marbeck's eye, but plodded on.

'Well now, perhaps we might lay some plans after all,' Marbeck resumed. 'For it may be your wife can be left out of the picture – if, as you say, she has no knowledge of the design.'

He waited, eyes forward, as they tramped the Kent Road. Bermondsey was falling behind, and in the fading light the tower of St Saviour's could be glimpsed. Suddenly Burridge stopped, bringing his mount to a halt.

193

Marbeck stopped too.

'How can I trust you?' the paymaster demanded. 'You despise me ... you could promise the earth, and lie with every breath.'

'That's true,' Marbeck agreed.

A pause, then: 'What would I have to do?'

'Merely play yourself. Deliver your report ... it would help if you appeared overjoyed at the apparent success of the enterprise. In any case, it wouldn't be for long. Our people will be close by.'

At that the other blanched. 'I'm not a fighting man. If weapons are drawn, I—'

'You'll be protected,' Marbeck broke in. 'But I make no promises.' He waited, then as an afterthought added: 'The inn: you haven't told me where it is.'

'It's the Dagger, in Holborn.'

Having made his decision, Burridge looked up and met his eye. It was the last piece of information Marbeck needed; the paymaster knew that he could now be surplus to requirements. His fate was in his captor's hands.

'Is it, indeed?' Marbeck allowed his surprise to show. 'I confess it's the last place I would expect ... but that makes it a good choice. Then, one nest of rogues and thieves is as good as another. No wonder Meeres takes armed guards with him ... I didn't think it was to protect himself from you.'

With that he turned, gave Cobb's reins a

tug and walked him on towards Southwark. Ahead, a train of packhorses ambled towards them, heading out of the city. Burridge drew his own mount forward, hurrying to catch up.

'Where are we going now?' he demanded. 'What will—'

'I do with you?' Marbeck broke in. He thought for a moment. 'I think we'll go to church.'

The other stared. 'Do you jest?'

'Not at all. We'll go to St Andrew Undershaft, by Aldgate. I hope evensong isn't over before we arrive.' Straight-faced, he turned to Burridge. 'There's no need to look so dismayed; we won't go inside. We'll merely wait for someone.'

He would have turned away, but a thought struck him. 'I'll tie your mule's reins to my horse's tail,' he added. 'Merely as a precaution, you understand. For dignity's sake you may remain unbound ... I'm counting on you not to make any difficulty. Is that fair play?'

Burridge barely nodded. But then, Marbeck had to admit, the idea of the man attempting to escape now was somewhat absurd. He looked the very image of defeat.

FOURTEEN

In Marbeck's old chamber at the Boar's
Head by Whitechapel, he and Nicholas Prout
sat in silence. Below them the inn roared and
roistered, while a breeze rattled the window-
panes. A single candle flickered, almost went
out, then recovered.

'By the saints, what a farrago this has
been,' the messenger said at last.

Marbeck said nothing. It was the day after
his return to London, and of turning his
prisoner over to Prout. They had spoken
only briefly outside the church: the man had
agreed to meet him the following evening,
after he had gathered news. Now, having
heard Marbeck's account in full, he was subdued.

'Llewellyn was more than a good intelligencer,' he went on, his eyes downcast. 'He
was a friend.'

'I came to regard him as one, too,' Marbeck said.

'Yet you achieved much together.' Prout
looked up, and there was respect in his gaze.
'The news is not all dire ... indeed, I believe

the Papists' scheme has failed utterly.'

'Then the landing of the Infanta did not take place?'

Prout hesitated, then said: 'It seems her ship never sailed. She never even left the Low Countries.'

Marbeck gave a start, and a look came over his face which Prout didn't like. Drawing a breath, the messenger began to speak quickly. 'I've spent the day gathering reports, from several sources. You couldn't have known – Drax and his people couldn't have known either. The voyage was aborted ... I don't know why. Perhaps the Archduke reassessed the risks of invasion, and forbade it. Perhaps even the Pope forbade it...'

But he broke off as Marbeck got abruptly to his feet. Breathing hard, he took a turn about the dingy chamber, then faced the other man. 'What has Master Secretary to say about it?' he demanded.

'Master Secretary doesn't know yet,' Prout replied, without expression. 'He's gone from London, to meet King James on his journey south. He left on Sunday.'

Suddenly Marbeck felt very tired. Turning away, he went to the bed and sat. The messenger, seated on a stool nearby, watched him uneasily.

'What of Drax's regiment?'

'Melted away by now, I expect. There's no news of the man himself.'

Marbeck stared, and in his mind a suspicion arose. 'You're mighty well informed about it all, Prout,' he murmured. 'I only returned last night. This intelligence you've gathered...'

'I had someone follow you,' Prout admitted. 'He was in Folkestone, Dover too...' He met Marbeck's gaze frankly. 'Cecil would expect nothing less.'

Marbeck was silent.

'This matter goes far beyond you and me,' the messenger went on. 'The safety of the realm is at stake – and you and Llewellyn have played a part in preserving it. Drax's army is in tatters ... men turned on their officers, from what I hear. One was killed in the melee ... a Captain Feaver. Did you know him?'

After a moment Marbeck gave a nod. 'But no word of Drax?'

'Likely he escaped by ship. To France, perhaps.'

'What about Burridge?'

Prout gave a shrug. 'We have him in the Gatehouse. I could bring Sangers in, put the fellow to the question. But I doubt there's much more he can tell us.'

'So it only remains to catch Sir Roland Meeres, and put him to the question too,' Marbeck said. But at once a frown creased the other's brow.

'I'm uneasy about that,' he said. 'How can

you be certain it's Meeres? We've only the paymaster's word – he could be lying, or simply mistaken.'

'I've a strong feeling he is neither,' Marbeck said.

'A feeling?' Prout's frown deepened. 'I need more than that. Meeres was seen as a force for good, in the Queen's last days. Even Master Secretary trusted him, to a degree ... the man has friends in the Council. I would need hard evidence before I lay charges.'

Now Marbeck was frowning too. 'I've already outlined my scheme,' he said. 'Burridge will do his part – you need only threaten him. A trap can be sprung, this very night...'

'It might be too late,' Prout argued. 'News of the explosion near St Radigund's, and of the mayhem that followed, has reached London. The plotters had their sources ... they may have guessed more, and taken steps—'

'All the more reason for us to go ahead,' Marbeck persisted. 'Whatever rumours Meeres has heard, he'll be desperate for news. Burridge is his link with the events down in Kent.'

'That's true, but...' The messenger looked uncomfortable. 'I have no authority for this. Sir Roland Meeres is a Privy Councillor. If it came to a struggle and he were wounded, let alone killed—'

'Damn you, Prout!' Marbeck cried. 'A pox

on you and your caution – what is it you fear? Meeres getting a bump on the head, or you receiving a drubbing from Master Secretary?'

The messenger bridled. 'You know better than that,' he retorted. 'I've already taken risks, bringing you and the others together as I did. I care not for my own place – but the dangers are numerous—'

'Indeed they are!' Marbeck threw back. 'One of your party's dead, and I'm lucky not to have died with him. Meanwhile John Chyme's gone north, perhaps into danger...'

'Chyme will do his work!' Prout said angrily. 'You know the man well enough. And aren't you forgetting the Earl of Charnock, and his part in all this? He's been sighted near Berwick with a hundred Scots ... they say he's following in the King's wake as he journeys south, gathering more followers by the day. Any danger to James Stuart comes from the north, not from phantom landings by Spanish princesses—'

'What did you say, Prout?'

There was a silence, in which Prout seemed to regret his words. Hasty speech was unlike him. He opened his mouth again, saw Marbeck's expression and closed it.

'Are you telling me all my efforts were wasted?' Marbeck demanded, his voice ice-cold. 'That Llewellyn died for nothing? That I almost lost my life too – for nothing?'

'Of course not,' Prout replied. 'I've said you played a part – a heroic one—'

'By the Christ!'

The messenger fell silent; he knew better than to argue. He sat rigid as Marbeck leaped up. But instead of starting towards Prout he seized the nearest object – a rickety table, on which stood the remains of his supper – and threw it against the wall. There was a crash of splintering wood, while dishes flew everywhere. Turning furiously he caught up another object, then saw it was his lute. His chest heaving, he put it down again and turned on the messenger.

'Do your worst,' Prout said. 'I'll not draw blade against you.'

They eyed each other, as they had done a short time ago, though to Marbeck it felt like weeks: the grizzled messenger in his sober clothes and Marbeck in black, his eyes blazing. 'Or ... perhaps you'd care to wait a while,' Prout added quietly. 'For I would go now to St Dunstan's Hill, and tell Llewellyn's sister what's happened to her brother. Also that, since nothing's left of him, there's no body for her to bury.'

A moment passed, then it was over; Prout knew it before Marbeck slumped down. But when he raised his eyes again, there was a look in them that brooked no refusal.

'I will go to the Dagger in Holborn this night,' he said. 'If you want no part in the business, well and good. I merely need two or three good men, well armed. And a warrant from you, to have Burridge released into my charge.'

Prout made no reply.

'When this man is taken – whether it's Meeres or someone else – you can convey him in secret to wherever you choose,' Marbeck went on. 'The Council need know nothing of it, nor need Master Secretary, until the prisoner's been questioned. Then you may take the whole tale to him. It will be Cecil's choice as to how he deals with him, and with Charnock too – or King James's choice, perhaps. He's well used to plots being hatched by his own countrymen, is he not?'

Calmer now, he waited. He knew Prout would see the sense of the argument. But when the man spoke at last, his words came as a surprise.

'I'll have Burridge released,' he said. 'But into my custody – and I will set the snare. The men can be found, but they'll be under my orders – are we agreed?' Receiving a curt nod, he let out a sigh. 'Well then – how long do we have?'

'Two hours, perhaps,' Marbeck answered. 'It's long enough.'

Slowly, the other got to his feet. 'But not long enough for me to visit Mistress Llewellyn first. Unless I were to deliver my news in haste, and leave her in her grief...' He looked away. 'I won't do that. The task must wait.'

'If you wish me to visit her instead...' Marbeck began, but the other shook his head. He started to go, then paused. 'I want this man taken alive. Will you give me your word upon that?'

But Marbeck was barely listening. Without another word, he got up to take his sword from under the bed.

They assembled in the dark on Holborn Bridge, with the murky waters of the Fleet River below. From thirty yards behind them, by the corner of Snow Hill, sounds of revelry floated from one of the notorious inns of the Ward of Farringdon Without, the Saracen's Head. But the eyes of Marbeck, Prout and their fellows were fixed on Holborn Hill, and on the lights of a tavern of even worse repute. The Dagger was a gambling-house, a haunt of coggers, foists and others of unsavoury reputation. Marbeck could hardly wait to enter it.

Three soldiers of the Crown accompanied them, armed with pistols; men whose discretion Prout trusted. He himself wore a sword and poniard, as did Marbeck. The sixth member of the party was Thomas Burridge, white-faced and tense as a whip. He remained silent as the intelligencers spoke together, finalizing plans they had already laid. He knew his part, as he knew that his fate depended upon what followed. He was to enter the inn and take the back stairs, to the private room where Meeres awaited him. He was dressed in outdoor clothes and carried the pay chest, which was now empty. He would behave normally: how much the plotters had learned of the events down by the Kent coast, nobody knew. The gamble was, Burridge would have Marbeck with him.

Prout had been against the idea, but Marbeck was deaf to his arguments. He was dressed as a soldier, and would pose as one of Drax's men who had accompanied the paymaster to London. While he distracted Burridge's superior, Prout's men would take their stations. Then at Marbeck's signal – three heavy blows on the door – they would burst in with pistols ready. There would be no time for those inside to ready their own weapons. Though what might follow, neither Marbeck nor Prout cared to discuss. Prout feared a pitched battle, and suspected that Marbeck privately relished the notion. The look on his face suggested he was in no mood for restraint.

And now at last, the talking was done. Marbeck and Burridge started forward while the others hung back – and suddenly the paymaster began to shake. Stifling a curse, Marbeck half-turned to him.

'You're not in danger. Our men know what

to do – you'll be bundled out of the door as soon as they're in the room.'

Burridge wet his parched lips. 'You don't know my master,' he said plaintively. 'If he thought I'd betrayed him—'

'He won't have chance to do anything,' Marbeck broke in.

To that the other said nothing; and in any case, the time for delay was over. They were at the inn door, whence noise spilled into the street. Two young men brushed past them and hurried inside, allowing a reek of beer and tobacco fumes to flow out. Marbeck caught the door and stepped in after them. Close on his heels, Burridge followed.

As expected the place was crowded. Easing their way through the press of drinkers and gamblers, Marbeck and the paymaster passed from the main room to a passageway, and thence to a flight of stairs. There was a rear door, which was bolted. Marbeck glanced about to ensure no one was about, and quickly unbolted it. Then he was ascending, allowing Burridge to go ahead.

On the landing were several doors, dim light showing under them. But Burridge, swallowing audibly, indicated a door at the end where no light showed. At Marbeck's prodding he walked forward and gave a complex series of knocks: two sets of three, one set of four, then two of two. Finally he opened the door and entered, Marbeck close behind. But the moment they were inside the darkened room, both of them froze. Burridge gasped as a shape loomed up, grabbed him and thrust him forward. Marbeck remained motionless: another figure had appeared from behind the door, and was pressing something sharp into his back.

'Who's that with you, Burridge?'

A voice from the gloom ... Marbeck glimpsed someone seated at a table, his face in shadow. The window of the chamber was curtained; there was no other furniture. He sensed another man, standing near the seated one. Three guards altogether...

'He's one of Drax's men.' Shakily Burridge moved forward, clutching his pay chest. Placing it on the table, he stepped back. 'He came with me to deliver the tidings. There's...' He gave a cough, then ploughed on. 'There have been momentous events...'

'Have there?' The voice was cold, yet apparently calm. 'Do you mean to tell me that all went smoothly in Folkestone?'

'I do, sir,' Burridge answered quickly. 'The regiment performed well – the colonel is most pleased. There will be despatches to follow ... I hurried back as soon as my work was done—'

'Liar!'

The word cut Burridge off in mid-flow. With a gulp he began to step back further, then thought better of it. Marbeck remained still ... but one hand was in his pocket. Slowly, with an imperceptible movement, his fingers closed round the tailor's bodkin.

'Bring the other one here,' the shadowed man said, whereupon Marbeck received a shove. Unhurriedly, he moved towards the table. His night vision was better than they would have expected: he could see the seated figure, muffled in heavy clothing. On the table before him, beside Burridge's pay chest, lay a poniard with a jewelled handle.

'You are...?' the man enquired.

'Duggan, officer of horse.' Glancing about quickly, Marbeck saw the men shifting position. Apparently disregarding Burridge as a threat, they were closing in on him instead. His pulse quickened.

'Have you tidings for me, too?'

'That depends who I'm addressing,' Marbeck said.

There was a stir, but nobody spoke. His hand gripping the bodkin, he added: 'If you're Sir Roland Meeres, I will speak. However, since I cannot see you—'

But he broke off, wincing; the guard had stuck his dagger through doublet and shirt to prick Marbeck's spine.

'The explosion, and the fire...' Suddenly, the man's voice was shaking. 'Tell me what happened by St Radigund's,' he went on. 'And quickly!'

His men had formed a rough semicircle

about Marbeck. A few feet away he could almost hear Burridge trembling. He paused, then said: 'You mean when the armoury was destroyed?'

There was no reply.

'That was unfortunate,' Marbeck went on. 'A spark igniting some spilled powder ... the guards were careless. Yet the colonel refused to let that spoil his plans. Why would he?'

He spoke as calmly as he could, though his ear was cocked towards the doorway. He thought he heard a creak – and one of the armed men heard it too. The fellow half-turned; it was the only chance Marbeck would get, so he seized it. Ducking aside, he drew out his bodkin and struck at the guard who had prodded him. The fellow let out a yelp and staggered, whereupon Marbeck lunged for the door and banged his fist on it three times – then everything happened at once.

The door flew open, and everyone was shouting. Bodies crashed into the room; there were grunts and oaths – but when a pistol thundered, its flame a vivid flash in the semi-darkness, there was a sudden hiatus. Someone fell with a cry – but from the doorway, Prout's voice rang out.

'Hold, in the name of the King! Our fire-arms are primed! Fall to your knees and lay down your weapons, or face the conse-quences!'

A silence followed, filled with possibilities. Men breathed heavily in the gloom ... Marbeck glimpsed the leader, on his feet behind the table. But Prout's men pushed forward, forcing the others back. Nearby, someone was whimpering. Then mercifully came a blaze of light: Prout had brought in a lantern, and all was revealed.

Two of the guards were on their feet, glaring at the interlopers. One held a dagger, the other a smoking pistol ... but seeing fire-arms pointed his way, he dropped it at once. The other one fell to his knees, his face ashen. Their commander had fallen back – and now Marbeck recognized him. Once a much-feared performer at the Queen's birthday tilts, Sir Roland Meeres had become a pinched, white-haired old man. Eyes blazing, he crouched by the wall like a cornered wolf, one hand gripping his jewelled dagger. For a moment he looked as if he would protest ... then he looked into Marbeck's face, and blanched.

'What is it you see, Sir Roland?' Marbeck said gently. 'Your death awaiting you?' He drew his sword sharply and levelled it at the knight, who froze.

'Stop!'

Prout pushed forward through his men. As they made way he handed one the lantern and drew his own sword, his eyes sweeping the room. He and Marbeck exchanged looks: there was relief on the messenger's face. Meeres's eyes flew towards him, then back to Marbeck. But it was finished; both his followers were kneeling, apart from the one Marbeck had attacked. He sat on the floor, hands to his face. Blood oozed through his fingers...

But it was he who whimpered – and at the same moment both Prout and Marbeck realized it. With a curse Prout turned towards a corner, but Marbeck knew what had happened. With one eye on Meeres, he looked round ... to see Burridge lying in a heap, blood welling from a wound in his chest. His grey-blue doublet, which Marbeck remembered handing him by a roadside in Kent, was soaked with gore. But his face was calm, the eyes open; briefly they flew upwards, towards Marbeck. Then without a sound, his life slipped from him.

But Marbeck saw his expression before his eyes closed, and understood; the paymaster's last emotion had been relief.

FIFTEEN

Some hours later Marbeck was slumped in a boat, being rowed up the Thames; and he was seriously drunk.

The riverbanks drifted by, dimly illuminated by the skiff's lantern, but he barely saw them. Images, along with fragments of speech, swam before him: Sir Roland Meeres being frog-marched out of the Dagger like a common criminal; his men following, their hands bound; Prout at his most officious, issuing orders ... and above all the face of Thomas Burridge, gazing up as his eyes closed. Blearily Marbeck looked at the boatman, who was straining grimly at his oars.

'If you're like to vent your guts, I'll ask you to lean over the side,' the man muttered. 'I was a fool to take you ... you should be sleeping that bellyful off somewhere.'

'I said you'll have double your rate,' Marbeck answered. He fumbled in his doublet. 'You want it now?'

'When I get you to Chelsea,' the other said; then he grunted. 'Bad news, was it? Money trouble, women...?'

But Marbeck was trying to focus. He remembered walking away from Prout, going back over Holborn Bridge and entering the Saracen's Head. After that, things became somewhat hazy.

'Where did I hail you?' he asked, squinting at the boatman.

'Bridewell Dock,' came the reply. 'Do you not remember?'

There was a bailing can lying in the bottom of the skiff. Seizing it, Marbeck held it over the side until it filled up, then poured freezing-cold Thames water over his head. He shook himself, and took several deep breaths.

'Feel better?' the boatman asked sourly.

'I believe I do.'

'Scroop House...' The man frowned at him. 'Are you sure that's where you want to go?'

'Quite sure,' Marbeck replied. 'And I don't care for further conversation – can we settle on that?'

The other gave a shrug and lowered his head, while Marbeck leaned back against the stern. His eyes closed; he pictured Celia, sitting in her evening chamber playing at cards. It pained him to remember that he had neglected to write to her from Cambridge; as he had from Huntingdon, and even from London. She had trusted him to find her son, and he had done so – but then he had failed her. What had become of the boy he had no idea. His mouth tightened; of all the ways in which he had disappointed Celia over the years, this was the worst. He thought of going north again, of tracking down Isaac Gow and his followers, but feared it might be too late. As for further plots against James Stuart ... he sighed. Others should look to the King's safety. After all, he had been an outcast as far as Sir Robert Cecil was concerned; his fists clenched at the mere thought. He opened his eyes, and saw the boatman eyeing him uneasily.

'We're almost there,' the fellow said, jerking his head over his shoulder. 'See?'

Marbeck looked, and saw the stone steps ahead. 'What hour is it?' he asked.

'Past midnight.' Quickening his stroke, the other began to pull towards the landing-stage. Marbeck watched him for a moment, then found his purse and tugged it open.

'Will that repay you for your trouble?' he asked. The boatman turned, and his eyes widened: Marbeck was holding up a silver crown. 'I ask pardon for being a tiresome passenger,' he added, and placed the coin on the seat beside him. Thereafter, neither of them spoke again. Soon Marbeck was walking unsteadily up the steps of Scroop House, and the boat was disappearing downstream.

For once, and somewhat to his surprise, Celia was abed when he arrived. But her servants admitted him, while looking askance at his condition. He was given a small chamber along the landing from hers, and left to himself. So with some relief he peeled off his wet clothes and crawled into the bed. Within minutes he was asleep, and did not awake until dawn ... whereupon his first sight on opening his eyes was Celia bending over him wrapped in a morning-gown, her hair loose about her face.

'Did you come to bring news?' she asked. 'Or are you merely in hiding?'

'Both, I think,' Marbeck said sleepily. He lifted the covers, but she did not move. Then his eyelids drooped; in a moment he was asleep again.

When he awoke for the second time the morning was advanced. He gave a start, and looked to see that he was alone in the bed. But sensing a presence, he sat up to discover Celia sitting nearby. She was clothed in a dark gown, her hair carefully dressed.

'I know I should have sent you a report,' he said. 'I've no excuse to offer.' When she made no reply, he added: 'I saw Henry and spoke with him, but he wouldn't hear me. He said—'

'I've heard from him,' Celia interrupted.

Marbeck fell silent.

'He sent me a short letter; from where, I know not. It came some days ago ... I waited, hoping you would send word, for I was at a loss what to do. I still am.'

'What did he write?' Marbeck asked.

'That he was on the verge of a great undertaking, and that one day I would be proud of him.'

'Is that all?'

'Not quite. He also said he would not use his father's lands or title. And he bade me search my heart, and look to my own future. He ended by owning his duty to me and to his sister, as a loving son and brother. Then there was only his signature...' She looked away. 'I did not recognize it ... even his handwriting looked odd. It was a letter from a stranger.'

Her voice was flat, as if feeling had been drained from her. Marbeck lowered his gaze, wondering what to tell her.

'And yet you talked to him,' Celia went on. 'When?'

'Three weeks ago, in the countryside near Cambridge.'

'What was he doing there?' But when he hesitated, her eyes narrowed. 'You'd better tell me all,' she added. 'And don't spare my feelings – not even a little.'

So he drew a breath and told her; though he left out the substance of his talk with Edward Poyns in the inn at Huntingdon. By the time he had finished the tale his mouth was dry; seeing a pitcher of water on the night-stand, he left the bed and went over to it. Having drunk thirstily, he turned and saw Celia slumped in the chair with a hand to her face. His instinct was to comfort her, but instead he crossed the room and picked up his clothes. Once in shirt and breeches, still damp from the previous night, he went to her.

'I'll go and look for him,' he said. 'I'll go today.'

'Will you?' Celia raised her head. 'And if you cannot find him?'

'I will find him.'

'This man Gow...' She hesitated. 'You think he has bewitched Henry – that he's somehow in his power?'

'To his followers Gow is priest, father and prophet too,' Marbeck said. 'So in a manner he has power over Henry – or at least has clouded his thinking.'

'And what do you think he wishes to do? Gow, I mean.'

Her eyes peered sharply into his: as he feared, she had guessed more than he'd told. He hesitated, whereupon suddenly she stood up.

'I want the truth, Marbeck.'

'I think he wishes to make an attempt on the King's life,' he answered after a pause. 'And that his people – Henry included – deem it their duty to carry the scheme out.'

In silence they faced each other. He wanted to reach out, but held himself back. 'Yes

'... that would make sense,' she said softly. 'To make up for everything he sees wrong with England ... to atone for his father's failings as well as his own, he wants to take part in this great undertaking, as he calls it. Now I understand his letter.'

'But it may come to naught,' Marbeck said at once. 'Our people are aware of the threat – as we stand here, despatches go north to Sir Robert Cecil. The King will be protected from any danger...'

'As the Queen was,' Celia broke in. 'Yet her saddle was smeared with poison, she was shot at, came within inches of a dagger-point—'

'Yet she died in her bed, of old age,' Marbeck persisted. 'And the King's a wily Scot, who's survived plots galore. Do you truly think Gow could get near him?'

'Perhaps,' Celia said. 'Many flock round the King, from what I hear. He rides about his new domain as if it were a country park, dubbing new knights as fancy takes him. What if Henry...'

Suddenly she caught his eye: for a moment, he had betrayed his own fears. The look in his eyes was gone in an instant, but she had seen it.

'You think Henry could be the one to do the deed,' she said. 'As the son of a nobleman who lost his life on the field of battle, he could approach the King and be welcomed...'

'He would be stopped,' Marbeck said firmly. 'Now we know of the danger, people will watch for him. You must not dwell upon this – you'll drive yourself to madness.'

'I am mad already – do you not see it?!' Suddenly she was shouting, turning her fear into rage. 'Mewed up like a Bedlamite, waiting for news and getting none! Meanwhile all of London looks north, while the Queen's body rots at Whitehall. The past is dead – Scots plaid is the new fashion!'

'That's true,' Marbeck said. And now he did reach out, to take hold of her arms. 'Yet Master Secretary will keep his head, as he will keep order.' He drew a breath, then: 'I'll ride to him myself, and see him face to face.'

She said nothing, but nor did she push him away. They stood in silence; outside he heard gardeners at work mowing. 'And I'll track Henry down,' he added. 'I will bring him here to you, or take him back to Oxford – whatever you wish.'

'Oxford?' Suddenly, her eyes filled with tears. 'I fear it's too late for that; the dean of his college will refuse him re-admission.'

Marbeck shook his head. 'He will reconsider. There are men of substance I can call upon, who'll speak for Henry.'

'If he wishes to go back.' Celia sighed. 'His letter reads like a last testament ... a farewell to us all.' Then she sagged at last, and let her head fall on his chest.

But now his resolve was firm. Once again he had a purpose, that mattered more than foiling hare-brained plots in Kent, or snaring traitors like Meeres. Uppermost in his mind was not preserving the life of the new King of England, France and Ireland; but that of a confused boy, who happened to be the son of a woman he loved.

By midday he was back in London; an hour later he was in the saddle, riding the North Road to Highgate and beyond.

The roads were busy, but that was to be expected. At first Marbeck cantered, then he galloped, letting Cobb have his head. He passed groups of riders going in the same direction; some were noblemen with substantial trains, others rode alone. By late afternoon he had covered the distance to Hitchin, where he stopped to feed his horse and take a hasty supper. The town was bustling, and as with every other settlement he passed through, all eyes looked northwards. King James had left Gateshead, the gossips said, and was moving down to York, where he would be a guest of the Council of the North. As he pressed onwards, Marbeck recalled that the Council's President was Lord Thomas Cecil, Sir Robert's half-brother; likely that was where Master Secretary would go, to meet the King.

Now he forced himself to consider his strategy. He knew Prout had sent a despatch to Cecil, by fast courier. Before Marbeck even arrived, the spymaster would at least know that he had acquitted himself well as a loyal servant of the Crown. Surely he would not deny him an audience? The ruin of William Drax's rebel army and the capture of Sir Roland Meeres would add weight to his case. He had seen Prout briefly before leaving London, and learned with relief that Meeres had confessed to being part of the group of Catholic plotters which included Drax – and, as they had suspected, the Earl of Charnock. What Meeres refused to do, however, even under threat of torture, was name the source of their funds: the one whose wealth had driven the scheme, even made it possible. It seemed even the ringleaders were in awe of him. The matter rankled with Prout, as it did with Marbeck. That was a trail yet to be uncovered, but for now it must wait.

As the light began to fail he spurred Cobb to greater effort, and to his satisfaction reached Huntingdon that same night. He had covered more than sixty miles. In the short time since he was here, however, it seemed the town had swollen in size. There was no room at the George, or indeed any other inn. Travellers thronged the streets and taverns, while some were even camped out-side the town. Finally Marbeck recrossed the river to Godmanchester where he was able to get oats for Cobb, though no stabling. Having gathered what news he could, he walked the horse out of the town and found a ruined barn where he spent the night. In the morning, stiff and cold, he was back in the saddle, riding on to Newark-on-Trent, where he was lucky enough to find an inn. There both horse and rider rested, in prepar-ation for the last stage of their journey; tomorrow they would reach England's second city, York.

But that night, matters took an unexpected turn.

Having washed himself and eaten a wel-come supper, Marbeck was in his chamber preparing to retire when someone knocked on the door. In breeches and shirt he went to open it, only to start in surprise. There stood a man he had almost forgotten; at first he could not even recall his name ... then it dawned.

'Rowan?'

The other barely nodded, leaning on the door-frame. He was more than merely tired: he was utterly spent. 'Somehow, I thought you and I might cross paths again,' he said.

Marbeck stood aside to let him enter, and at once the man slumped down on the bed. Looking up, he managed a thin smile.

'Where are you bound, northward?' he asked. 'That's where half the country's heading, from what I see.'

Having looked him over, Marbeck went to a table, poured out a mug and took it to him. 'This was mulled, though it's cooled now,' he said. 'But it's wet, and well spiced.'

Rowan took it gratefully and drank almost to the dregs, while Marbeck found a stool and brought it over. 'What do you do in Newark? he asked. 'More, how did you know I was here?'

'I didn't,' came the reply. 'I've been using the town as a base these past days ... following up scraps of what I would have called intelligence, but which always turn out to be false.' He wiped his mouth and gave a sigh. 'It was a relief to see a face I recognized.'

'I heard of your trouble with Isaac Gow,' Marbeck said, after a moment. 'Are you still looking for him?'

'Still looking.' The other sighed again. 'Who'd have thought a man like that could give someone like me the slip – and with such ease?'

'He had help,' Marbeck replied. 'And he's cleverer than he looks. That coughing fit—'

'Oh, that was real.' Rowan drained his mug and set it on the floor. 'He's not a well man ... even when I lost him on the way to Hitchin, he wasn't faking. His friend –that old scarecrow Silas. He seized the chance, and got him outside.'

'And his people were following?' Marbeck asked sharply.

'So it would seem.' The other peered at him. 'I remember now – it was that boy you were trying to rescue, wasn't it? One who'd tagged along with Gow...'

'Henry Scroop.' Marbeck stiffened. 'Have you had any word of him?'

The other shook his head. 'Gow's people scattered ... the trail went cold almost at once.' He let out a sigh. 'I'm done with it all. I'm not a man who likes to admit he's beaten, but...'

'Your man – the guard who was with you...' Marbeck began, but Rowan merely grunted. 'He's gone back to London. He said he'd make a fair report, but he'll just try to cover his back. That's what everyone's doing just now, is it not?'

Marbeck couldn't help a rueful smile. 'Then it looks as though you and I are both outside the pale,' he said. 'Though I won't bore you with my story just now ... you look like a man who needs some rest.'

Rowan nodded. 'Might I share your chamber? My purse is light – a corner will do.'

But Marbeck was already on his feet. 'Take the bed,' he said. 'I'll order a supper for you ... things will look better tomorrow.'

He took up Rowan's mug and went to

the door. But even as he opened it, a sound made him turn. The man had already stretched out, and was falling into an exhausted sleep.

SIXTEEN

'I knew you were Marbeck, as soon as I saw you,' Rowan said. 'That day in the magistrate's house near St Neots. Perhaps it's meet you should learn my name – for you know it's not Rowan.'

They stood in a meadow outside Newark, letting their horses graze in the sunshine. It was the morning after the man had appeared at Marbeck's door in a sorry plight, but having slept and eaten he was much refreshed. The intelligencers had agreed to exchange news, for they soon realized they shared a common purpose: to find Isaac Gow and, so Marbeck hoped, Henry Scroop along with him.

'Then who are you?' Marbeck asked.

'I'm Barleyman.'

He recalled the name from years back, in the time of Sir Francis Walsingham. Barleyman had been under a cloud: it was believed he'd once sold intelligence to Spain. The slur was later found to be false, and the man entered Sir Robert Cecil's service, since which time he had served the Crown well. He was

225

a man who needed to prove himself, it was said, time and again.

'You'll recall last night, when I said you and I are both outside the pale,' Marbeck said after a moment. 'Shall we trade confessions?'

'You mean compare grudges?' the other asked wryly. 'Or lay bare our guilt?'

'I mean swap confidences. Though for policy's sake, I'll still call you Rowan.'

Marbeck returned the other's smile, and soon they were talking. Rowan had indeed had his troubles, since losing Isaac Gow en route for London. He'd heard of sightings of the man, always further north. They had led him to Nottingham and Lincoln, and now to Newark. In turn Marbeck told his own tale of recent weeks, which surprised his companion. But when he mentioned John Chyme, of whom he'd had no news, Rowan nodded.

'I heard rumour of a newcomer amongst them – a young man. The group you encountered at Cambridge and Huntingdon is much altered – I think some of them have deserted Gow. Though I believe the boy's still with him, as is Silas. Perhaps Chyme succeeded in worming his way into their company.'

'We must find them, and quickly,' Marbeck said. 'I'm told the King is nearing York. And if Gow's heading north...'

'Yet I've been chasing shadows for the past fortnight,' Rowan said with a sigh. 'They're more like a robber band than a company of zealots. Gow spreads false rumours of his whereabouts, he has sympathizers who provide shelter ... he may even use disguise.'

'So what brought you to Newark?' Marbeck wondered.

'A piece of intelligence that's yet to be exhausted,' the other answered. 'There's a doctor in this town, a barber-surgeon, who's been in trouble in the past for making angry pronouncements about the Queen, the bishops, indeed, anyone who isn't of the Calvinist persuasion like him. I thought he might know of Gow's whereabouts, so I visited him yesterday, but he claimed he'd never heard of the man. I mean to try him again.'

'Then might I try instead?' Marbeck suggested.

The barber-surgeon's premises were in a narrow street close to Newark's market square. An hour later Marbeck presented himself in a guise he had not used before, that of a devout Puritan, seeking out a fellow devotee. At first however his plan almost stalled: the good doctor, who went by the name of Slowpenny, claimed he was setting out to visit a patient. Hence Marbeck was obliged to plunge into extempore.

227

'By the good saints, sir – have you no heart?' he cried. 'I've come fifty miles looking for tidings, and you say you're too busy to greet one of the faithful?'

The other blinked. He was a flinty little man, clean-shaven and clad from head to foot in dusty black. 'Who are you, and what do you want with me?' he asked. They stood in the doorway of his home, Slowpenny with a high-crowned hat in his hand. Marbeck wore a plain black cloak and no sword and carried a similar hat, which he had managed to find on a stall. Twisting its brim in feigned nervousness, he bent closer.

'I hoped you might have news of a friend,' he said. 'I went to join him in the Gogmagog Hills by Cambridge, but he had gone ... I've spent weeks trying to find him.'

The doctor gave a start, and a look of suspicion appeared. 'There was someone else here yesterday, asking questions,' he murmured. 'I told him I'd never heard of that man, and I'll say the same to you—'

'What man?' Marbeck broke in. 'I've named no names. I came here because I was told you were one of faith and soberness. One brave enough to challenge the squalid reign of Elizabeth Tudor – to speak the truth as written in scripture.'

The other hesitated, and a touch of pink appeared on his cheeks; he was not immune to vanity after all. 'Yet I fail to see how I can help you,' he answered. 'You're asking for news I cannot give...' And he would have moved to the door, had Marbeck not stayed him.

'I merely wish to find him, and hear him preach,' he protested. 'To converse with him, as I would have at Gogmagog – where's the harm? I believe you're a man of principle, but also of charity. Can you not at least send me away with some hope? Point me towards good Doctor Gow, that I may clasp his hand as I yearn to do!'

But Slowpenny remained stony-faced, and merely nodded towards the door. So with an effort, Marbeck produced his last card. It was a Ballard trick, of course: focus your mind upon a painful memory from childhood, the old player had once told him, and the tears will come. So screwing up his face, he forced himself, and was rewarded by his eyes filling and drops coursing down his cheeks. To his relief, the ruse worked.

'Great heaven...' More in embarrassment than in sympathy, the barber-surgeon relented. 'Brother, this will not do ... you'd better come and take a restorative.' He led the way to the rear of his cramped premises. Marbeck sat on a stool, shaking his head and wiping his eyes, while the other fussed about, preparing a mix of powders and liquids.

'You are most kind, doctor.' Marbeck took

the cup from him and sipped the foul-tasting brew. 'My weakness confounds me; our leaders of old, like the great Calvin, would be ashamed.'

'No doubt.' Slowpenny looked uncomfortable. 'See, I must go soon. You may rest here a while – but with regard to the other matter...' He shook his head. 'I deem you a believer, yet I fear to aid you. Our brother Isaac – yes, I will name him – has been sore pressed in recent weeks. Arrested for no good reason, pursued after he bravely escaped—'

'Arrested?' Marbeck looked horrified. 'No ... that is too hard to bear! But can I not join him, and share his tribulations? At least tell me in which direction I should go, dear friend – will you not do that?'

A moment passed; he held his expression, of earnestness mingled with deep concern, until at last the barber-surgeon sighed and pointed through the window. 'You'd best journey north,' he said. 'There's a house on the edge of Brampton village that belonged to a friend of his – the Tyrrell house. I know not if he is there still, for he moves about a great deal. But you may get news...' He shook his head again. 'I pray you're in time, for our poor brother is sick ... yet one day he shall be raised in rapture. God preserve him!'

'Amen...' With a sigh, Marbeck stood up.

'I'll go at once.'

He placed the cup of medicine in Slowpenny's hand; the man took it absently, then saw that it had hardly been touched. He glanced up, but all he saw was Marbeck's back disappearing through the doorway.

Brampton was fifteen miles away. On Cobb, Marbeck could have reached it by noon, but he was obliged to go slowly, Rowan's horse being as wearied by recent exertions as its rider. The two reached the village by mid-afternoon, and after watering their mounts, obtained directions to the Tyrrell house. But as they left the main road and turned onto a track that led through fields, they slowed down instinctively.

A large timbered house had appeared ahead. This had been a farmstead, Marbeck saw, but it was run-down, and he was reminded of the place at Gogmagog; there was the same silence, the same air of watchfulness. There were no mules, however, nor smoke from the chimney. He and Rowan walked their horses to the front of the house and halted. No one appeared, so they dismounted and approached the door; both sensed that something was wrong.

'Let me go first,' Rowan said, and drew his sword. Marbeck loosened his in the scabbard, his eyes sweeping the house. They mounted a step, Rowan lifted the latch and

threw the door wide. It opened with a creak
... and as one, they stopped dead. Stretched
out across the hallway was a man who appeared to be in the throes of agony. As they
stared, he raised his head and gazed implor-
ingly at them.

'Help me ... for the love of Christ...'

Sheathing his sword, Rowan went forward.
Marbeck followed – and recognition dawned. 'This man was with Gow at Gogmagog,'
he said.

The front of the man's doublet was covered with vomit. 'It works through me!' he
gasped. 'I'm slain, like the others...' His
hands clawed his stomach. 'It burns ... hor-
rible!'

'He's been poisoned,' Rowan said, but
Marbeck gave a start. 'Others?' he echoed.
'Henry...'

He listened, but there was no sound.
Quickly he moved along the hallway, peering
through open doorways. Rowan came after.
At the end was a wide chamber, lit by the
afternoon sun; they hurried in – and froze.

Two men were sprawled by a large table,
where the remains of a meal lay. One Marbeck recognized immediately: the oldest of
Gow's company, white-haired Silas, whom
he had last seen in the house by St Neots.
The other ... he breathed out in relief: it
wasn't Henry Scroop. Then dismay over-
came him.

The man was John Chyme.

'By heaven ... what foul business was done here?'

Rowan stood beside Marbeck, dumbfounded. Silas had seemingly expired where he sat, half-drooped across a bench. His eyes were open, while his hands clutched his stomach, like those of the man in the hallway. Chyme had apparently got up from the table and staggered several feet before collapsing on the floor. There were traces of vomit about his mouth.

'All poisoned?' Marbeck looked at the table, noticing several overturned cups from which red wine had spilled. Then he knelt beside Chyme, feeling the great artery in his neck. There was no pulse, but the body was barely cold. The young man – handsome still, but clad in the plain clothing he had donned to infiltrate the company – looked as if he were merely asleep. With a heavy heart, Marbeck bent his head.

'What in God's name was this – a last supper?'

Rowan was sniffing one of the wine cups. He gestured to the dishes, some of which were untouched. 'The food's cold,' he said. 'I'll wager it happened hours ago...' He gave a start, as a cry came from the hallway. Marbeck turned, tearing his gaze from the body of his friend.

'Let's hear what the other can tell us,' he

murmured.

The man was where they had left him, whimpering with pain. As they knelt beside him, he turned a haggard face to Marbeck. 'Gone...' he breathed. 'He threatened to leave us before ... he trusts no one now ... not even Silas. He said we'd break bread together, for the last time...'

'The boy – Henry.' Marbeck lifted the man's head and cradled it. 'Where is he?'

'Gone too...' came the hoarse reply. 'He won't leave him...' The man's face creased in anguish. 'He must have known ... he didn't drink...'

'The wine,' Rowan said. When Marbeck turned sharply, he added: 'Laced with poison: I'm certain of it.'

'Poison...' The dying man gazed at them. 'Aye ... 'twas in our company! What fools we were to believe all he said – we were charmed, as by a sorcerer!'

Marbeck glanced at Rowan, who shook his head: the fellow had not long to live. 'Where has Gow gone?' he asked sharply. But there was no answer, only a grunt of pain.

'You must tell us,' Marbeck persisted. 'For the boy's sake, if nothing else...'

'To perdition!' The man's breathing was laboured, and there was terror in his gaze. 'Where he would have led us, too. God save us all...' His eyes closed; the last member of Isaac Gow's flock let out a hoarse breath, then went limp. Marbeck laid his head on the floor and stood up heavily, while Rowan gazed down at the prone figure.

'Let's assume the worst, then,' he said at last. 'Shall we on to York?'

Marbeck barely nodded.

There was no time to waste, but a long ride lay ahead of them, and already the day was waning. So reluctantly they decided to leave the following morning, when the horses would be fully rested. There was time for a search of the ill-fated farmhouse, but it yielded nothing. There was also time for Rowan to find the constable in Brampton, and tell him of mischief at the Tyrrell house to be investigated; though to the man's dismay he would not stay to tell more. Having found an inn at Gainsborough, some seven miles further north, they ate and slept, leaving the village at dawn.

There was little to be said that day. The green flatlands of Lincolnshire sped by; by afternoon they had crossed the Humber, and entered the East Riding of Yorkshire. Their progress was good, and as they rode up the valley of the River Ouse, there was an opportunity for talk. Both men were preoccupied with the discovery of the day before, but for Marbeck the matter was graver. The death of John Chyme, let alone the danger Henry Scroop might now be in, weighed heavily upon him.

'You truly think Gow intends a plot against the King's life?' Rowan asked. Having watered the horses at the last village, they were now walking them. From Selby they intended to make speed, and reach York before evening.

'I believe so,' Marbeck answered. 'Indeed, I've suspected it since I saw the rage in the man.'

'He deems himself a martyr,' Rowan said. 'He seeks death ... but what of the boy?'

Marbeck didn't answer for a while. He was recalling the letter Henry had sent to Celia; now, its portent was grim indeed. 'Edward Poyns thought Gow was using him in some way,' he said, then shook his head. 'I know not. He said Gow was mad enough for anything.'

'Well, he seems to want Henry's company, or he'd have poisoned him along with the others,' Rowan said grimly. 'And I let that devil escape! If anything happens to the boy – let alone the King...'

'Racking yourself is no use,' Marbeck said shortly. 'If anyone has cause to do so it's me. I could have asked Prout to let John Chyme go with me into Kent ... he could be alive...'

'Or blown to smithereens, along with your friend Llewellyn,' Rowan countered. When Marbeck said nothing, he went on: 'You're right: this will avail us nothing. Let's find the

King's party – whether he's at York, or further off. No doubt our crookback master will be nearby, whereupon I'll demand an audience with him; and I mean to demand it, if I have to fight my way to him.'

He turned to Marbeck, who merely shrugged and gathered up Cobb's reins. 'Are you ready?' he asked.

For answer, Rowan put his foot in the stirrup and mounted.

Once in the saddle they started to trot, then to canter. A further ten miles lay ahead, but the light was good. Soon they were speeding along the North Road again, until on the brow of a low hill they stopped to gaze ahead. There in the distance, the outline of Clifford's Tower could be seen, and to the left, that of St Peter's.

So at last Marbeck and Rowan entered the great city of York, to a peal of bells and an air of high excitement – and very soon they learned the cause.

It was Saturday the sixteenth of April; and James Stuart had arrived a day before them.

SEVENTEEN

King James, the sixth of Scotland and first of England, had been welcomed at York with great show of loyalty by the mayor and populace. With the King was a large train of followers: noblemen, servants and hangers-on, both Scottish and English. Others were arriving by the hour, to swell the crowds; the city was packed, with people flocking from far afield. The royal party was lodged at the King's Manor, on the north-west side of the city by Marygate: the seat of the Council of the North. Here too were the Cecils: Lord Thomas, the Council's President, and his half-brother, Sir Robert. That same evening, Marbeck sent a message in cipher to Master Secretary, begging him for an audience on a matter of gravest importance. He sent it by a man he recognized, one of Cecil's own household who, encouraged by a generous tip, promised to deliver it to his master soon. After that, there was little to do but wait.

There was no room anywhere, of course; every inn, tavern and alehouse was filled to bursting point. The two intelligencers managed to get fodder for their horses and a supper for themselves, but only by paying high prices for both. Finally, to escape the throng they walked along the river by St Martin's. Night had fallen, and torches stood along the bank.

'If Gow is here, he'll be hard to find,' Marbeck observed. 'But if he intends mischief he'll show himself at last, disguised or not. I only hope we recognize him.'

'I'll recognize him – have no fear upon that,' Rowan said.

They walked in silence, among strolling couples and larger groups, picking up snatches of conversation. The King had been stag-hunting on the moors, someone said; he was a great man for the chase. Another remarked on the coarseness of his Scottish followers, as rough in manners as in dress. Someone else spoke of James's awkwardness; rumour had it he did not enjoy formal ceremonies. That was unfortunate, a man nearby said, for tomorrow he had to endure another. Overhearing this, Marbeck glanced at Rowan.

'We must find out where that will be. Likely it's at St Peter's ... the Minster.'

'Perhaps he means to dub a few more knights,' Rowan suggested, with a sardonic look.

They had walked westwards almost to the city wall, and the ruined St Mary's Abbey.

Behind another wall was the King's Manor. It would be well guarded, Marbeck knew; but the thought of a large public ceremony on the morrow made him uneasy. The monarch was always exposed on such occasions: an opportunity for Isaac Gow to make his move. He was musing upon it, when he felt a tug on his sleeve.

'I think someone here knows you,' Rowan said.

He turned sharply – and his heart sank. Walking towards him was none other than his former master at Barnes: the bumbling courtier, Sir Thomas Croft.

'Richard Strang, as I live and breathe!'

'Sir Thomas...' Marbeck managed a bow. 'An honour ... and such a surprise.'

'So I observe.' The knight, dressed in a garish suit of yellow and crimson, looked him up and down. 'I would have words with you, concerning the way you left my house without even a farewell. You were remiss, Strang – and insolent!'

'So I was, sir...' Marbeck forced a contrite look. 'Yet I had family business that would not wait. But surely you'll not begrudge a loyal subject wishing to set eyes on our new King?'

The other grunted, and his gaze fell on Rowan, who stood stiffly to one side. 'Is this a kinsman of yours?'

Marbeck hesitated, but mercifully Rowan

came to his rescue.

'Merely an acquaintance, sir,' he said amiably. 'Master ... Strang and I travelled together, to see His Majesty. There's to be a great occasion tomorrow – at the Minster, we hear...'

'Then you hear falsely,' Croft retorted, with the air of one who was in the know. 'The King will preside on the green before Marygate, when poor citizens and yeomen may have sight of him. They say he will touch the sick, as did the great monarchs of old.'

'Indeed...?' Rowan inclined his head, but both he and Marbeck had stiffened. 'That will be ... a joyous event.'

'How does the Lady Margery, sir?' Marbeck asked quickly. 'Is she here too, or...'

'She is not,' Sir Thomas answered. 'She remains at Barnes with our family. Speaking of whom, you have much to do, Strang, to repair relations with Lady Alice. She's been out of sorts since you went off in such a precipitate manner.'

'I'll visit her and make amends,' Marbeck said. 'Yet I trust another tutor may be found. Such are ten a penny.'

'So they are, now I think upon it.' Sir Thomas sniffed, clearly thinking he had spent long enough talking to men of no importance. With a final glance at them both he started to go, then frowned. 'Just where is it you're from, Strang?' he asked. 'Somewhere here in the north, isn't it?'

'Not here exactly, Sir Thomas,' Marbeck answered. 'Nowhere you would know...' but the man was already striding off. They watched until he was out of sight.

'So, who is Lady Alice?' Rowan asked, raising his brows. Marbeck merely sighed.

The Sabbath dawned fair but chilly, with a breeze blowing down from the moors. Unable to find accommodation, the two intelligencers had spent the night in a stable with their horses, after bribing the ostler to let them bed down on the straw. As the city stirred into life they went to an ordinary, the first customers of the day. Over a breakfast of porridge and stewed fruit they made their plans. Marbeck had walked the city streets the previous night, picking up what news he could.

'Croft might be mistaken about the King touching sick people to heal them,' he told Rowan. 'From what I've learned, he thinks such old practices mere superstition ... and he shrinks from contact with ordinary folk.'

'He's an odd fellow,' Rowan said. 'Learned as a judge, I hear, yet slobbers like a beggar.' He thought for a moment. 'We'll join the throng – but first we should go to the manor and accost Crookback Robert.'

'You mean bluff our way in?' Marbeck

looked sceptical. 'None can get near the house. He has my message ... I've said I'll wait near the manor, if he should send for me.'

'A pox on him,' Rowan muttered. 'Whatever happens, on his head be it.'

Soon after they parted, having agreed that Marygate should be their meeting point. Rowan would look about the city, while Marbeck walked out by Bootham, a busy way lined with shops and stalls. Here he paused: to his left stood the gates of the King's Manor. But the guards eyed him keenly, and he would not linger; after the encounter with Sir Thomas Croft he had no wish to draw further attention to himself. He moved on, mingling with those gathering for Sunday worship; church bells were clanging from several directions. Beyond Bootham were meadows, and a windmill beside the road. Here he stopped, looking southwards towards the walls, and the broad green before Marygate. Already men were setting up barriers, and close to the gatehouse itself a low platform had been erected, with a padded chair for the King. People would pass before him and kneel, to present gifts and petitions. Whether any would feel the royal hand laid upon them to cure their ills, Marbeck doubted; that custom had long since fallen out of favour.

He walked by the creaking windmill, its

sails turning in the breeze. His intention was to survey the green and choose the best vantage points for himself and Rowan. But at that moment a commotion arose from Bootham: cheering, along with a clatter of hooves. He retraced his steps, to stand by the roadside as others were doing. It seemed a party had emerged from the manor – and quickly, he realized he was about to get his first sight of James Stuart. The heads of riders could be seen above the stalls ... but when they approached, Marbeck's reaction was one of surprise: could that unsmiling, rough-bearded man in the centre really be England's new King?

Yet there was little doubt that it was James himself. His horse was a fine thoroughbred and he sat it well, even with a hooded falcon on his wrist. With him rode other noblemen; some finely dressed, others in plainer garb, also carrying falcons. So the King was going hawking, in sight of the people; from habit Marbeck looked around keenly, but saw only cheering bystanders, bowing and doffing hats. The monarch paid them no heed, but merely stared ahead. Marbeck glanced at the other riders ... and froze: towards the rear, sitting somewhat awkwardly on a black hunting horse, was Sir Robert Cecil.

His first instinct was to step forward and hail him, but he knew the notion was foolish: there were armed guards riding behind, their eyes scanning the bystanders for any sign of trouble. In any case the group were already past, heading out to open country. Soon they were merely a distant body, raising a cloud of dust. Standing at the roadside, he cursed silently.

'Tha's no call to look downhearted, sir,' someone nearby said in a thick Yorkshire accent. 'His Majesty will sit before Marygate this afternoon, and ye may see him at your leisure.'

Marbeck turned to see a sturdy fellow in workaday garb, and summoned a wry grin. 'So I hear, master,' he said. 'What's the occasion? Will the King make more knights, or touch the sick as some say?'

'I know not,' the man answered. 'There's to be a pageant and speeches – as if we needed any more o' them. Yet some are indeed bringing their sick folk here, in hope ... is there someone ailing in your family?'

With a shake of his head, Marbeck walked off.

He found Rowan later, and the two of them talked in a tavern in Coney Street. But there was little to add to what they had already learned. The King, it seemed, would spend a few more days in York before moving on to Doncaster. It occurred to Marbeck that Master Secretary intended the sovereign to break his journey at the Cecil family's seat at Burghley, near Stamford.

'Aye, he'll entertain the King's party in style,' Rowan agreed. 'And strengthen his influence all the while ... you can wager he has his eye on a peerage.'

'Meanwhile, I take it you've seen no sign of our Puritan friend?' Marbeck asked, to which the other shook his head.

'Yet I'm certain he's here,' he said, almost to himself. 'Call it the victory of hope over reason, if you will. But I've spent so long pursuing the varlet, I believe I can smell him. I've come close before...' He looked up sharply. 'It ends here in York, Marbeck. I can't continue in this way ... I'll arrest that man, or perish in the attempt!'

With that Rowan took his cup and drained it, as if to seal the vow.

'Then let's take positions on the green,' Marbeck said. 'I pray the sun keeps shining – and that luck shines on us, too.'

By afternoon the ground before Marygate was a mass of people, of all ages and stations. City dignitaries dressed in their finest clothes were gathering about the royal dais, presided over by the mayor, Sir Robert Watter. Further off, behind wooden palings patrolled by marshals with staves, ordinary folk thronged in their hundreds, which soon became thousands. Among them the intelligencers moved unnoticed. Rowan was dressed in a plain cloak, with a hat pulled low.

Marbeck had no cloak: his sword was at his side, and he wanted ease of movement.

But as the day wore on and the King had still not appeared, both men grew restless. They kept apart, ignoring one another, though now and again Marbeck caught sight of his fellow, always close to the platform. He himself preferred to rove about, observing people and hearing the gossip. His eyes soon fell on those who, perhaps from mere desperation, had brought sick relatives with them. They were a heart-rending sight: the lame and the diseased, from babes in arms to elderly folk being helped along by others. It angered him that these people were doomed to disappointment; the impression he'd formed was that King James would not allow them near him. He recalled Nicholas Prout's words, when they had sat in the rain, in the gallery at the Boar's Head: how the new King would drive the people apart...

A great cry went up, shaking him out of his reverie. There was a surge towards the platform, and at the same time a fanfare of trumpets rang out. Peering over heads, Marbeck saw the King arrive at last wearing a tall hat, velvet cloak and jewelled chain, guarded by halberdiers. His followers were about him: lords, knights and mere gentlemen. He couldn't see Cecil, but was sure he would be among them. He did glimpse Sir Thomas Croft, a gangling figure towering above others. Soon the party had placed themselves before the crowd, and the King took his seat. People cheered, shouted and waved hats. The royal trumpeters blew another fanfare, to bring silence more than anything else, whereupon the mayor raised his hands and called out.

'God save our royal sovereign James: King of England, Scotland, France and Ireland!'

A roar went up. Marbeck looked round: those with sick relatives were pressing forward, making their way to the barrier. Uneasily he threaded his own way, eyes sweeping the crowd; but there was no sign of anyone who looked like Isaac Gow, let alone Henry Scroop. He caught sight of Rowan, not a dozen paces from the King, and knew the man was as tense as he was.

'His gracious Majesty...'

There was another cheer; the mayor lifted his hands again, struggling to be heard. 'His gracious Majesty,' he repeated, 'in his mercy, has agreed that citizens in sore need may come before him. If it is meet and fit, he may place his royal hand upon their person, in honour of his state and in knowledge of the blessed power of kings, that they may with God's help be healed forthwith!'

There were cries of approval. Yet Marbeck saw several people crossing themselves openly; the old religion was strong here. Tales of ancient times, when Edward the

Confessor had first touched the sick, were not forgotten. Easing forward, he saw the marshals forming a passageway to the platform: if anyone did intend harm to the King, he reasoned, there were men to prevent it. He realized his hand had gone to his sword-hilt, and hurriedly removed it. But nobody noticed: all eyes were on the King in his chair, and those who were at the front, desperate to have their kinsfolk touched. He sighed; one thing he shared with James Stuart, if rumours were true, was a deep scepticism in the efficacy of such a process. But those folk carrying children or assisting the old clearly believed ... He looked away, to observe others near the platform. No weapons were in evidence: such would easily be spotted by the guards ... and suddenly, doubt overwhelmed him.

Would someone like Isaac Gow – madman or not – truly attempt such a desperate act? It occurred to Marbeck that he had allowed fancy to run away with him. Had he become caught up in Rowan's obsession with the man's capture? Indeed – had Rowan not become somewhat unhinged these past weeks, tormenting himself for allowing Gow to escape? He strained his eyes to see his fellow intelligencer, but he was nowhere in sight. Frowning, he began to push his way through the crowd, occasioning a few rebuffs in the process. People jostled for sight of the sick, the first of whom were lining up between the rows of marshals. Now he was near the front ... he caught sight of Cecil, standing beside the King. For a moment he thought Master Secretary had seen him too, but the man gave no sign.

A murmur went up: a woman with a child in her arms was allowed forward. Humbly she approached the King, and fell to her knees. Marbeck couldn't hear what was said, but he saw the sovereign's lips move, presumably in commiseration. All eyes were on mother and baby, and now a silence fell. Suddenly it seemed the same question had risen in every mind: would this stand-offish monarch, who was said to shun contact with all but his family and favourites, put such notions aside and touch the ragged folk before him?

He did – but quickly, and with a gloved hand. Another murmur rose: surely this was not the way? People turned to one another, muttering – but Marbeck's eyes were on the platform. He saw the woman with the child being ushered away, and understood. This was but an exercise in majesty ... a new king striving to show himself one with the people. It was a pageant in itself – as much of a show as those that would follow it. His mouth set tight, he looked hard at Sir Robert Cecil, and knew. Who else but Master Secretary, weaver of intrigue, would have planned it?

The monarch had to be seen in the best light ... all England would hear of how James in his humility had touched the sick on his progress south.

And yet, the sick still waited in hope. Another woman had approached, leading two children by the hand. They too knelt, to receive some empty words and a touch of the King's glove. Then they were led aside, as an old man limped forward, leaning heavily upon a raggedly dressed boy. The man used a crutch, and took a long time to reach the platform. The marshals glanced at him, then looked to see who was next in line. The boy stumbled and dropped to his knees before the King, seemingly overwhelmed by the occasion. The old man bowed but stayed upright, struggling to keep his balance. There was a moment as the King spoke up, bidding him come closer. People strained to see and hear, heads bobbing...

But Marbeck gave a start, and every sinew in his body tightened. He shouted, but few heard. He elbowed people aside, and got blows in return. Some turned to look, and fell back at sight of a man with hand on sword. Then he was at the barrier, struggling to climb it.

'Stop that man!' he shouted. 'He's an assassin!'

Someone loomed to block his way, but he downed the fellow with a blow. Then he was

251

over the paling, advancing towards the platform – and at once marshals started towards him. But his eyes were on the lame figure, who was no cripple at all – and on the boy, who was suddenly on his feet. The King and those around him had now realized the danger, and a cry of dismay flew up: the old man's crutch had suddenly become a blade. Half of it was thrown aside, and steel flashed in the sunlight ... Isaac Gow, eyes blazing, lurched towards the monarch.

For Marbeck, time slowed to a snail's pace. He drew his sword, knowing he was too late. Burly arms seized him ... He thrust at someone, but his stroke went wide. There were screams from all sides ... He saw figures in his path, and a blur of movement. He thought he heard Rowan shout ... He even had time to glimpse Sir Robert Cecil, a look of horror on his features. And then to his amazement, something else: the boy – who was indeed Henry Scroop – appeared to be grappling with Gow, struggling for possession of the man's blade. Locked as in a dance, the two impostors fell to the ground, to be overwhelmed at once by guards.

But now Marbeck too was held. He shouted again, and it was Henry's name he called ... then he was falling, bodies pressing him downwards, pinning him as if he were a madman. Someone kicked him in the ribs, someone else tore his sword from his grasp

... He lashed out, but was overwhelmed. It was over: breathless and half-dazed, he was yanked to his feet; then he was being march-ed away, with a great roaring in his ears.

It sounded as if the crowd were shouting, *Hang him!*

EIGHTEEN

York Castle was damp and cold, its old walls echoing to the sound of footfalls. Marbeck was frog-marched down a passage to a small cell and shoved inside, so violently that he fell to his knees. The door squealed shut, and a key rasped in the lock. Then he was alone, with a tiny window too high to see out of and a pile of straw in one corner. Getting to his feet, he went to the door and vented his rage by hammering on it. But there was no answer except a distant shout of approval, perhaps from some wretch who was in a similar position.

Anger and frustration overwhelmed him. He had tried to save the King, only to be taken for an assassin himself. Cursing roundly he kicked the heavy door, bruising himself in the process. He felt for his poniard, but it had been taken from him along with his sword. He searched his doublet, and found that even his bodkin was gone. There was the lute-string in his waist-band ... but as he stood there in the gloom, he knew he would get no opportunity to use it. Fighting despair, he sank to the floor.

Vivid in his mind was Gow's attempt on the King's life, which seemed to have failed – at least, he hoped it had. He was amazed by the clumsiness of it: the man who had managed to elude Rowan, to disappear for weeks and then re-emerge in disguise, face to face with the monarch, had seemingly been confounded at the very last by Henry Scroop, of all people: the boy who worshipped him. What lay behind it Marbeck could not know, but it hardly seemed to matter now. He himself, no longer trusted by Master Secretary, had been dubbed a traitor, and would face interrogation whenever the King's servants chose. The injustice nauseated him ... though he had a memory of Sir Robert Cecil's face, as he stood behind the monarch. Would he not interpret Marbeck's actions differently? And what of Rowan? Had he not come forward to defend him?

He breathed deeply, pressing his hands to the cold floor; this was no use. For the moment he could do nothing but conserve his strength. Sooner or later he would be called to account ... He smiled grimly: when that time came, he would have his say. After a while he stretched out on the straw; there was a rustle and something scurried away, but he paid it no heed. Instead he fixed his eyes on the little square above and watched the afternoon turn to evening, then to dusk.

Finally, because he could do no other, he slept.

The squeal of a key woke him. He sat up, his eyes going to the window: dawn had broken. As the door opened he got to his feet, events of yesterday crowding his mind. He was cold, stiff and hungry. Half-crouching, he prepared to face his captors ... but at sight of the figure who appeared, he drew a breath of relief.

'Thanks be to God ... I thought they'd used you as they did me,' Rowan said.

Marbeck stared. His fellow intelligencer looked tired and pale, and there was a swelling at his mouth that spoke of blows received. But he was no prisoner: he even wore his sword. A guard stood outside while Rowan came into the cell.

'Are you hurt?' he asked anxiously. 'I've been up half the night, haranguing everyone from the Sheriff of the Castle to his potboy. It's an outrage you were treated in this manner.'

'The King...' Marbeck found his voice. 'Did they—'

'He's unharmed,' Rowan answered at once. 'Gow's a prisoner, in this very dungeon. It was the boy saved him – did you not see?'

But Marbeck sat down heavily on the floor, relief sweeping over him. He sighed, and gazed up at his fellow. 'Then … they don't think I tried to attack the sovereign?'

'Not any longer. Not after I'd told my tale half a dozen times, finally to Master Secretary himself.' Rowan's irritation showed. 'But it's all been laid forth now, and he's satisfied. In any case, it seems he has Prout's report – had it for days. And he knows about Drax and Meeres, and the Earl of Charnock too.'

It was becoming a great deal to take in. Marbeck started to raise himself, but at once Rowan put a hand out. 'Let me aid you,' he said. So Marbeck took his hand, and was pulled to his feet. The other did not let go; and in his eyes, there was something like contentment, born of sheer relief. They clasped each other, and Rowan even managed a smile.

'So it has ended in York, as you vowed,' Marbeck said.

With a nod, Rowan released his hand. 'For you too, I think. When you've eaten you'll get your wish: an audience with Master Secretary. Though I wouldn't expect too much.'

'I don't,' Marbeck said. 'All I want is the chance to ask a few questions. After that I care not what happens…' His face clouded. 'But what of Henry? Is he arrested too?'

'He is.' Rowan turned to the door. 'And he's unhurt, despite everything. It's best you have it from our master ... Shall we get ourselves out of this stinking hole?'

It was midday before Marbeck was finally admitted to see Sir Robert Cecil. He was not taken to the King's Manor, but to another room in the castle. Though his accommodation had improved beyond measure: he had eaten breakfast, washed, and enjoyed the feel of fresh clothing. Rowan had brought his pack and left him, having things to do, he said. So rested and refreshed but smouldering with anger, Marbeck awaited the call, and was at last conducted to an upper chamber, well appointed and bright with hangings. Master Secretary, his face expressionless as usual, was seated behind a table, propped up on a woolsack. To Marbeck's surprise another man was with him: elegant, richly dressed and vaguely familiar. It took a moment for him to realize that this was Sir Robert's half-brother, Lord Thomas Cecil. So – his master wanted some support. He made his bow to both men and waited.

'But he's quite young,' Lord Thomas said, raising his eyebrows at Marbeck. He was on his feet, dwarfing his hunchback brother. 'I pictured a middle-aged swaggerer, with battle scars and all. Is this the man who tried to take on an army, in defence of our blighted nation?'

Master Secretary cleared his throat. 'I'm

relieved to see you well, Marbeck,' was all he said.

Marbeck's reply was a faint smile.

'The Lord President of the Council...' Cecil indicated his brother. 'His Lordship has come to convey His Majesty's gratitude for your actions yesterday. Now that all's been said and sifted, I think at last we have a true picture of events.'

'I'm pleased to hear that, sir,' Marbeck said. He glanced at Lord Thomas, and was surprised to see a half-smile on the older man's face. 'I did what I could.'

'And you should have due reward,' his Lordship said. 'I'm asked to give you this, with His Majesty's thanks.' He produced a purse, and waited for Marbeck to walk forward; but he remained where he stood.

'I want no reward, my lord,' he replied. 'Only my rightful wage – and some speech with Sir Robert, about certain matters between us.'

Sir Robert Cecil stirred. 'We'll talk of that,' he said. 'But I advise you to rein in your pride, lest you forget yourself...'

'Oh – forbear that, sir,' the Lord President broke in. Marbeck blinked: the man almost appeared to be enjoying himself. What had passed between the two he could not imagine, but he quickly revised his earlier notion; it now looked as if Master Secretary disliked his brother being present.

'He has a right to feel indignant, does he not?' Lord Thomas went on. 'He foils a plot down in Kent – even if it was doomed before it started – then hurries up here to prevent a madman from murdering the King, only to find himself arrested! In his place, I wager I'd feel somewhat displeased too.'

Silence fell. Through an open window Marbeck heard guards drilling, and the distant cries of street-sellers; it was Monday morning, and York was returning to normal. Blank-faced, he eyed Master Secretary, taking some satisfaction from the man's discomfort.

'Yet what's done is done,' Sir Robert said finally. 'Isaac Gow is a prisoner, and will be conveyed to London...'

'The boy, sir.' Marbeck interrupted, more sharply than he intended. 'Henry Scroop ... he's but a foolish youth, who was bewitched by Gow. I swore to his mother I would find him...'

'His mother?' Lord Thomas spoke up. 'Do you mean Lady Scroop, the widow of Sir Richard?' When Marbeck indicated assent, the man showed his surprise. 'And what, precisely, are your relations with her?'

'She's a friend, my lord,' Marbeck answered. 'I've known her son since he was a boy – he's no murderer, I would swear it.'

'He served a regicidal traitor – he should die with him.'

Sir Robert snapped out the words, showing anger at last. But Marbeck stood his ground. 'Did he not stay his hand, though?' he countered. 'I saw him myself, struggling to take the blade from Gow ... I'm certain the boy had no knowledge of his true intent. The man had poisoned his mind – Henry was frightened and confused. He's not been himself since his father's death.'

'Perhaps so.' Master Secretary remained stony-faced. 'Yet we cannot let his actions go unpunished.'

Marbeck pictured Celia in her anguish, the last time he'd seen her. With a heavy heart, he sought to shape his argument further ... then he stiffened: the Lord President was looking fixedly at him.

'These actions were committed here in the North Country, were they not?' he enquired, turning his gaze on his brother. 'Hence, I think I am the proper authority.'

Another silence; Marbeck lowered his eyes. He sensed a current of hostility between the two Cecils: the sons of the former Lord Treasurer, Sir William, but by different wives – and as unlike as could be. With hopes barely alive, he waited.

'Indeed,' Master Secretary said. 'Yet I should remind you that the deed was done within the King's presence. It's treason – we must await His Majesty's pleasure in this.'

'Oh, very well ... so be it.'

Quickly Lord Thomas appeared to come to a decision. With a curt nod to his brother, he started for the door. Marbeck bowed; but when he looked up, the man was holding out the purse again.

'If not for the Crown, then take it for my sake,' he said.

So Marbeck took it. Meeting his lordship's eye, he sensed that the man understood his feelings. He murmured his thanks, whereupon the other turned briskly and went out.

'By the Lord Christ,' Sir Robert exclaimed, as soon as they were alone. 'I'd like to hang you from the walls of Clifford's Tower, Marbeck – as is the custom here, I'm told.'

'For traitors, sir, from what *I'm* told,' Marbeck said mildly. 'And I am not one of those.'

They eyed each other. 'Prout's sent me a full account of all that happened in the south,' Cecil resumed. 'Even the harshest of men could only applaud you for what you've accomplished – you and others...' He paused. 'Llewellyn's loss cuts me deeper than you know. He served my father once.'

After a moment Marbeck inclined his head. 'John Chyme's death cuts me in the same manner,' he said.

At that his master showed irritation. 'But I should have been told! I would not have sanctioned the mission. Prout over-stepped his powers – in every respect.'

262

'He believed we were about to be invaded, sir,' Marbeck replied. 'As did I ... and Drax's regiment was no phantom army.'

'Well, I'd not meant to speak of that now,' Cecil replied abruptly. 'The entrapment of Meeres was your work, and I commend it. Yet Drax remains free – as does the man who supplied the money for their enterprise. By now, it's more than likely he too has fled – we may never learn who he was.'

Marbeck frowned. 'And the Earl of Charnock?'

A look of contempt crossed Cecil's features. 'A fool, if ever there was. He did naught but trail in the King's wake, swearing blood and thunder. His force – such as it was – melted away as soon as word came that the Infanta hadn't arrived. Nor would she have done: I could have told them that from the start. Do you truly think the Spanish have any stomach left for invasion? Now the Earl's held at Berwick, which he'd sworn was the furthest south King James would ever ride. He'll go to the block – and few will mourn him.'

In silence Marbeck took in the information. His mind went back to his chamber at the Boar's Head, when he had slammed a table against the wall, and Prout had sat and watched him. His own words came to mind ... had it all been for nothing? He looked at Master Secretary, and found the man's eyes upon him.

'You think you've been harshly treated,' he said.

Marbeck didn't answer.

'I needed to be certain of something, that's all...' Cecil gave a sigh, and glanced down. For the first time Marbeck noticed a sheaf of papers, stacked on the table before him. 'There's no room for sentiment where the safety of the realm's concerned,' the spymaster added briskly, looking up again. 'Hence, I had to await the results of some intelligence of my own.'

Now Marbeck began to understand. 'Then it's true that someone denounced me,' he said, containing his anger with difficulty. 'Had you called me in, sir, I might have been able to answer that charge—'

'The Queen was dying,' Cecil snapped. 'Everything was in the balance. You were—'

'Of small importance? I realize that, Sir Robert. But had I been shown the accusation, it's likely I could have saved you a deal of effort.'

He waited, whereupon Master Secretary seemed to relent. 'Perhaps,' he allowed. 'But in any case, I've satisfied myself the charge was malicious...' He picked up a paper. 'This was intercepted, taken from a captured Spanish courier back in January. It's addressed to you – thanking you for your intelligence, which led to the capture of the

English agent Thomas Luce. A reward of two hundred escudos is promised.'

Cecil laid the paper down, and allowed Marbeck a moment to take in the words, which hit him like a blow to the vitals. 'But Luce wasn't captured, was he?' he began. 'The last I heard he was in France...'

'He was,' the spymaster broke in. 'He died – but not in a Spanish prison as I feared. It's taken me months to get to the bottom of it, but it seems he was killed in a whorehouse brawl. He always was a hectoring fellow.'

'Then who says otherwise?' Marbeck wanted to know.

'There's the rub,' came the reply. 'The letter's signed Juan Roble.'

The name hung in the air; Marbeck exhaled, a curse on his lips.

'I said it was malicious,' Master Secretary went on. 'This despatch was meant to be intercepted. It's a trick to get you arrested as a traitor, and sow doubt among us into the bargain. Clearly Roble still burns for revenge, after you broke his circle of agents a while back. You'll recall the details better than I.'

'I do,' Marbeck said at last. 'Though I confess I'm surprised the truth didn't occur to you sooner – sir.'

'I told you, I had to be certain,' Cecil retorted.

Neither of them spoke for a while. For

Marbeck memories flooded back, of the desperate search for Juan Roble's double agent, which had caused mayhem among the Crown intelligencers in the year 1600. That the Spanish spymaster should have waited this long to take revenge surprised him ... but then, who could fathom such men? He looked up and found Master Secretary's gaze upon him; at times, Marbeck failed to understand him, too.

'So – you may sleep easy in your bed again,' Cecil said dryly.

'That will be a refreshing experience,' Marbeck replied.

The other fell silent. He wore a familiar look, one that signalled the end of their discourse, but Marbeck wasn't finished. 'Have you had any word from Edward Poyns?' he asked. 'It was he who pointed me towards Gow's designs...'

Cecil shook his head. 'I've heard naught from Poyns since he went to Wisbech Castle.' Then almost as an afterthought he added: 'Since you're at something of a loose end, Marbeck, perhaps you should return to London and seek him out. Speak with Prout, too – tell him I'll have words with him as soon as I return. Just now I have other matters to attend to. The King will leave York tomorrow for Doncaster ... is there anything further?'

For a moment Marbeck thought of trying

to plead Henry Scroop's case again, but knew that it was useless. Then, what had he expected? With an effort, he bowed and turned to go. But as he did so, the spymaster cleared his throat pointedly.

'I mean to interrogate Sir Roland Meeres myself, at a later date,' he said. 'But I won't object if you look in on the man first, on some pretext ... it can do no harm.'

With a nod, Marbeck made his way out.

A few minutes later he was walking the castle walls in the clear air. Below him the river glittered in sunshine, dotted with small boats. He gazed southwards to open country, trying to collect his thoughts. His anger had evaporated, to be replaced by grim disappointment over the fate of Henry Scroop. He had found the boy at last, but once again was unable to help him. How he might break the news to Celia, he did not know.

Soon afterwards, however, he was surprised to receive a somewhat cryptic message by one of the castle guards. He was leaving the place, intending to retrieve Cobb and prepare to journey south, when the man waylaid him. He should make his way to Micklegate Bar within the hour, he was told, in readiness for escort duty. There was no written instruction, and the man would not say whence the order came. Marbeck's first thought was that it was from Master Secretary, before dismissing the notion. So in some puzzlement he collected his belongings and went to the stable near Goodram Gate, where he paid the reckoning from the purse the Lord President had given him. Then he saddled Cobb, and led him out through crowded streets.

Several times he thought he was recognized, as the swordsman who had burst out of the crowd by Marygate, seemingly to attack the King; shouts of *Hang him!* came uneasily to mind. But none accosted him, and with some relief he passed over the Ouse Bridge to Micklegate ... only to stop in surprise.

Two figures appeared ahead, standing beside saddled horses. One was Rowan; the other, looking pale and thin as a waif, was Henry Scroop.

NINETEEN

'Here we must part,' Rowan said. 'I've a prisoner named Gow to take to London, and I'm taking no chances. They've given me an escort of four men, just in case.'

He smiled, though Marbeck barely noticed. He was gazing at Henry, who refused to meet his eye. But the boy was changed: he saw it at once. There was anger and sullenness in his expression, but there was shame there too.

'Am I to escort a prisoner, too?' he asked Rowan.

'Not quite; you're to take our friend here back to Oxford,' his fellow intelligencer answered. Reaching into his sleeve, he produced a sealed document. 'This is a letter for the dean of Exeter College, instructing him to readmit Henry as a student by order of the Crown.'

In some disbelief, Marbeck took it. 'Whom should we thank for this sudden mercy?' he wondered. 'Not Master Secretary, surely...' Whereupon a memory arrived, of Lord Thomas Cecil's face as he had taken the purse from him; now, he understood.

'That must remain a matter of confidence,' Rowan said.

He was holding the reins of his horse, which shifted its hooves, restless to be on the move. Marbeck turned again to Henry, and after a moment the young man raised his eyes.

'I'll go with you,' he said in a dull voice. 'I'll make no trouble, but I don't wish to talk.'

Rowan and Marbeck exchanged looks. Then with a nod Marbeck stretched out his hand, which was taken firmly by the other. 'God speed you to London,' he said.

'And you to Oxford,' Rowan answered. Then he mounted, and with a last glance at them both rode back across the bridge into the city.

Marbeck watched him go, before turning to Henry. 'Have you got everything you need?' he enquired, and received a nod in return. 'Then we'll try to make Gainsborough by nightfall ... there's a passable inn I know. Thereafter we have a ride of more than a hundred miles ahead of us – can you manage that?'

Without a word the youth turned and put his foot in the stirrup. He had a good chestnut horse, which had no doubt been supplied by the same powerful man who had obtained his freedom. Marbeck recalled His Lordship's words, in the castle chamber: it seemed Lady Celia Scroop was known to him too. With a lightness born of relief, he too climbed into the saddle and grasped the reins. This day, which had started so badly, was ending in ways he would never have imagined.

And only then did he realize that Henry was no longer wearing his ragged disguise, nor the black garb of his former brethren, but a sober doublet and breeches of fawn. Wordlessly the two of them shook reins and rode out onto the Old North Road, heading south towards the fields of Lincolnshire.

Marbeck allowed two days for the journey from Gainsborough to Oxford, though he could have gone faster. Henry rode well, he saw, but he had no intention of forcing the pace. They said nothing throughout the entire first day, and Marbeck merely bided his time. He believed he understood the young man's feelings; but not until that night, when they were installed in the George Inn at Huntingdon, did he confront him.

He had chosen the resting place deliberately. It was roughly halfway along their journey, but he would have stopped there anyway. Not far away, more than three weeks earlier, he had found Isaac Gow's company, and attended the meeting in the wood which had ended so abruptly. There was no need to remind Henry; the boy understood well enough. Having eaten supper, he was about to walk off to their shared chamber when, to his alarm, Marbeck steered him into the tap-room and sat him down. The drawer appeared, and he ordered spiced ale for himself. Then he looked at Henry and waited.

'I don't want anything,' he said. 'I'm weary...' He glanced at the drawer who stood nearby. 'Tell him so.'

'Two mugs, then,' Marbeck said to the man, who started to go. Whereupon with a frown, Henry lifted his hand.

'No, I'll take Canaries ... sugared a little.'

The drawer looked at Marbeck, who nodded. But the moment they were alone, the youth turned on him. 'What do you intend, to get me soused?' he demanded. 'I'll have none of it – I drink to help me sleep, that's all.'

'That's wise,' Marbeck said.

They sat in silence, while the room gradually filled with townsfolk. Someone started singing an old Yorkshire air, and someone else joined in. Marbeck drank a little, then stretched his feet out towards the fire, recalling that he had sat in this very spot with Edward Poyns. Henry tasted his cup of Canary wine and stared at the table. Finally he eyed Marbeck and said: 'If you want gratitude, I shall disappoint you.'

'I don't,' Marbeck told him. 'All I want is for you to take up your studies again, and put away what's past.'

The youth made no reply.

'I spoke to someone you know,' Marbeck added. 'Thomas Garrod. He was saddened at the way you shunned your friends.'

Henry gave a start. 'You'd no right to delve into my affairs.'

'I went at Lady Celia's behest. Had she no right either?'

'A pox on you – you're determined to treat me as a fool!'

The words came in a burst of anger. One or two people looked round, but since Marbeck appeared unruffled they lost interest. To Henry he said: 'I don't think you're a fool. I think you were restless and unhappy, not knowing what to believe or whom to trust. Gow appeared, and—'

'Yes – now it comes!' Henry stared fiercely at him. 'I was a lamb, led by the nose and destined for sacrifice. I was drunk with love and friendship ... my new family!'

'Some families are by nature worm-riddled, and bound to destroy themselves.' Marbeck eyed the boy grimly. 'I went to the farmhouse at Brampton, with Rowan. We found the bodies of Silas and another man – and John Chyme's, too. Likely you knew him by another name; but he was a brave man, and a friend.'

At that Henry frowned. 'John ... the newcomer?' A bleak look came over his pale features. 'He came to betray us ... Isaac said so.' When Marbeck said nothing, he added: 'Yet if he was a friend to you...'

'He worked for the Crown,' Marbeck said sharply. 'And in doing so he lost his life. As others have done, because of that man you venerated – and what was his aim? What was it for, will you tell me that?'

'He swore he would be a martyr for England,' Henry said, after a pause. 'Those who followed him would share his rapture, on that great day...'

'And you would be one of them,' Marbeck said. 'I saw the letter you sent your mother ... anyone who read it would know you were prepared to die. Can you not guess what torment it caused her?'

Quickly Henry picked up his cup and drank. Breathing hard, he put it down ... and Marbeck saw his hand shake. 'I was ready to die,' he said finally. 'Yet not in the way you think ... Isaac told me we were going to denounce the King before a crowd, so they would know him for a secret Papist who would turn the country towards Rome.' He spoke rapidly, his face taut. 'I didn't know he meant to kill him; nor did I know his staff had a blade inside – I swear it. Yet no one believes me.'

'I believe you,' Marbeck said.

Henry eyed him, but did not answer.

'And you stopped him – thereby saving the

King's life. But you shouldn't be surprised if those serving His Majesty see it differently. They're afraid for their own positions, and their own necks.' Marbeck wore a wry look. 'They allowed an assassin to get close, hence they want to see you executed along with Gow. I'd expect nothing else of them ... You're fortunate that one important man showed mercy, and set you free.'

The youth picked up his mug again; but without drinking he set it down. 'You serve the Crown too...' He looked away, unwilling to meet Marbeck's eye. 'I'll admit I owe you much, yet it comforts me not. I see nothing before me but an empty plain, filled with dead things. You can return me to Oxford, present that letter and see me readmitted, but it matters little. I come from brutal stock ... the son of a liar and a rakehell.'

'Yet one who died bravely on the battlefield, fighting alongside his men,' Marbeck said after a moment. When Henry made no reply he added: 'Now you have assumed his lands and his title ... and you have the chance to use them differently. Is that nothing – or is it that you deem yourself unworthy?'

The boy stared down at the table. 'You know I am,' he said.

But Marbeck shook his head. 'I've yet to form a judgement on that. I'll wait until you've completed your degree and returned to your family. It's what you do in the coming years that matters...'

He broke off; Henry looked so forlorn, he half-expected him to weep. But instead the youth looked up suddenly. 'Isaac poisoned the wine at Brampton,' he said. 'He didn't tell me – he left my cup untainted. Even Silas, who was always loyal, he no longer trusted. I thought I was honoured – that he valued me above the others, to be with him at the end. But I see I was merely his instrument, to help him to the King.'

A moment passed. The singers had ended their song, and were arguing about what to sing next. For now, Marbeck thought, all seemed to have been said. Looking away from Henry he drained his mug, whereupon the boy stood up.

'I'll go to bed now. I'm unused to riding so far in a day.'

Marbeck nodded. He watched him walk from the taproom towards the stairs, then leaned back as the drawer appeared.

'Will you take another, master?' he enquired.

'I believe I will,' Marbeck said.

The following evening, having delivered Henry Scroop safely to the doors of Exeter College, he found an inn on the other side of Oxford and took his first proper rest in days. In the morning he called for inkpot, quill and paper and penned a letter to Celia telling her that all was well, and that Henry was a student again. He left out the details, letting her know he would tell more later. Then he stowed it in his pack, intending to have it delivered as soon as he reached London. Soon afterwards he was in the saddle once more, with time to collect his thoughts.

In the final moment by the college doors, he and Henry had had little to say to one another. The youth was subdued, but no longer as hostile. When Marbeck asked if he wished him to convey any words to Lady Celia, Henry said he would write to her with a promise to return home at the end of the term. Thereafter they parted, without any words of farewell. Yet despite everything, Marbeck sensed some stirring of purpose in him; or had he merely wished it? With a sigh he put the matter aside, and turned his thoughts towards London.

He was back by afternoon, walking Cobb down Bishopsgate Street with the din of the city ahead. Carts rumbled by, there were shrieks from Bedlam hospital and beggars shuffling out of the gatehouse. With a full purse at his belt for once, he thought of finding a good chamber in a good inn, instead of returning to the Boar's Head. Then he remembered his lute was there; so he drew rein, dismounted and turned into Houndsditch. The street was crowded, with people

pressing about the fripperers' stalls. He led
Cobb past the gun-foundry, turned by St
Botolph's into Whitechapel, then stopped.
Walking towards him, head down in a reverie, was a figure he could never mistake. He
waited until the man was abreast of him,
then stood in his way.

'Were you looking for me, Prout?'

Nicholas Prout started as if someone had
pulled a dagger on him. 'By the heavens,' he
began, 'I thought you were...'

'Dead? Not yet ... though I had something
of a scrape in York. Have you ever been
there?'

The other shook his head. 'I wasn't looking
for you, though I'm relieved ... Are there
tidings?'

'Indeed there are,' Marbeck replied.
'Where shall we talk, at the Boar's Head?'

Prout waved the question aside. 'Have you
seen Master Secretary?'

'I have.' Marbeck put on a frown. 'He's
most displeased with you.' The other flinched, and he almost laughed. 'I expect he'll
forgive your recent lapses, though I'm not
certain he'll excuse your taking so many
matters upon yourself. I was strong in your
defence, I should say.'

'To the devil with you, Marbeck,' Prout
muttered.

'Let me go to my chamber,' Marbeck said
amiably. 'Once I've stabled my horse and

made sure my belongings haven't been filched, I'll tell all. Are you still holding Sir Roland Meeres at the Gatehouse prison, by the way?'

'I am – for I can do naught else,' Prout retorted. 'He should be taken to the Tower, yet I've not—'

'The authority,' Marbeck finished.

The other frowned. 'Why do you ask – do you wish to question him? Is there a warrant from Sir Robert?'

'Tonight after supper,' Marbeck said. 'If you'll meet me at Westminster, we'll converse. Will that serve?'

And without waiting he tugged the reins and led Cobb away.

The old gatehouse of Westminster Abbey had been a prison for centuries, and was in a poor state of repair. Yet here some of the most celebrated prisoners of the Crown had been held, including Sir Roland Meeres, who was now confined in an upper chamber. Marbeck and Prout passed down a gloomy passage to a tiny room used by the turnkeys, where they were left alone. Whereupon the messenger, who'd had time to think since their meeting by St Botolph's, put on a hard look. 'I've waited long enough,' he said. 'Tell me what's occurred since you and I last parted – the whole of it.'

So Marbeck drew a breath, and told him.

By the time he had finished, Prout was seated on a bench with his back to the wall, and an expression that was glum even for him.

'By all that's holy,' was all he could say.

'So, we're in something of a quandary,' Marbeck said. 'Neither of us has the power to interrogate Meeres, as a Privy Councillor, unless we find some means to persuade him to talk willingly. Yet one thing that would restore both you and me to Master Secretary's good favour would be to get him to name this financier who put up the money for Meeres and Drax to hatch their little enterprise.'

'I'm aware of that, Marbeck,' Prout muttered. 'Yet short of putting the man to hard question, I see no means to make him spill anything. He's a widower, his children grown and scattered. There's little leverage.'

'Save in the matter of his religion, and his cause,' Marbeck observed. 'What if I were to address him, dwelling on the fate that awaits the Earl of Charnock? The prospect of a traitor's death, in all its detail, would chill any man's blood.'

'He cares little for threats, from what I've seen,' Prout said. 'He still has rank and influence. He demands a public trial before the Lord Chief Justice, when he'll have his say.'

'Can we not be fanciful?' Marbeck suggested. 'Tell him Drax is caught and has spilled everything; that his only chance of mercy is a full confession...' An idea struck him. 'Or, what if we claim the Pope has denounced Meeres as an upstart who acted without sanction ... that he may even be excommunicated?'

Prout looked sceptical. 'He'd never swallow that.'

'He might, if a priest were to take the news to him.'

They eyed each other. Marbeck had brightened, but Prout was shaking his head. 'If you mean to take on another of your theatrical roles, it'll fail,' he said. 'The man got a good look at you in that room over the Dagger – he'd see through such a ruse in no time.'

Marbeck thought – and the answer came at once. 'Is Edward Poyns in London still?' he enquired.

'Poyns? I saw him a few days back...' Prout stiffened. 'Do you suppose he could carry it off?'

By the following morning it was arranged. Edward Poyns, whom Marbeck had last seen in Huntingdon, was tracked down by Prout to his lodgings in Silver Street. There the two intelligencers talked until late, constructing a small interlude to play before Sir Roland Meeres. Marbeck would maintain a role as

281

Crown pursuivant, while Poyns would take that of a Catholic priest, released from prison on licence to visit Meeres. When that was at last decided, and news had been exchanged, both of them rested for what was left of the night. Marbeck had left the Gatehouse without ever seeing Meeres, but now as London sprang into life he met Prout again by the entrance. With Marbeck was a slight, stooped figure in a priest's hat and cassock. A pair of spectacles was perched on his nose, and there was a bruise on his cheek made by the skilful application of soot and walnut juice. Prout took one look at him and grunted.

'You know what's required of you,' he muttered.

'I do, Goodman Prout,' Poyns replied, fingering a silver crucifix at his neck. 'It would go better if I had an Agnus Dei, and a stole. But this was all I could get.'

Prout turned to Marbeck. 'I can't be there, hence I must put my faith in you,' he said.

Marbeck merely nodded. And soon afterwards the two intelligencers were inside, walking behind a turnkey up a narrow stair. The door at which the man halted was unlocked; he even knocked politely, before a voice from within bade him enter. Marbeck and Poyns exchanged looks: noblemen often lived in high style in prison, provided their funds held out. Some had servants with them, and food and wine brought in daily, even enjoying the company of their wives at times. But the room which Marbeck and Poyns entered was small, furnished only with a bed, table and padded stool. There was a single occupant: well dressed, though somewhat haggard in appearance. As the turnkey stood back to let them enter, the man stood up – then recognition dawned.

'I'll not speak with you,' he said to Marbeck. His eye fell on Poyns, and a frown appeared. 'Who's this?' he demanded of the gaoler. 'What trickery do they attempt now?'

'No trickery,' Marbeck said. He looked round at the turnkey, who took the hint and disappeared. The intelligencers waited until his footfalls receded, whereupon Marbeck closed the door carefully.

'I hear you need a priest, Sir Roland,' he said with some contempt. 'Here's one they've let out for an hour, before he's returned to the Marshalsea. Will you receive him, or shall I take him away? It's a matter of indifference to me.'

He waited. So did Poyns, with a look of mingled fear and concern on his face; then he spoke – but in Latin.

'*Loquemus lingua Romana,*' he said in a reedy voice, fixing his eyes on the prisoner. '*Hinc grassator non comprehendabit.*'

Marbeck stiffened, and though he understood perfectly – *let us speak the Roman tongue,* Poyns had said, *so this ruffian won't understand* – he feigned incomprehension.

But Meeres gave a start. *'Es sacerdos, veramente?'* he asked quickly, and received a nod in return.

'Sum ... Te succereram—'

'Stop that!' Marbeck glared at them both. 'Speak English, you devils!'

'Very well...' Poyns gulped. 'I ... I was merely soothing this man in his predicament.'

A moment passed; Meeres had asked Poyns if he was really a priest, and received an affirmative answer. Marbeck retained his angry look – until at last, to his relief, the prisoner sat down again. 'Do you intend to stay?' he demanded in a surly tone. 'Can't he and I have a minute to ourselves?'

'Later, perhaps...' Marbeck eyed him stonily. 'For now I'd like to ask you some questions – may I proceed?'

The other hesitated, then looked at Poyns in his cassock. 'What's your name, Father?' he asked.

'Tobias Marchant, sir,' Poyns answered, bobbing. 'Newly removed from Wisbech Castle. I'm pained to see you in such straits ...Will you not placate this man, so I may do my office?'

Meeres hesitated, then let out a sigh; as did Marbeck, in silence. His scheme was about to bear fruit.

TWENTY

'You realize, Sir Roland, that you will be the last one to die,' Marbeck said. 'William Drax is in flight, the Earl of Charnock is captured. In time they'll both be dragged to Tower Hill on hurdles, to be hanged at the gibbet and taken down alive. Then their privy parts will be cut off, their innards opened and their bowels pulled forth to be burned before their eyes...' He paused, with a look of mock concern. 'Do you wish to meet that fate alone?'

There was no answer. Meeres sat rigid, his chest rising and falling rapidly. Nearby Poyns stood, his face transfixed in horror. To Marbeck he said: 'May the Lord forgive you ... you're no better than the wild beasts in the Tower—'

'No doubt.' Marbeck threw him a bland look. 'But remember your place here, priest. Any more insolence and you'll receive further treatment, of the kind you found in the Marshalsea.'

Poyns put his hand to his fake bruise and winced. Meeres looked shaken, but remained silent.

'There's nothing to be gained by holding back now,' Marbeck went on. 'All I want is the name of the man whose money allowed you to launch your venture, then I'll leave you. The entire scheme has failed – but you know that. Indeed, it was a fool's breakfast from the start. The Pope never sanctioned the enterprise – there's even talk of excommunication.'

'Lies!' Poyns raised a trembling finger, pointing it at Marbeck. 'I cannot keep silent at such falsehood ... and you're a blasphemer, to speak of the Holy Father in such a manner! This man here will receive his due rites, as a courageous defender of our religion—'

'A what?' Marbeck forced a scowl; for an instant, his admiration for Poyns's acting had almost thrown him. 'I told you to keep silent, you Papist cur...' Stepping forward, he gasped his arm. 'Perhaps we'll dispense with your services until it's time for those last rites you speak of—'

'No!'

Suddenly Meeres was on his feet again. 'This is a man of God, who's borne your savagery long enough!' he cried. 'Let him alone, for I'll tell you nothing! But when it comes to my trial, I'll waste no time in naming those who've stepped beyond their office...'

He broke off; Marbeck had thrown Poyns

a look, which his fellow understood even as he shrank from him. To the prisoner, he turned a face of anguish. 'Sir Roland ... I fear there may be no trial,' he muttered, shaking his head. 'They'll slay you here on some pretext – attempting escape, perhaps...' He turned on Marbeck. 'Why should I not speak the truth? You can do naught but separate me from my body – whereupon I will find joy everlasting, which you will never know!' Near to tears, he crossed himself. 'Forbear to fight them, Sir Roland,' he begged. 'It matters little now. Tell them what they want to know, for the man you will not name has forsaken you – can you not see it? He walks free, while those who put themselves in danger pay the price! I can do no more than pray for you – pray for us all!' And with that, he dropped to his knees and bowed his head.

A silence fell. Meeres looked aghast, his eyes going from Poyns to Marbeck and back. He sank down on his stool, while Marbeck put on another angry expression, as if Poyns had said too much. He placed his hand on his sword-hilt, threw a withering look at Meeres, and counted to ten...

'His name's Spinola,' the man said hoarsely.

Marbeck froze, then raised his eyebrows.

'Augusto Spinola, from Genoa ... the *argentarius.*' Meeres sighed and lowered his gaze. 'Now for the love of God, will you let me make my confession? For my life's done, and there's naught to keep me on this earth.'

He looked up with a bleakness born of despair. 'England is broken, and the forces of evil are at her gates,' he mumbled. 'James Stuart will betray us, and burn one day in the pit that's prepared for him – as will you and your kind. Now leave me – and may God have mercy on you!'

Another moment passed; then to Meeres' dismay, Poyns got abruptly to his feet. The prisoner stared – and saw at once how he'd been outwitted. Words failed him; all he could do was gaze at the bogus priest, as he removed his cassock to reveal an unwashed shirt and a pair of striped breeches.

'Well, that wasn't so difficult,' Poyns breathed, wiping his brow with a sleeve. 'Shall we leave Sir Roland in peace?'

Prout was waiting on the ground floor of the Gatehouse. As soon as the two appeared, he started towards them.

'Well, have we a name?' he demanded.

'We do, thanks to a fine performance on Poyns's part,' Marbeck answered. Suddenly, he felt elated. He gave the gist of what had happened, whereupon the messenger's jaw dropped.

'Spinola? Surely not ... why, he lent gold to the Queen's Council.' He frowned. 'Meeres has spun you a tale.'

'I think not,' Marbeck said. 'I know the truth when I hear it.'

Poyns nodded. 'I too believe it,' he said.

'Well, likely it will be a formality in any case,' Prout said, after a moment. 'If it was Spinola, he'll surely have fled by now.'

'But you at least will know it was he,' Marbeck said. 'You may search his home – he might have left evidence. Something to tell Master Secretary when he returns, isn't it?'

Despite himself, Prout was looking relieved. 'I suppose ... Spinola has a great house in Broad Street, as I recall.' He was rapidly becoming his former self. 'I'll gather an escort, force an entry...' He was about to go, then checked himself. 'And you'd better come along too – both of you.'

By noon the party had assembled by the pump in Threadneedle Street, a short distance from the Royal Exchange. Before them was Broad Street, where stood the town house of one of the richest men in London. Yet Augusto Spinola, who claimed acquaintance with some of the crowned heads of Europe, had always been a shadowy figure, rarely seen outside his well-guarded residence. He was frequently abroad, and had other properties outside the city, rumour said. The man did business in many fields: wool, lead, timber and alum – yet there was one commodity in which he dealt above all else: money. He was an *argentarius*, Meeres had said: one who managed silver and gold for others, and somehow made it work in his favour. There was no word in the English language for such men, as yet; but it was well known that in Italy and Germany certain powerful figures were forging new ways of doing business. Several times throughout the morning, Thomas Burridge's words had echoed in Marbeck's head: *Men like them live by money as others live by their toil ... their fortunes multiply as if by sorcery...*

'Bartolemeo Renzi,' Poyns was saying. 'He's foremost among moneylenders, is he not? I'd have laid odds he was our man – I'd barely heard of Spinola before Meeres named him.'

He and Marbeck stood apart from the group: three armed pursuivants were being given their instructions by Prout. They all carried swords, and the messenger had a pistol. The intelligencers wore their rapiers and poniards, and the party had already attracted attention. But it was too late for a dawn intrusion, and being impatient for results, Prout would not wait until nightfall.

'I'd barely heard of the man either,' Marbeck replied. 'But Drax's paymaster said he was hired through Renzi. He would know Spinola, and could have recommended the man to him – one who was easily bought.'

'But then, what man doesn't have his

price?' Poyns asked.

Marbeck touched his arm: Prout was nodding at them. So in broad daylight the six men moved off up the street, to stop outside the iron gate of Spinola's residence. The front was deceptively narrow, someone said: the house stretched back a long way, as far as the gardens of Gresham House. Nobody was certain whether there were other entrances to the property, so Prout despatched one man to look. Then he tried the gate, which to his surprise was unlocked, and they were soon nearing the front door. But already, disappointment threatened.

'The courtyard's unswept,' Marbeck observed. 'There's nobody here ... we would have seen servants by now.'

'I care not,' Prout said shortly. 'I want the place ransacked, every closet turned out, floorboards lifted.' But for propriety's sake, he banged on the door before trying the latch. It was locked, so the guards would force it. Meanwhile Marbeck and Poyns stood back to survey the shuttered windows.

'I've seen places like this in Lombardy,' Poyns said. 'Cool in summer, warm in winter. They know how to build.'

'Do you see that?'

Marbeck pointed, and moved to a window at the corner of the house. Prout's attention was on the door, which his men were about to break. Poyns came over to examine the shutters.

'Someone's forced an entry here,' Marbeck called to Prout. 'Do you want to look—'

But a crash of splintering timbers interrupted him, as the front door gave way. The guards piled in, while Prout looked impatiently at the intelligencers. 'Thieves, most likely ... let's get inside.'

They followed him into the darkened house. At first little could be seen, until the shutters were opened. Then as light flooded in they saw that everything – furniture, mirrors and portraits – was covered with sheets. The guards pulled some of them off, revealing finely carved chests, tables and presses. Tapestries hung from floor to ceiling, though there was little in the way of plate or ornaments. Nor, Marbeck noticed, was much dust raised.

'They left recently,' he said. 'No more than a week...'

But Prout, unusually animated, was already striding off. 'Look in every room,' he said over his shoulder. 'Open the chests – break locks if you have to.'

The intelligencers exchanged looks. 'There is a man trying to salvage his reputation,' Poyns said wryly. 'Shall we aid him?'

Without much enthusiasm they set to work; but as Marbeck had feared, the search brought little result. Augusto Spinola had removed himself, along with his family and most of his wealth. The only items that remained were those too large or too heavy to be carried away quickly. A cursory examination of the room with the damaged shutter also proved fruitless. Thieves had apparently broken in some time ago, but had no doubt departed with little to show for their efforts. From there, the two intelligencers moved to a large kitchen, where at last they found evidence of recent habitation. The place was untidy, with dirty pans and dishes lying about. In the great fireplace the ashes were cold, the turnspit silent. Poyns poked about on shelves, then turned to Marbeck.

'Do you smell that?'

'I believe I do...' Marbeck looked to a corner, where stood a large copper still. He smelled herbs and alcohol.

'No, bacon ... well cured, too.'

Poyns was bending, peering under a low table where there was a small keg. He pulled it towards him, lifted the lid and wrinkled his nose. 'Not fresh, but edible if you're hungry enough...' He glanced up at Marbeck, who recognized his expression. He had seen it before, at the deserted farmhouse by Gogmagog, when his fellow had looked up from a fireplace where papers had been burned.

'Let me guess – something doesn't feel right,' he said. 'So what think you: someone stayed here after the household fled?'

For answer Poyns stood up. 'It's worth

considering. Shall we look upstairs?'

They left the kitchen and walked along a passage to the entrance hall. In one room they could hear the guards clattering about, moving things aside. From another doorway Prout appeared, then gave a start. They all looked round as a door by the stairs opened. The third guard appeared, who by the look of him had climbed through a hedge.

'There's a back gate into the gardens,' he said, out of breath. 'A fair sight ... statues, and ponds with carp and all.'

'Is that all?' Prout snapped. 'This isn't a sightseeing foray.'

'If you let me finish,' the man retorted, 'I'll tell you there are more rooms, opening off a covered way – a colonnade, like in the Exchange. One looks like the master's private chamber. No windows and an iron-bound chest, but it's empty.'

Disappointed, Prout muttered under his breath, whereupon Marbeck spoke up. 'We think someone's been using the place,' he said. 'And not just thieves...'

'Or even beggars,' Poyns put in. 'Otherwise, they'd have left more sign.'

'The upper floor, then,' Prout said to his pursuivant. The man nodded and went off to the stairs; as he ascended, the messenger faced the other two. 'Have you found something?'

'A barrel of bacon,' Poyns said with a

shrug.

'Bacon?' The messenger glared.

'Just a notion I have.'

There was a bang from the room nearby, followed by a squeal of hinges; the guards had forced a lock. With a grunt Prout turned ... then stopped in his tracks. Poyns froze too, but Marbeck swung round, his eyes going to the staircase. They had all heard it: a muffled cry, followed by a thud.

'You men, out here!' Prout shouted, reaching for his pistol. But even as the guards appeared Marbeck was climbing the stairs, loosening his sword as he went. Poyns was behind him, light of foot. The two scanned the landing above, but there was no one in sight.

'Wait!' Prout shouted from below. But his men were quicker to act, their boots thudding on the steps. Marbeck gained the top floor and looked round. Light spilled from open doorways, but one door was closed. He glanced at Poyns, who nodded. Hurrying forward, they placed themselves on either side of it, then Marbeck kicked the door in. Sword in hand he rushed inside ... and stopped; the room was empty, save for a pile of soiled bedding and a broken chair. Poyns was already off, hurrying to the next room. Marbeck followed, almost colliding with the first guard at the stair-head. The man was drawing his sword, eyes darting about...

A groan; whirling round, Marbeck ran in its direction, to the farthest doorway. It was the main chamber spanning the front of the house, and there was noise within. He gained the entrance – and almost fell over.

The guard was lying on the floor, sprawled on his back, his mouth working feebly as blood gushed from his neck. Marbeck looked up … and his heart thumped.

'I might have known,' William Drax said, in a voice as cold as marble.

For what seemed an age, they gazed at each other. The former commander of the rebel army, whom Marbeck had last seen at a table toasting victory, was crouching balefully, rapier in hand. He was dishevelled and dirty, but the same pitiless eyes bored into Marbeck's. His blade, Marbeck saw, was stained with blood. He breathed hard, holding the man's gaze: *the one they called the Basilisk* … nor did he turn when Poyns and the guards hurried up behind him. Somewhere Prout was shouting, but nobody listened. For there was another movement from nearby. As one man the Crown's servants whirled round towards it – but too late.

Lieutenant Follett, in shirt and breeches, his face disfigured with burns, leaped from behind the door like a crazed animal. His sword flashed and found its mark: the first guard fell with a gasp, blood welling from his chest. The second lifted his own blade, but

wasn't nearly quick enough: the young officer merely ducked under his arm and struck
again, slashing the man's neck. The guard
reeled and fell against the wall, before
sprawling beside the body of his companion.
All three men down ... in the doorway, Poyns
stared in disbelief.

'Now the odds are changed,' Drax said.
There was no mistaking his intent; he even
smiled. 'And I rejoice that we may finish it
here,' he added. 'For there's a reckoning to
be paid, is there not?'

'Perhaps there is,' Marbeck said at last.

They eyed each other: four swordsmen
now, their breath loud in the empty room.
Sunlight flooded through tall windows, dust-
motes glittered ... but Marbeck suddenly
lowered his sword, stood to full height and
relaxed.

'Will you allow me a moment?' he said.
When nobody moved, he went to the door.
Bending, he pulled the body of one guard
roughly aside: the man was dead, and could
hardly object. Having cleared the doorway,
he seized the heavy door and started to close
it – just as Prout arrived out of breath.

'What are you—' he began, but his words
were lost as Marbeck closed the door on him
and drew a heavy bolt across it. Then he
turned back to the others.

'Shall we play?' he said.

Poyns nodded.

TWENTY-ONE

Once, when Marbeck was a boy, he had been bold enough to challenge his fencing master on a point of honour. 'You didn't give me time to ward, Master Ralph,' he had said indignantly. 'Didn't you say a gentleman would signal when he was ready to begin the bout?'

'I did, sir,' Ralph had replied. 'Yet suppose the one you're fighting isn't a gentleman, but a ruffian who means to spike you and take your purse ... what would you do then?'

In the years since, Marbeck had recalled his teacher's words many times, though seldom as vividly as now. He had fought for his life before, but rarely against an opponent like William Drax. The man was not only desperate; he was a murderer, as cunning as he was cruel. Marbeck had seen it at their first meeting, in a forest in Kent. And as soon as the two engaged, he knew he was locked in a duel to the last.

At first it was routine fencing: thrusts and parries, each probing for the other's weaknesses. Drax attempted a few bolder strokes, which Marbeck warded easily. But the man was a fine swordsman, he saw, which sharpened his mettle. Drax soon manoeuvred him to a position where the sunlight might dazzle him; but by jabbing and feinting, Marbeck forced the other round. Then the two veered back and forth, their breath coming faster. Words had ceased to be of use. The Shade of Death hovered in the room; it would be but a short time, Marbeck knew, before it decided where to alight.

He tried not to think about Poyns, though he couldn't help hearing him. The little man and Follett were engaged in a terrible struggle at the other end of the dusty room, gasping and snarling like fighting-dogs. It was no fencing bout, but a feral struggle. Poyns was not a skilled swordsman like Marbeck; the thought troubled him. Follett was enraged and, like Drax, a man with nothing to lose. Poyns had been right about intruders: the forced shutter was explained. How long the two fugitives had been hiding here Marbeck didn't know, but it made sense: Drax had come to Spinola seeking the means to leave England – only to find that his sponsor had fled.

These thoughts flew through his mind as he fought, darting across the bare boards, neither man yet gaining the upper hand. But both were tiring: Marbeck's hope, albeit a slim one, was that he could disguise his weariness enough to trouble his opponent. Soon he might need to pull a Ballard trick from his repertoire ... he was running over the notion, when Drax tried a ruse of his own. He stumbled suddenly, putting his free hand out to steady himself. Marbeck hesitated, but only for a half-second: Drax's blade flew up, missing his face by a whisker. Ducking aside, he slashed the man's exposed arm, and was rewarded by a hiss of pain. But at once Drax was up, blood on his sleeve, thrusting as before.

Grimly Marbeck set to again. Swords clashed and rang in the room; a scene of carnage already, with the guards' bodies piled by the doorway. Then he grew aware of a thudding, and realized it had been there from the start: Prout was shouting and pummelling the door, but the stout bolt held. Marbeck ignored him, narrowly avoiding another lunge from his opponent. He smelled the man's breath, sour and sharp...

A cry from across the room. He gritted his teeth, but dared not look. He knew Poyns had been hit; it only surprised him that it hadn't happened sooner. He heard a raucous laugh: Follett scented victory, and was going for the kill. His anger stirring anew, Marbeck struck Drax's next thrust aside savagely, and at the same time reached for his poniard. The other man had none, he saw: why had he not noticed? But the thought had barely occurred, when there came another cry that jarred his nerves. A helpless anger welled up in him: Poyns was about to die, and he could do nothing for him...

There was a crash of breaking glass that startled all of them. Shards sparkled and flew across the room, whereupon there was a shout from outside, through the broken window.

'Yield, by order of the Crown! There can be no escape ... throw down your weapons!'

'For pity's sake, Prout,' Marbeck muttered, gripping the handle of his poniard. Inside the room four figures gasped and staggered in the sunlight, swords flailing, narrowly avoiding the bodies of the guards. Blood ran across the floor, dark and shiny. One of the men was still alive; Marbeck heard him wheezing. He dodged another thrust from Drax, after which the fellow attempted a crosswise sweep – and in that fleeting moment Marbeck saw his chance. He parried the man's blade, and at the same time brought his poniard up – whereupon his right foot slid from under him, and to his dismay he found himself flat on the floor.

He lay there for what seemed seconds. There was time to notice the ceiling, painted blue and dotted with stars; a common enough conceit, in imitation of the famous Star Chamber. There was also time to feel something wet seeping through his breeches:

he had slipped in blood, of course. Winded, but still holding rapier and dagger, he looked up and saw his opponent standing over him. There was an ugly grin on Drax's features, which were streaked with sweat and grime. Marbeck saw his blade, shining and deadly. He braced himself to roll away – when there was a grunt, and a sudden movement to his left. But even as it registered he saw the look of surprise on Drax's face ... and the next moment the man was falling, his hands grasping empty air. His sword whistled by Marbeck's ear, then clattered to the floor.

Panting, Marbeck forced himself to a sitting position and saw what had happened. The guard lying nearest – the one who still lived – had seized Drax's heel with his hand and tripped him. The rebel commander, out of breath, was lying on his back turtle-fashion. Half-dazed he looked round, then struck out savagely. But the blow was wasted: the guard – the one Marbeck had almost collided with at the stair-head – was in his death throes. With a sigh the fellow went limp ... but he had saved Marbeck's life. And in a moment Marbeck was on his feet, the point of his sword at Drax's throat.

'Lie still,' he breathed.

Drax looked up, his eyes bloodshot. 'End it,' he said, in a voice drained of emotion. Marbeck held his gaze ... then frowned. Though aware of noises across the room, he had been so intent on his own struggle he had barely listened. Now he risked a sideways glance – and drew a sharp breath.

Poyns was on his knees, blood everywhere, his sword arm hanging uselessly; even as Marbeck looked, the weapon slipped from his hand. Follett, his face livid with rage and triumph, loomed over him. His arm rose, blade shimmering in the sunlight. Poyns gazed up helplessly; three other pairs of eyes were riveted upon the scene: a grim tableau of execution. Marbeck heard his fellow gasp – but in that second he acted. His left arm flew up, launching his poniard like a dart; with a soft thud it embedded itself in Follett's side.

There followed an odd sound; neither cry nor gasp, but a collective groan from the mouths of three men: Poyns, giving vent to his relief; Drax, because he saw that all was lost; and Follett because he was in pain, and numb with shock.

But the young lieutenant stayed on his feet. His sword arm dropped and a puzzled frown appeared, as he gazed down at the dagger protruding from his ribs. Blood stained his shirt: once an expensive garment, with bands of fine lace at cuffs and neck, now torn and soiled. He regarded the wound, his eyes went to Marbeck ... then his knees buckled, and he sank to the floor. There he remained, his and Poyns's positions reversed. Shakily, the little man got up.

'Yield – this is my last warning. We have ladders – we'll force entry!' Prout shouted from below.

Marbeck didn't look round, but kept his sword pressed to Drax's throat; and for the first time he saw fear in the man's eyes. 'End it now, for Jesu's sake,' he repeated; though it was a plea rather than a threat.

But Marbeck shook his head slowly. Eyes still on Drax, he spoke to Poyns. 'Will you unbolt the door? Then call to our friend outside, and tell him to come in.'

Crunching on broken glass, Poyns crossed the room, slid the bolt back and threw the door wide. From downstairs, voices sounded. He turned round, his eyes on Follett, who had slumped to a sitting position. Then the little man winced with pain, pressing a hand to his wound; blood dripped from his sleeve.

'Where did they get the ladders?' he muttered weakly. He peered down at Drax. But Marbeck leaned over his victim and spoke low.

'I met Sir Roland Meeres today. I was obliged to remind him how traitors are executed; to focus his mind, you understand. If the King's Council is merciful, perhaps they'll allow you a soldier's death – but I wouldn't wager on it.'

Hatred filled Drax's eyes. His gaze went to

his sword lying nearby ... but Poyns stepped forward and kicked it beyond his reach. He went to Follett too and kicked his away, though the man was in no condition to move. Blearily he looked up at the two intelligencers, and then an odd smile appeared. Marbeck frowned – then suddenly understood.

'Stop him!' he cried.

Poyns looked round. 'Stop what...?'

But he was too late: Marbeck knew it even as Poyns saw what was happening. He started towards Follett, but the man's hand was at his mouth. As Poyns grabbed it he threw his head back and swallowed the poison. In his hand was a glass phial, but it was empty. He let it fall to the floor, a grim smile on his face. Then he fell backwards, his body twitching. The intelligencers could only watch until he died.

A moment passed; then Poyns went to the broken window and leaned out. 'We're done here,' he called. 'Will you come up?'

When evening fell, Marbeck was back at the Boar's Head.

He was exhausted, though not too tired to indulge himself in a bath. Such a request was unknown at the inn, but when he named a price the place sprang into life. A half-butt was found, scoured hastily and carried up to his chamber, while servants laboured to bring pails of heated water. Finally, stiff and sore, he peeled off his sweat-stained clothes and lowered himself into the glorious brew. Herbs had been strewn in the tub, and a ball of scented soap provided. A feeling of bliss descended on him. Even the Queen had rarely indulged herself in such a manner, he remembered; perhaps now that James Stuart was King, such occasions would be rarer still.

'Will there be aught else, Master Strang?'

Summoned from his reverie, Marbeck looked round to see one of the inn's regular wenches standing there, regarding him with a brazen smile; for a moment, he was tempted.

'Most kind, Bridget,' he answered, leaning back in the tub, where a cloth was placed on the rim for a headrest. 'I'll pass this time ... but if you'd care to hand me my belt, I may find you something for your trouble.'

Bridget didn't hesitate. Going to the bed, she picked up his belt and saw the purse tied to it. But when she hefted it expertly, her mouth fell open. 'Jesu! You're a bold one to let anyone see a bung as heavy as this, especially at the Boar's Head...' A wicked grin appeared. 'Why, I could cut it and be off before you got out of that barrel.'

'You could,' Marbeck said. 'But what would they say downstairs, when you fled into the yard with a naked man in pursuit?

They'd think you'd tried to cozen him.'

'You'd not be the first to give chase in such a manner,' Bridget retorted. 'And who cares what they think?'

But when he smiled, she couldn't help return it. She brought him his purse, which he unlaced. Coins fell on to his hand, from which he selected a half-angel. The woman gave another start – but when he looked up, she was pointing not at the money but at his arm.

'How did you get such scars?' she asked.

'A long story,' Marbeck replied, and proffered the coin.

With a nod she took it. 'I know what's the cause of all this,' she said suddenly. 'You mean to go to the Queen's funeral, do ye not? Thursday next, they say.'

'All this?' Marbeck looked blank, then realized she meant his taking a bath.

'Lords and gentlemen will follow the hearse,' Bridget went on. 'And half of London will stand and gawp ... not me, though.'

'No?'

'Nay – it's naught to me who sits on the throne. Nothing will change, save there'll be more men about the Court than ladies...' She frowned. 'But you're a lute-player, are you not? Has someone important hired you, or some such?'

'You might say so,' Marbeck told her. 'Now, no affront intended, but will you leave a man to enjoy his soak?'

She went out, whereupon he exhaled and closed his eyes. The sweet-scented water enveloped him like warm silk. Images flew up: Poyns walking unsteadily from Augusto Spinola's house and sitting down in the courtyard, the shock of his ordeal only now striking home. Guards bearing the bodies of their dead comrades out into the sunshine and laying them in a row, grim-faced at the sight. Prout wandering about, his face filled with shame. The body of Lieutenant Follett had also been brought out, to be dumped unceremoniously on a handcart. Lastly came the prisoner William Drax, bound and hemmed in by Crown officers. The man had kept his eyes down, his face expressionless. Only once had he looked up, to meet Marbeck's eye before he was bundled away. But in that second Marbeck saw the man's dismay, and was reminded of a similar look on the face of Sir Roland Meeres, in his cell at the Gatehouse.

He had walked away then, to stand by the gate. Here, in the splendid house in Broad Street, the Papist plotters might have met with their purse-holder: a Genoese whom few people had seen, yet who had financed a scheme that might have handed England to a foreign power. Now the place stood empty and abandoned, used in the final turn as a refuge for one of those same plotters. The three men who had put the scheme into action faced a terrible death; yet he who had made it possible was gone. Then, such people generally got themselves clear, Marbeck mused; that slippery commodity, justice, often favoured the richest, if not the fleetest of foot.

He breathed deeply, hearing the sounds of revellers gathering in the inn downstairs. Briefly he opened his eyes, his gaze falling on his lute in the corner. He planned to dispose of it soon, along with the identity of Richard Strang; a man who would soon become notorious, he suspected, for being the only person in memory to take a bath at the Boar's Head.

Slowly a smile formed; he leaned back again, water lapping his body, and thought of Celia; but his eyelids drooped. As he drifted into sleep an odd notion occurred: that he might become the only man in England who had ever drowned in a bedchamber. But the notion passed, and in minutes he was snoring.

He never heard Bridget, when she stole into his room later and found him sleeping peacefully. With her was another woman, painted, perfumed and wearing a very low-cut gown sprinkled with fake jewels. The two stared.

'I fear to wake him,' the newcomer muttered. 'I thought you said he'd be out of that tub by now, and open to persuasion? There's few men can say no, when they get a sight of my dugs.'

'We'd best go,' Bridget said after a moment. 'He's a tired fellow, anyone can see.'

'Yet did you not speak of a full purse?' the other said. 'I'll look if you won't...'

But Bridget was tugging at her sleeve. 'You blowsy old callet,' she said sharply, 'are you grown deaf? I said he gave me sixpence. He's but a lute-player, can't you see?' She pointed to the instrument, whereupon her companion gave a sigh of impatience.

'Then why do you waste my time?' she demanded. 'I'm for downstairs – are you coming or not?'

EPILOGUE

Queen Elizabeth's funeral took place on the twenty-eighth day of April, some five weeks after her death. A great host followed her body, on a chariot drawn by four horses caparisoned in black. On the coffin was a wax effigy of the monarch, splendidly dressed and wearing a crown. The way from Whitehall to Westminster Abbey was short, and not all those who witnessed the procession were sorrowful; the last years of the Queen's reign had been hard, and many looked to a new beginning. Marbeck, standing with Edward Poyns near the entrance, had few strong feelings either way.

'I thought the King would keep clear until this was over,' Poyns observed. 'I hear he's at Hinchingbrooke by Huntingdon, as guest of the Cromwell family. Do you know the place?'

'I remember it,' Marbeck said. His memory went back to when he sat on Cobb, gazing at the fine manor house; it seemed an age ago. He and his fellow were standing

311

among the onlookers, watching black-clad nobles and servants pass. Poyns's right sleeve was empty, his arm strapped to his body beneath his doublet. After a moment he gave a sigh, and turned to Marbeck.

'I'm away. Since no one appears to need me now, I mean to pay visits.'

'As do I,' Marbeck answered.

So with a brief embrace they parted. Marbeck watched the slight figure disappear into the throng, then walked off in the other direction. He skirted the crowd, the abbey and the great huddle of buildings that made up Whitehall Palace, to emerge a short while later on Millbank. Here he took the ferry across to Lambeth, where Cobb was waiting, saddled and laden with his pack, and his lute in its case. He had paid a boy to hold him; as he appeared the lad handed him the reins and doffed his cap.

'So the Queen is laid to rest now, master,' he said. 'Were many tears shed?'

But Marbeck merely shrugged, and got himself mounted. Soon he was riding leisurely upriver, reaching Barnes within the half hour. Some distance from Croft House he dismounted and tied the horse to a fence. Then he made his way to the wicket-gate, to pass through the vegetable garden into the kitchen as had once been his habit. Servants were about, and the wenches recognized him at once.

'Master Strang – what do you here?' one asked in surprise. 'We heard you were dismissed.'

'So I am,' he said with a smile. 'I came to see the Lady Alice – is she here?'

The women exchanged looks. 'I believe she's in the rose garden,' another said. 'Yet do you think you should be there...?' But she broke off, for Marbeck was already going.

He found the girl sitting on a bench, under a cherry tree laden with blossom. To his relief there was neither nurse nor maid present, only a gardener at work some distance away. As Marbeck approached Alice gave a start, and leaped to her feet.

'Richard Strang ... Where have you been? I waited, yet you never returned!'

Drawing close, Marbeck halted and made his bow. 'I came to tender you my apology for that, my lady,' he said. 'And to enquire whether you still study the lute, or the virginals as your mother wished.'

The girl stared at him, as if deciding whether to be angry or not. Finally she put on her prim look.

'I learn the virginals. My teacher is old, and sour as a green plum. My brother has a teacher upon the lute, but I'm not allowed. They have taken my instrument and put it away, I know not where.' She brightened

313

suddenly. 'Do you wish to return as my tutor? I could ask my father...'

'I regret I cannot,' Marbeck told her. 'But I had a notion you might like to have a gift; a token of our days together. Will you honour me by accepting it?'

Her eyes widened: until now she hadn't noticed the case strapped across his back. When he unslung it and held it out, her hand went to her mouth. 'You wish me to have your lute?'

'I do,' Marbeck answered. 'There's no one in England to whom I would rather give it.' He waited, until finally the girl stepped forward and took it in both hands.

'You are a true friend,' she said quietly.

'As you are to me, my lady,' Marbeck replied.

A moment passed. The gardener was regarding both of them curiously, while from the direction of the house came voices.

'Now I must leave again,' Marbeck said, summoning a smile. 'Please present my respects to your father and mother.'

But Alice's face fell. 'Oh ... I cannot,' she said. 'Or at least, I can to my father, when he returns from the north country. But my mother is gone into Essex, to her family's estate. Palmer is gone with her.'

'Palmer?' Marbeck raised an eyebrow ... then he understood. 'Do you mean the steward?'

314

The girl nodded.

'Well then...' A wry smile tugged at his mouth, but he resisted it. 'Pray pass my respectful greetings to Sir Thomas. I trust he'll find a place at the court of our new King, when he finally arrives.'

The girl bit her lip. 'He already has, I think,' she said. 'The King's party will stay at Sir Robert Cecil's house in Hertfordshire soon ... My father is gone there before him, to help make ready.' She looked at the lute, which she had been holding at arm's length; now she clasped it to her slim body.

'I thank you, most heartily,' she said.

'There's no need to,' Marbeck replied. Then he made his bow and walked off. At the entrance to the rose garden he turned, to see Lady Alice standing where he had left her. She waved, and he returned the gesture. Then he was striding away from Croft House, to retrieve Cobb from the roadside.

He glanced up: the sun was almost at its zenith. He could ride anywhere; all England was open to him, for he had no duties. Perhaps he no longer had a future in Master Secretary's service; just now, it hardly seemed to matter. But he turned eastwards, leading Cobb along the path towards the Putney ferry. If the ferryman would take the horse across, he could be at Chelsea by noon. If he refused, Marbeck would have to find a barge and pay extra, or even ride as far as London Bridge.

But then, that didn't seem to matter too much, either.